# Constable Around
# the Park

NICHOLAS RHEA

# Constable Around the Park

ROBERT HALE · LONDON

© *Nicholas Rhea 2004*
*First published in Great Britain 2004*
*Paperback edition 2005*

ISBN 0 7090 7570 7 (hardback)
ISBN 0 7090 7622 3 (paperback)

Robert Hale Limited
Clerkenwell House
Clerkenwell Green
London EC1R 0HT

The right of Nicholas Rhea to be identified as
author of this work has been asserted by him
in accordance with the Copyright, Designs and
Patents Act 1988

*A catalogue record for this book is available from the British Library*

2 4 6 8 10 9 7 5 3 1

Typeset in 11/14pt Baskerville by
Derek Doyle & Associates, Liverpool.
Printed in Great Britain by
St Edmundsbury Press Limited, Bury St Edmunds, Suffolk.
Bound by Woolnough Bookbinding Limited.

# Chapter 1

A large proportion of my Aidensfield beat lay within the boundaries of the North York Moors National Park. This is quite distinct from the Yorkshire Dales National Park the nearest boundary of which is some forty miles to the west of my former patch. Even today, people are confused by the fact that North Yorkshire contains two national parks, each with its own distinct features. The Yorkshire Dales are many miles to the west of the North York Moors and include the Pennine range of hills, otherwise known as the backbone of England, while the Moors occupy a patch of high ground very close to the north-east coast. The two national parks are separated by the broad Vale of York which contains the market towns of Easingwold, Thirsk and Northallerton and also carries the main London–Edinburgh railway line as well as the A1, otherwise known as the Great North Road. There is a fine view of the Vale of York from the summit of Sutton Bank which is near Thirsk on the A170. Some claim this is the finest view in England and it was once said a person could stand on this site to watch a steam train leave York and continue to observe it until it arrived at Darlington some forty-five miles to the north.

The North York Moors National Park was created in 1952, the year I joined the police service, and it covers 553 square miles (1432 square kilometres) with an outline surprisingly similar to that of Australia. It includes England's largest area of open heather and the greatest area of woodland cover of any English national park. In addition, it has some of the country's finest coastline, not to mention a wealth of ancient abbeys, castles and country estates, a surviving steam railway, a Roman road, an historic Roman Catholic village said to have been missed by the Reformation, a church crypt dating to the time of William the Conqueror, Fylingdales Ballistic Missile Early Warning Station, the home of England's first poet, the scene of the first-ever flight by a man, and the scene of the first German aircraft to be shot down in World War II by no less a person than Group Captain Peter Townsend. He was known for his ill-fated romance with HRH Princess Margaret.

There is much more of course and it takes a long time to explore and enjoy everything within the national park, but there is a similar galaxy of fascinating places just beyond its boundaries, such as Whitby with its ancient whaling, fishing and jet industries, plus an abbey where the system for determining our date of Easter was established in AD 664. Further down the coast there is Scarborough whose spa waters gave birth to England's first seaside resort, while inland there are the beautiful Howardian Hills with their showpiece, Castle Howard, still remembered for its role in the 1980s hit TV series, *Brideshead Revisited*. To the south, is the ancient and remarkable City of York, and to the north there is the thriving connurbation of Middlesbrough and other Teesside towns, along with historic Durham and bustling modern Tyneside.

In a large circle around the park's boundaries is a collection of England's most charming market towns such as Pickering, Kirkbymoorside, Helmsley, Thirsk, Stokesley, Guisborough and Loftus, while the region's most interesting villages are either within the park or very close to it. They include Thornton-le-Dale, Goathland, Grosmont,

Lastingham, Rosedale Abbey, Hutton-le-Hole, Robin Hood's Bay, Staithes, Runswick Bay, Hackness, Ravenscar, Danby, Westerdale, Castleton, Glaisdale, Egton Bridge, Ugthorpe, Osmotherley, Hawnby, Coxwold, Kilburn – and others, with, of course, Aidensfield. In spite of the national park now being more than fifty years old, and in spite of its well-organized publicity, there is still, in the minds of some, considerable confusion about its functions. Some tourists believe it is akin to a corporation park in a town, or even a theme park as evidenced in these comments – 'Excuse me, Constable, but what time do the moors open?' 'Look, that bird's escaped from somewhere!' It was a pheasant. 'Why can't I light fires on the moor?' 'Is that a real village down there or is it a museum?' 'Let's get a postcard from this shop so we know where we've been.' 'Do you have electricity in your house, and can you get daily papers here?' 'Fancy building that castle so close to the railway line.' 'Which is the way to Devon?'

Many seem to think the national park belongs to the nation but in fact most of the land within its boundaries is privately owned, even if it does include some fifteen hundred miles of public footpaths. It is the task of the national park authority to enhance our appreciation of the countryside, to preserve natural beauty and to encourage others to respect those who live and work within the area. The latter is not easy – an uncle of mine encountered a party of ramblers on his private land; there was no public footpath through the area and he politely pointed out this to them. Their apparent leader retorted, 'So what? It's a national park, isn't it?'

It is perhaps unfortunate that the word park has so many different meanings – think of car-park, leisure park, business park, science park, game park, deer park – so it is not difficult to understand why some people are confused by the name of national park. Generally, though, the word

park implies a place of recreation, either public or private, and most parks are now geared in some way towards the needs of people.

Far back in history, however, parks were created for animals, deer in particular. Deer parks were the very earliest, being areas of forest appropriated for use by all animals of the chase but particularly deer. The very first was at Woodstock in Oxfordshire, created by Henry I in 1123. (Woodstock was once claimed to be the home of Alfred the Great.) The name comes from the Latin *parcus* or the French *parque*. It was the lawyer Manwood who defined a park as 'a place of privilege for beasts of venery and other wild beasts of the forest, and of the chase.' A park differed from a chase or a warren in that it had to be enclosed and I have an eighteenth-century law dictionary which states that, to constitute a park, the following are required: (a) a grant thereof; (b) inclosures by wall, paling or hedge, and (c) beasts of a park such as doe, buck etc. If all the deer were destroyed, then the area was no longer considered a park. Similarly, if all the fences were removed, it ceased to be a park – it was vital that it did not 'lie open'. Having qualified as a park, the area could then be licensed as such and this had to be done by the king. It was by the king's grant or prescription that an area was designated a park, and no one could create a park without such approval. And, of course, a park could only be dissolved by the king under Letters Patent.

Because a park was such an important area of countryside, it was strongly protected, not only by its boundary fences but also by the law. Lots of offences could be committed by damaging walls, fences or hedges, or by stealing and killing deer and other beasts of venery. They were not, however, governed by that wealth of forest laws which eventually led to the legislation on poaching, but instead were protected by the common law of the country. This was less

ferocious than the forest laws because it allowed ordinary people certain rights within the park, for example taking timber; or allowing pigs to feed there.

Many of London's early parks remain to this day, although their original purpose has been overtaken by modern requirements. Battersea Park, for example, did not appear until Victorian times when the Queen empowered the Commissioners of Woods to form a royal park there. Green Park was enclosed in the reign of Charles II, but in 1717 was reduced in size by George III because he wanted to enlarge the gardens of Buckingham Palace. Hyde Park, perhaps the best known, belonged to the monastery of St Peter, Westminster, and it was enclosed to form a park in 1545. There were cottages here until 1655 and later, Queens Anne and Caroline enclosed further portions. Regent's Park was once afforested and the public were not admitted until 1838, while Victoria Park was another of Queen Victoria's creations. It was formed in 1841 when 290 acres of land were bought at Hackney for transformation into a royal park.

In the north of England there are still many parks, some open to the public and others in private hands. A few retain their original purpose, albeit without the hunting, and one superb example is Studley Royal near Ripon which magnificent park with its herd of deer is renowned across the world. Others include Lambton Park in County Durham, with Blansby Park near Pickering, and Duncombe Park at Helmsley, both in North Yorkshire; others have long since vanished. Now, of course, the national park caters for the public, even if it does not have boundary fences or deer hunting as part of its legal status, attracting visitors rather than huntsmen.

From a police point of view, the influx of visitors has caused some problems – there is an increase in the volume of tourist traffic with the resultant pressure on car-parking space particularly in small villages and narrow lanes; there is a massive increase in the amount of litter; problems with ramblers leaving field gates open so that livestock can stray; visitors getting lost on the moors necessitating search parties; complaints from residents about ramblers peering through their cottage windows or even entering their gardens; thefts from cars parked in picturesque places; damage to wild plants, and vandalism to objects like dry stone walls. Apart from the damage caused by climbing over dry stone walls, lots of tourists seem to think it is perfectly permissible to help themselves to a few stones for their rockeries. This is not so – it is theft with a ten-year imprisonment as a maximum penalty.

There is one story of a tourist in his car stopping to ask a Yorkshireman of the moors for directions back to Middlesbrough. The Yorkshireman noted the other's car was full of things the tourist had looted from the moors – heather, stones and even some flowers and shrubs.

'Can I take this road back to Middlesbrough?' he asked.

'You might as well,' the moorlander retorted. 'You seem to be taking everything else.'

Every store, café, pub, car-park and other attraction within the national park can produce its own hilarious stories of unworldly and ignorant townies and yet those same places recognize the fact they cannot survive without them. Around each Easter, therefore, the residents of the park's pretty villages grit their teeth, repaint their properties and settle down for another long summer of coping with grockles, gaupers and emmets, the private and rather rude names given to the worst of the tourists. It is a fact that many who live in the tourist areas rarely venture out of their homes during the busiest times quite literally, we hand over our countryside to the incomers.

In my time as the village constable of Aidensfield, the police also awaited the tourist season with apprehension.

There was some cheerful anticipation at the thought of seeing pretty women in their summer outfits, but there was more than a little trepidation too. Each year we wondered what problems the new influx of tourists would thrust upon us. It was like waiting to face an outpouring of boisterous children from a school; waves of them bearing down and threatening to swamp anything and everything that stood in their way.

Each year, hordes of tourists descend upon quiet areas in cars, caravans, buses, trains, moor bikes, pedal cycles and even on foot. Individually they are usually charming and delightful. *En masse*, however, they can be terrifying and frustrating, the frustration coming from having to go about one's daily business while they obstruct one's progress on the roads or in the shops. And it happens every day from Easter until the end of October. For the tourists, it is just a day out or perhaps a week's holiday; for the residents it goes on and on for months. It is little wonder that some residents are heartily fed up by the end of the tourist season, even if they have pocketed a useful income from them, it being a fact that many places cannot survive without tourists.

As police officers responsible for the security of several tourist honey-pots, Ashfordly's finest made sure they checked procedures for dealing with lost and found dogs, lost and found children, lost and found ramblers and anything else that might get lost or found, especially with a human aboard such as rubber dinghies being swept out to sea or gliders coming down on remote moorland. It's amazing how irresponsible and stupid some adults can be when on holiday or exploring the countryside.

We made sure we had sufficient 'No Parking' signs and traffic cones to deter motorists who thought they could park anywhere so long as it cost them nothing, and we swotted up our procedures for dealing with any incident that might occur, however rare and unusual it might be, and likewise

11

the regulations which create the multitude of minor offences we might encounter.

For example, it was amazing how many people came to the moors for a holiday, then dropped dead, committed suicide or merely fell off a cliff. It meant that someone, usually the police, had to tidy up after them. The offences we might encounter regularly included dropping litter, various grades of vandalism, malicious damage, truancy, various parking or driving regulation infringements, cycling offences, abuse of noise restrictions, breaking the laws on drinking alcohol, especially in the street, committing a public nuisance (i.e, urinating in the street), the abandonment of animals and animal cruelty or breaching performing animals regulations, or breaking a host of rules governed by numerous 'Ages Fixed by Law' (what one can or cannot do until reaching a certain age). We had to cope with dogs worrying livestock on agricultural land, footway offences, highway regulations, the use of obscene language or obstructing private entrances or farm gates. There were problems with fake charity collections, the theft of wild plants or taking birds' eggs, the civil trespass laws, the rules about using bridleways, bomb disposal procedures (it was amazing how many hikers managed to find unexploded bombs on the moors), brawling in cemeteries, children smoking cigarettes, the misuse of air weapons or other guns, people acting as clairvoyants with intent to deceive, others leaving holiday accommodation without paying – and many, many other matters of a criminal or nuisance value.

I must stress, however, that most tourists and day-trippers were utterly charming and a delight to deal with on a personal level; there was no complaint against them.

On the other hand some were dreadful, the pits of humanity who came to inflict themselves and their doubtful deeds upon our countryside. In between, there were the stupid ones who often caused as much, if not more, chaos than truly obnoxious types. When such visitors arrived at the same time and in the same place, in very large numbers, they were more than a problem, they were a menace. Due to the questionable and unsocial behaviour of a minority, it is not surprising that some visitors are upset by the reception they receive from country dwellers, but they should try to understand the stress placed on rural people, day in, day out, year in year out, by a daily dose of inconsiderate visitors. Quite often, as a policeman, I would find myself acting as a kind of arbitrator between a disgruntled countryman and a bewildered tourist.

Sometimes there were misunderstandings on both sides, sometimes there was anger and blame on both sides, and sometimes it was the fault of either one or the other as the protagonists vented their anger on the first available person. And sometimes, it was no one's fault at all. But, in spite of all our grumbles and grouses, these were all minor hiccups when considered in the full light of the hectic influx of thousands who helped to form the daily routine of a popular national park. In most cases, these hiccups were usually forgotten by the following weekend. Certainly they were forgotten by the next tourist season.

Among the stories that have come my way are the following: a motorist pulled up at my side as I was patrolling the road which runs along the top of West Cliff at Whitby. This is a splendid road with wonderfully extensive sea views and the man climbed from his car to ask, 'Which is the way to the Italian Gardens, Constable?'

'Italian Gardens?' I puzzled. 'There aren't any.'

'Are you new here or something? I know they're here somewhere, on this cliff face.' Clearly the man had a short fuse. 'Really Constable, your bosses should make sure you know your way around before they turn you loose on the street!'

'I do know my way around,' I replied, as calmly as I could. 'I was born nearby and went to school here; I've worked

13

here since I was sixteen and I know there aren't any Italian Gardens.'

'Look,' he said. 'I'm not stupid; it's that new one-way system that's thrown me. They're here somewhere. I've been coming to Scarborough for years and I know the Italian Gardens are up here somewhere, the entrance is from the top of this cliff.'

'This isn't Scarborough.' I smiled as charmingly as I could muster.

He paused and I could see the look of gradual dawning upon his face.

'Not Scarborough?' His voice was quiet now.

'No, this is Whitby. There are some Italian Gardens at Scarborough, on the south cliff, but that's twenty miles from here. You're in the wrong town, sir.'

He did not apologize or make any further comment, but merely returned to his car without a word and drove off. I hope he found his way to Scarborough, but even now I find it difficult to understand how he thought he was in Scarborough when all the signposts on the roads heading into town indicated he was approaching Whitby.

That, however, is a small error when compared with an unfortunate couple who hailed me at seven o'clock one summer evening as I sat in my Mini-van on a lofty moorland lay-by. I was collecting messages via my police radio and that was a particularly good place for reception. I had noted the necessary details in my pocket book and was preparing to leave when the small car arrived. It was a Ford Anglia in a shade of pale green and contained two people, a man and a woman who were, I estimated, in their mid-fifties. It eased to a halt only a few yards away and at first, I took little notice of it – lots of drivers pulled into this lay-by for a break, or to allow them time to have a snack, or merely to admire the view.

In this case the man climbed out and, rather stiffly, made his way towards me.

'Excuse me, Constable.' I did not recognize the accent; he was speaking English but I was not familiar with his brogue. 'Is this the way to the coast?'

'Well, sir, it's not a direct route,' I had to warn him. 'But you can reach the coast from here. It's over there,' and I pointed to the distant east. 'You see that horizon beyond the moors? The coast is over there, about thirty-five miles from here. An hour or so's driving once you get on to the main road. I can direct you to the main road from here; once you're on the main road it's a simple route.'

'Another thirty-five miles!' he groaned. 'I'm not sure we could stand that . . . we've been on the road for hours and hours . . . we never seem to get there.'

'Which part of the coast are you heading for?' I asked.

Our Yorkshire coastline is considerable, stretching from the mouth of the River Tees near Redcar in the north to the mouth of the Humber in the south, eighty miles or so as the seagull flies, with the resorts of Whitby, Scarborough, Filey and Bridlington along the way. I wanted to be sure he departed in the right direction.

'St Agnes,' he said, 'We're going to St Agnes.'

For a moment or two I was baffled. To my knowledge, I had never heard of St Agnes, certainly not as a coastal town or village in Yorkshire. Could it be further south, in Lincolnshire, or further north in either Durham or Northumberland?

'I'm sure we don't have a place called St Agnes along our coastline,' I had to tell him.

'Oh yes, there is; it's only a very small village,' he said. 'Very quiet, just as we like it. You get a wonderful view along the coast from the Beacon just above the village and the artist, John Opie, was born there, you know. We're interested in art, you see, and especially his work . . .'

'Have you a map?' I asked.

'No,' he shook his head. 'No, we haven't a map. I never

use a map. We got directions from a friend. It was very simple, she said, just head for the A1 and turn south towards London, then look out for signs for the A30 and follow it all the way.'

'Where is St Agnes?' I asked. 'What's the nearest large town? Do you know?'

'Oh yes, it's between Newquay and St Ives, just off the A30. I've followed the A1, just as she said, but we haven't found London or the A30 yet, but as it's been a long journey – I knew it would be a long journey of course – I thought I'd better get off the A1 and head for the coast. I asked a man the way to the coast at the filling station on the A1 about an hour ago and he said head this way, so here we are.'

'Am I right in thinking you are heading for Cornwall?' I asked with as much sympathy as I could muster.

'Oh yes, definitely. St Agnes is on the northern coast of Cornwall, like I said, between Newquay and St Ives.'

'Have you any idea where you are now?' I asked, hoping to break the news gently.

'Well, no, not really, but if you say the coast is over there, I can't be too far away, can I?'

'This is the North Riding of Yorkshire,' I said. 'The coast over there is the Yorkshire coast, with places like Scarborough and Whitby. You're hundreds of miles from Cornwall, sir; you've come in completely the wrong direction.'

'But . . .' he looked puzzled and almost desperate. 'She said follow the A1 . . . so I did. I found the A1 without any trouble . . .'

'Where have you come from?' I asked.

By gently quizzing him, I discovered he had come from a small village in Norfolk and had been told to head for the A1 near Peterborough, then head south towards London, all the time keeping an eye open for directions to the A30 which led to the south-west from London. And he had set off without a map!

On reaching the A1 at Peterborough, it seems he had turned north instead of south, and had simply kept driving in the hope he would eventually find the signs showing him the way to the A30. Which, of course, he would never find in the north. And a kindly man on the A1, somewhere in the North Riding, had directed him to the coast. Here he was, looking as dejected as a spaniel which had had a bucket of water thrown over it, standing at my side contemplating the fact he was hundreds of miles from his intended destination. I was now faced with a couple who really looked as if they could not face driving another mile.

'Look,' I said hopefully, 'we have some lovely villages along our coastline, Robin Hood's Bay, Runswick Bay, Staithes, all favoured by artists . . . maybe you'd like to visit one of those?'

'Well, yes, we could, I suppose, if we're such a long way from Cornwall . . . I could ring the boarding-house to explain . . .'

'You must be completely worn out, you certainly look extremely tired,' I said. 'It might not be safe to drive any more. Why don't you stay overnight in Ashfordly? That's a market town about four miles from here, and tomorrow you could head for our coast and I'm sure you would find accommodation. And I would suggest you buy yourself a road atlas, so you can find your way to Staithes or Robin Hood's Bay, and then back to Norfolk.'

'I'll have a word with Audrey,' he said, and off he went for a chat with his wife.

They spent a few minutes in a huddle and then he said, with relief in his voice, 'Yes, we've heard such a lot about the Staithes group of artists, but we've never been this far north . . . so, yes, Constable, I think your suggestion is a good one. I don't think I could face another hour's driving.'

17

'A good decision,' I said. 'Just a moment.'

I radioed Alf Ventress in Ashfordly Police Station and said, 'Alf, can you call the Crown? I have a lady and gentleman here looking for good accommodation overnight. A Mr and Mrs. . . .'

'Brandon,' said the man. 'A double room. . . .'

'Hang on, Nick.'

There was a delay of a few minutes as Alf rang the hotel, but he replied with the news that a room was available and I said they'd be there in ten minutes – unless they got lost. In their case, I made sure they didn't, because I provided a police escort for them and led them right to the front door. As we chatted before they entered the hotel, Mr Brandon explained he had never used a map because he worked for the railways – most of his time as a young man had been spent in Norfolk, maintaining the railway lines without travelling away from the county, and even if he'd wanted a day out or a brief holiday, he simply jumped on to a train to make use of his concessionary ticket. That took him to wherever he wanted to be, even if it meant changing trains from time to time. A map was totally unnecessary.

Over the years, he'd never had to learn the geography of England and his short bout of schooling had not provided much help. On the day I met him, even though the signposts showed the way to Scarborough, it had never occurred to him that Scarborough wasn't in Cornwall. I suggested he obtain a map and that he learn to follow the roads by their numbers or follow the direction signs to a major town, rather as he might follow a railway line. He thought he could cope with that. Off they went into their hotel and I wondered where they would end their holiday.

A couple of weeks later, I received a lovely letter of thanks from the Brandons saying how much they'd enjoyed Staithes, Runswick, Whitby, Robin Hood's Bay and the entire Yorkshire coastline in that area. In fact, they were hoping to return next year to explore Scarborough and perhaps Filey – and they had bought a road atlas so they knew what delights lay around them, at every point of the compass.

Having completed that minor example of assistance to the public, it was time to resume my patrol. What lay ahead, I wondered? I had passed my promotion exams for the rank of sergeant; I had passed the promotion board and had even survived a spell of responsibility as acting sergeant, but I was still a constable patrolling my rural beat. What was my future? The truth was I had no idea. All I could do was wait my turn in the queue for promotion, and perform my varied duties to the best of my ability. It could take years – or might never happen at all.

# Chapter 2

I was completing a spell of patrol duty in Ashfordly because the small market town was suffering a shortage of police officers due to one constable being on leave, another being ill with flu and a third away on a refresher course. The sergeant was also away on a one-day Civil Defence course at Headquarters and he was expected back around six. From a police point of view, therefore, I had the town to myself even if I did share it with about 3,000 residents and a growing crowd of tourists.

Mine was a full day's duty comprising eight hours between 9 a.m. and 5 p.m.; I had sandwiches for my lunch at the police station and could pop back there on some pretext if I desperately needed a cup of coffee or a tea break. More than likely I could expect light refreshments from one of the friendly shopkeepers or hoteliers. Apart from a funeral scheduled to take place at the Anglican parish church a 3 p.m. I did not expect to be busy. My chief role was to patrol the town centre and market-place to cope with whatever happened, probably something like a visitor losing a wallet, or one wanting suggestions for bed-and-breakfast accommodation, or even someone anxious to know the history of the castle.

It was a brisk and blustery Tuesday in March, a day of sunshine broken by sudden squally showers whipped into mini-storms by the strong winds, but the pretty town was busy and traffic was pouring in as early as ten o'clock. I found myself having to perform the occasional spell of traffic duty to guide coaches through the traffic-ridden narrow streets, or to threaten some visiting car drivers with a ticket if they persisted in parking in silly places.

It needed just one car to be parked in the wrong place to bring the entire town centre to a halt, particularly when it became busy with buses, lorries and commercial vehicles trying to negotiate the tourist traffic. We knew which places caused the greatest problems. Some drivers actually moved 'No Parking' signs away from their sites in order to park, and we would respond with a ticket or the threat of having their obstructive cars towed away. It was a constant battle against thoughtless motorists but we managed to maintain the upperhand and keep the traffic moving.

On this particular day, however, I was not confronted by any obstreperous drivers and life was quite tolerable, enjoyable even as the cheerful tourists and happy residents went about their daily routines. Around half past ten, I succeeded in being offered a cup of coffee and a chocolate biscuit in the kitchen of a café – an act of generosity which lifted my spirits – and then at half past eleven I had to return to the office for half an hour, just in case the inspector or someone at Sub-Divisional Headquarters wanted to contact me. I had to leave the door open too, just in case a member of the public had any business to transact, such as producing a driving licence or insurance certificate, wanting to report a lost cat or found dog, or have their passport application signed. A notice on the board outside detailed our opening times if we were short staffed.

This visit enabled me to put the kettle on for a second break and, as it was boiling, I busied myself with some reports and paperwork which had to be despatched to Sub-Divisional Headquarters. And then the telephone rang.

'Ashfordly Police, PC Rhea speaking,' I had answered it immediately.

'Good morning, Mr Rhea, this is PC Stainley from Nottingham City Police, Enquiry Office. I have a request message for you.'

Request messages were part of our regular routine. Although there was no obligation for us to deliver these, it was done as a form of courtesy or public service because not every member of the public had a telephone. Most of our request messages were from hospitals asking us to inform relatives that a family member had been admitted due to an accident, or, in some cases, had died unexpectedly. Another regular form of request message came from families who were trying urgently to trace relatives who were on holiday – some of these were even broadcast on national radio, often with the vehicle registration number being given. Usually, of course, the precise reason for the message, or very personal matters were not publicized, the person sought being asked to telephone a relative or local police station for details.

'Right,' I said to PC Stainley. 'Fire away, I've got a pen and some paper.'

'It's from a Mrs Marjorie Carver,' he began, and followed with an address in Nottingham. 'She wants us to tell her husband, John Douglas Carver, that his father, George, has been taken to hospital with a serious illness and his presence is required at home immediately. It's an urgent request because Mr Carver, senior, is not expected to live for more than another forty-eight hours. It seems Mr Carver, junior, is staying at a country cottage in your part of the world. Bankside Cottage, Briggsby. He works for a clothing production company and is drafting a document, a proposal for the company being floated on the Stock Market.'

'I know the cottage,' I assured him. 'It's very remote and peaceful.'

'It seems he wanted somewhere very quiet to complete his work without being interrupted but there's no phone. Can you deliver that message for us?'

'No problem,' I said. 'It's just a couple of miles up the road. I'll go now.'

'Stress the urgency, please, I understand his father's in a very bad way. We got involved because he collapsed in the street.'

'I will,' I assured him and replaced the phone. I rang my Sub-Divisional Office at Eltering to inform them I'd be away for about half an hour while delivering an urgent request message, and said I would let them know when I returned. Moments later, I was in my official Mini-van and heading out of town. For the moment, Ashfordly's traffic would have to cope without traffic guidance from a uniformed arm-waving constable!

I knew my destination. Bankside Cottage was a delightfully rustic cottage tucked away in its own miniature dale on the outskirts of Briggsby. In former times, it had been a gamekeeper's cottage on a local estate. It had then been thatched but had since been re-roofed and modernized by its new owner, a local farmer who had been enterprising enough to purchase surplus cottages from the estate and turn them into holiday accommodation. Access was by an unmade track which was about half a mile long; this meant that Bankside Cottage, whose hillside site was ablaze with daffodils at this time of year, was hidden from view. People passing the road-end, or visiting the village of Briggsby, could not see Bankside; many passers-by and even local people were unaware of its existence. It was the perfect hide-away.

When I arrived, there was a black Hillman Minx parked outside and through a large window I could see a woman in the kitchen, evidently preparing lunch. She noticed my arrival and waved in acknowledgement, and I saw her mouth open and close as if calling to someone to come and attend to me. By the time I had parked and climbed out of my vehicle, a man was standing in the open doorway of the cottage. He was in his late forties, a burly individual in rolled-up shirt sleeves and corduroy trousers with braces. My immediate instinct was that this fellow did not look like a business executive. He looked more like an off-duty slaughterman or a butcher, or even a bouncer at a night club.

'Now then,' he said, as I approached him. 'Summat I can help you with, is there, Constable?'

'Are you John Douglas Carver?' I asked.

'No, that's not me,' he said. 'My name's Morgan. Stan Morgan from Thornaby.'

'Is there a Mr Carver here?' was my next question. 'From Nottingham?'

'No, Constable, there isn't, there's just me and our Josie.'

'When did you arrive?' I was momentarily flustered by this development. I had come to the right address, hadn't I?

'Last Saturday afternoon, and we're here till next Saturday; we have to vacate by half past ten. Why, what's your Mr Carver got to do with it?'

I felt obliged to explain briefly to this holidaymaker who listened carefully as I outlined the story, and he said, 'Well, Constable, all I can offer is to tell your Mr Carver if he turns up here, but I'm not expecting him, I don't know him and wouldn't know him from Adam if I set eyes on him.'

'Clearly there's been some mistake,' I said. 'Sorry to have troubled you, I'll go and have words with the cottage owner; he might know if Mr Carver is expected here or has been in touch.'

'No problem, Constable, sorry we can't be of help but, like I said, if he does turn up, I'll get him to contact his wife without delay.'

The farmer who owned Bankside Cottage was Joe Farrell

of Hazelside Farm in Briggsby and it was only a minute's drive away, so I headed for a chat with him. When I arrived at the farm, Mrs Farrell – Kay – was busy in her kitchen preparing lunch and before I could explain the reason for my presence, said Joe would be in any minute now. Why didn't I wait, and how about a nice cup of coffee, or even a meal if I could spare the time? It was a custom among moorland farmers for them to provide lunch – or dinner as they called it – for anyone who chanced to arrive around noon. I accepted a cup of coffee because the kettle was boiling, but declined Kay's offer of a meal on the grounds I had to do my best to trace Mr Carver. I asked Kay if she could help – she might undertake the administrative matters of their cottages although I didn't like to disturb her when she was in the throes of preparing Joe's meal.

'They came last year, the Carvers,' she told me, without consulting any notes or booking forms, and without breaking off her work. 'Two weeks, around this time of year, just before Easter. From Nottingham.'

'But not this year?' I put to her.

'No, although Mr Carver did ring me up but I had no vacancies for the time he wanted. This week in fact. Bankside was already booked and all my other cottages were full. I put him on to Moortop Cottages, they're at Gelderslack, Mr Rhea, Jane Burnett runs them. Stone Hall Farm. You know it?'

'I do.' I thanked her. 'I'll get myself up there straight away.'

'Why not ring from here? It'll save you a journey if he's not booked in; at least she'll be able to tell you whether he's there or not.'

And so I was shown into Joe's study, one of the ground-floor rooms which was full of paper and buff-coloured forms which seemed to spill everywhere from his ancient rolltop desk. Kay provided me with Jane Burnett's telephone number and I rang it. Being dinner-time, the Burnetts were in; she answered almost immediately.

'Hello, Jane, it's PC Rhea from Aidensfield,' I announced, for I had been to their farm on several occasions. 'I'm ringing from Kay Farrell's at Hazelside, I'm trying to trace a man who might have rented a holiday cottage and Kay thought he might have come to one of yours.'

'Well, yes, Mr Rhea, I'll help if I can. A few of our cottages are occupied already, even before Easter. So who is he?'

'He's called John Douglas Carver, and he's from Nottingham.'

'Yes, I know them, he and Mrs Carver are here, can I deliver the message for you?'

I hesitated. Mrs Carver was here? I thought she was in Nottingham, trying to trace him . . .

'Thanks, but I must deliver it myself,' I explained. 'It's an urgent and personal family matter. Would you know if they're in at this moment?'

'They are, Mr Rhea, I saw them drive past my window not more than ten minutes ago, and then saw the smoke rising from the chimney just a moment or two later, so clearly they intend staying in.'

'I'm on my way,' I said.

Joe Farrell was heading into his house for his meal as I was rushing away, and after a brief explanation of my presence, I left and hurried towards Gelderslack. It was almost a half-hour journey from Briggsby and by 12.30 I was turning into the clean farm yard at Stone Hall, Gelderslack. Jane Burnett was at the window of her kitchen which overlooked the yard. She spotted my arrival and waved me into the house. Like all the farms around here, this was dinner-time and her husband, Jack, was sitting at the table tucking into a mountain of mashed potato, roast beef, carrots and peas. Jane had just filled a plate for herself and was about to join him. I apologized for interrupting their meal.

'Rubbish! Sit down, Nick, Jane'll find you a plate,' invited Jack.

'No thanks, Jack, I've got urgent business with one of your holiday-makers.'

'They're in Rowan Tree Cottage, Nick,' said Jane. 'That's the second one past our barn, down the lane behind here, first turn left.'

And so I continued my quest and within five minutes was walking through a small white wooden garden gate, across a neat lawn and towards a green-painted door with a horse-shoe hanging in the upper centre. A smart Sunbeam Rapier was parked in the lane, so he – or they – was or were at home. I rapped on the door and waited; smoke was rising from the chimney and from within I could hear music play-ing, either from a radio or a record player. No one responded. I wondered if the music had drowned the sound of my knocking and so I repeated it, this time making a good deal more noise, but again no one responded. Had they popped out for a walk?

When a police officer gets no reply from the front door, the next stage is to try the back and so I began to walk back down the path, seeking the way around to the rear of the cottage, but as I walked away, I noticed someone at an upstairs window. They had clearly heard me and were now responding; a woman's face made a fleeting appearance at what was probably the landing window and then retreated. But I knew she had seen me. I returned to the front door, rapped again for good measure and waited.

The door opened and a dark-haired man in his mid-forties appeared; a young woman stood behind him, almost hidden by the shadows of the house. To say both were dishevelled is perhaps an understatement but he looked at me with more than a hint of antagonism in his eyes and said, 'Yes?'

'Mr Carver? John Douglas Carver?' I put to him, following with his Nottingham address.

'What if I am?' He licked his lips. I could almost feel his nervousness and embarrassment. A police officer knocking on your door is usually a sign of impending bad news, but it is infinitely more so when you are on a secret holiday and think your ruse has been secure.

'I'm sorry to have to bring you bad news, Mr Carver, but I have a message from your wife,' I said, stressing the word 'wife'. 'Your father is very seriously ill in hospital and is not expected to live. I have to ask you to contact home immediately.'

'Oh my God . . . oh dear . . . this is dreadful . . . yes, yes, of course, yes, but look Officer, er, this is very embarrassing, I mean, my wife . . . er . . . she doesn't know about er . . . this . . . but how did you find me?'

'We have our methods,' I said, deliberately letting him ponder the meaning of my words and the hidden message they contained. 'But my duty is now over. I'm very sorry to have to be the bringer of bad news like this, but I have delivered the message as requested. I shall report that to Nottingham Police. What you tell your wife is entirely up to you, Mr Carver.'

'There's no phone in this cottage . . .'

'There is a public kiosk in Gelderslack dale, near the chapel, Mr Carver,' and I turned to leave.

When I returned to Ashfordly, I rang PC Stainley in Nottingham and said, 'It's PC Rhea, Ashfordly Police. I have traced Mr Carver as requested, and delivered the message. He said he would contact his family without delay.'

'Thanks,' was his response. 'I can pass that on to his wife.'

Next I rang Sub-Divisional Headquarters to report my return to Ashfordly and said I would spend the following three-quarters of an hour in the office having my sandwich lunch before resuming my patrol. As I munched my ham sandwiches, I speculated that I could have been sitting in a cosy farmhouse kitchen enjoying a full meal of roast beef with all the trimmings, but apart from such enjoyable thoughts, I wondered if I was condoning John Carver's evident adultery. Did that make me party to his deception? Should I have done something to bring his conduct to his wife's notice? The answer is no. His personal behaviour was nothing to do with me.

I told myself I was not a private detective; my job was not to spy on him or to pass judgement about his marital affairs. My job was quite simple – to deliver a request message from his family and I had done that, nothing less and nothing more.

That modest task completed, it would soon be time to return to the streets of Ashfordly to see what other minor dramas awaited.

The only event noted in our diary was a funeral at three o'clock, that of an 80-year-old man called Ivor Barron whom I had not known and who, it seemed, had not lived in Ashfordly since he was a child. No one could recall him.

His funeral should cause no problems, other than a modest amount of traffic control, for an early-turn officer had already set out the necessary traffic cones and 'No Parking' signs. In that way, the entrance to the church had been safeguarded against indiscriminate long-term parking and the hearse could ease to a graceful halt immediately outside the lych-gate. I felt sure Mr Barron would have a smooth send-off.

With most funerals, it had been found through experience, that mourners and officials begin to assemble at the church at least half an hour before the start of the service. If there was something special about the funeral, perhaps if the deceased was a former mayor, bishop, famous person or some other character of renown when a larger than usual congregation was expected, then a greater time might be allowed for the final preparation of the church and grave-yard, for officials to assemble in advance, and for the mourners to arrive in calm circumstances with plenty of car-parking facilities.

Each funeral was dealt with on its merits, and although the police had no formal part in most of them, we did endeavour to be present outside the church or chapel both before and during the service. This was as a matter of cour-tesy and respect, and we did our best to ensure that things progressed with as much decorum as possible. Some might think it was an example of good public relations, designed to enhance the image of the police above all else, while others might think it was a cynical means of ingratiating ourselves with the public. Whatever the public perception of our courtesy role, we found our presence was generally welcomed by members of the deceased's families and by the respective funeral directors and clergy.

With this custom in mind, therefore, I finished my sand-wiches, told Sub-Division I was resuming my town patrol at 2p.m., and sallied forth to supervise the traffic near the church before and during Ivor Barron's funeral. I had plenty of time – the service was scheduled to begin at three o'clock and, to my knowledge, Ivor Barron was not expected to draw a large crowd. No one living locally knew the fellow; my own earlier and very discreet enquiries had shown he was not known to anyone in Ashfordly. He had no relatives in the area and the only thing the vicar could tell me was that the funeral was being organizied by a London firm of undertakers and that the dear departed had always expressed a desire to be buried in Ashfordly. He had been born here eighty years earlier but had left when he was five – return visits for holidays and the occasional business trip had cemented his love for his home countryside and even though he had lived away from Ashfordly for most of his life, he had asked to be buried here. And apart from that, the vicar knew very little.

The grave had been prepared by the Ashfordly gravedigger upon specific orders from the London undertakers, flowers had arrived at the church at their command too, the hymns had been chosen and notified by them and an Order of Service printed with his favourite music. And so, when I arrived outside the church just after 2p.m. for my first recce, I did not expect to see much activity. How wrong I was.

As I approached, I noticed a highly polished and large black limousine parked lengthways across the road, effectively blocking both carriageways of the rather narrow road a few yards from the church entrance. Two burly men were standing near it; each was dressed in a black suit, white shirt, black tie, black bowler hat and dark sunglasses. My immediate thought was – undertakers! My second was that their car had broken down as they were trying to turn it around in the middle of the road, and that it was marooned there. I was wrong in both cases.

'Problems?' I walked towards the two men. 'Shall I call a garage?'

'No problems, Constable,' replied one of them with a brief and rather thin smile. His London accent sounded very strong and rather out of place in this rural Yorkshire setting. 'No problems at all.'

His companion was waving his arms like a traffic policeman, guiding oncoming cars down a side road past the church. It led around the rear of the premises, past the graveyard and back on to the main road beyond. I noticed vehicles coming in the opposite direction too – clearly these characters had established their own traffic diversion system.

'But you can't leave that car there,' I said. 'It's blocking the road.'

'That's what it's there for, Constable.' The thin and

rather cruel smile was repeated. 'And if you walk around the corner past the church, there's another just like this, blocking the road from that side. We're keeping the church frontage clear for a funeral, you see. We don't want no incomers nicking our parking spaces, if you understand my meaning. And we're keeping other traffic on the move.'

'But the parking area's already been coned off. You can't do this, you can't block a road like this and set up your own diversion!'

'Constable, my son, we're taking no chances and we can do what we like. We'll clear the road when the funeral's over, then we'll go. No problems, like I said.'

'But you're obstructing the highway.' I tried to sound authoritative. 'You've got to get permission to close a road—'

'We gave ourselves permission, Constable. Now, if you want this funeral to go ahead without any fuss or bother, leave it to us. We'll cause no fuss, we just want Ivor to be buried in style, like I said, with no bother.'

'So who are you?' was my next question. I was already beginning to feel out of my depth here. I knew I had recourse to the Road Traffic Act and its wealth of powers; I could ask for their driving licences; I could book the drivers for obstructing the highway; I could ask for their insurance certificates . . . but this was a funeral when a sense of decorum must prevail. I had to try and find some middle ground, some acceptable compromise. 'So who are you?' I repeated.

'Friends of the deceased,' grinned the spokesman of the pair.

'Look' – I tried to be accommodating – 'I've no wish to be awkward especially as this is a funeral, but you can't take the law into your own hands—'

'Then push off, Constable, and leave us to see to things. You've no need to be here . . . we'll get Ivor into the church on time. We've seen to the parking arrangements for the

32

hearse and the flower cars, and the mourners – they're on their way now – so why don't you just go for a long walk and forget all about us?'

'I'm supposed to be on duty here, to make sure the funeral goes ahead without any problems.'

'Then you can take time off, we'll see to everything. We're in control. As I said, there are no problems, and there won't be, not with us in charge.'

I decided to walk around the church to see precisely what these characters had done, and at the other side, just out of sight of the first car, another large and highly polished limousine was parked lengthways across the carriageways with another two men nearby. Like the first pair, they were dressed in black suits, white shirts, black ties, black shoes, black sunglasses and black bowler hats. One of them was guiding oncoming traffic up a side road which I knew would take them back into town along a minor road which ran behind the church grounds. And the drivers of those diverted cars did not appear to be object-ing – they saw the obstruction with a man apparently in charge and seemed happy enough to drive around it. I began to think I was superfluous because I realized that our own official traffic cones had been removed. The road in front of the church was now totally clear on both sides, and there was ample overflow parking in the adjoining side streets. By now, of course, people in the local shops and offices were taking an interest, peering out of windows and doorways to watch these unusual proceedings. Not quite knowing what to do, I decided I should speak to the vicar or someone else who might be officiating inside the church.

I entered the churchyard through a side gate and made my way into the church. The organist was playing softly, rehearsing some of the music, and the interior was a mass of flowers where wreaths and bouquets had been placed along

33

each side of the wide aisle. It was more like the setting for a wedding than a funeral, but I found the vicar in the organ loft where he was discussing the final arrangements with the organist. Another man was there with them and he wore a dark suit, a black tie and white shirt, but no sunglasses and no bowler hat.

I had not previously met the Ashfordly vicar who had been here for some six months, but when he saw me, he moved away from the side of the lady organist to greet me.

'Gerald Benham,' he introduced himself.

'PC Rhea, Aidensfield,' I told him. 'I'm working in Ashfordly today.'

'Ah, good. Well, things seem to be going very well,' he smiled. 'Everything's in hand. I'm expecting the cortège to arrive about two minutes to three and the church will be full before that time.'

He checked his watch; it was quarter past two.

'You know the road outside here is closed?' I put to him. 'Some so-called friends of the deceased have taken it into their heads to block off the entire road around the south side of the church—'

'Don't interfere, Constable Rhea.' At this stage the other man came forward. 'I'm Detective Superintendent Eric Radcliffe, Scotland Yard,' and he extended his hand for me to shake.

'Oh, I see, well, good afternoon, sir, but I'm not quite sure what's going on.'

'Then let them get on with it, lad,' he smiled. Radcliffe was an affable character with a ready smile and a round, friendly face with dark-brown eyes. 'That's the advice I've given to Mr Benham, and that's the advice I'm now giving to you. By all means hang around to watch events, but don't try to get these characters to do as you wish: let them do what they want. It will work, you'll see. There'll be no problems.'

'So who are they?' was my next question, an obvious one.

'The Barrons,' he said. 'Gangsters from the East End. A big family of them. They're into protection rackets, drugs, prostitution, illegal supply of firearms – you name it, they're involved. Here, they will all dress exactly the same, that's to prevent us identifying them in any photographs. They know some of our men will be around hoping to see just which faces are here, it's one of the few occasions, like a wedding, where the whole family get together. They will whizz in very soon in their motorcade, see Ivor into his grave in what they regard as style, and then rush off in their limousines. I'm here to observe. They know I'm here, but it's their day: I won't interfere, and I won't upset them during a funeral, they know that.'

'You mean our local man, Ivor Barron, was a gangster?'

'He was. He was first cousin of the boss, the only family member living up north, an only child. He was taken down south as a boy and nurtured into their "family business" as you might call it. He became one of London's top gangsters. They reckon he killed ten or twelve rivals but we could never prove it.'

'I'm surprised I've never heard of him,' I said. 'The name meant nothing to me.'

'You wouldn't hear anything. They never go to court; we can never pin anything on them, and nothing they do ever gets into the newspapers. It's a family business which, quite literally, is kept under wraps. Not even the Income Tax authorities know what they do. They deal in cash, and nothing's ever put in writing. They're clever, Constable. So let them bury Ivor, it was his last wish to come back here. The minute it's over, they'll set off back to London. There'll be no funeral tea here, but they'll have some kind of celebration of his life in Soho tonight.'

Having been informed of this most unusual of developments, I returned to the street outside which was still totally devoid of cars.

'All right, Constable?' called the man to whom I had first

spoken when he noticed my reappearance.

'Yes, everything's all right,' I said, walking towards him. 'There's no problem.'

'That's just how we like it,' he said. 'We don't like problems.'

'It's odd that Ivor would want to return here after spending all his life in London.' I tried to make polite conversation.

'He always was an old softie, you know, a country lad at heart. You know he kept hundreds of hens on his spread outside London? Amazing, really. All the old ladies living nearby used to be given fresh eggs; he was very generous, was Ivor. Wouldn't take a penny for them. He gave eggs to the local hospital an' all. He reckoned eggs were very healthy, well, they didn't do him any harm, did they?'

He chatted amiably about Ivor and his country ways but never revealed anything of his criminal background. Then things began to happen. There was the toot of a car horn from the other waiting car, and the men near me sprang into action. Quite suddenly, like the leader in a procession of royal cars, a huge gleaming black Rolls Royce hearse cruised into sight followed by many other cars. The roof of the Rolls was covered in wreaths and so was every inch of spare space inside, beside and above the coffin. It was followed closely by five other hearses, none of which contained a coffin, but all of which had been adapted to carry wreaths. And then came the mourners' cars, all black, all polished and all cruising with people inside. There were dozens of the smart cars, just like a royal motorcade. I stood aside, beyond the limousine parked across the road and watched as the coffin-bearing hearse eased to a halt outside the lych-gate with the others behind. Black-suited men seemed to appear from nowhere and soon they were guiding the other cars into a parking slot. They did not park at either side of the road but parked in the centre, nose to tail and side by side until the entire area outside the church looked like the starting grid of a Grand Prix. But it was all done with great expertise and no fuss; people climbed out of the cars, brushed their clothes and went straight into the church. It seemed to me that the entire churchyard and area around it was full of men in black suits, dark glasses and bowler hats, with women in black suits and black hats too. At a signal from one of the men, I could hear the organ beginning to play and then the coffin was removed from the hearse by a team of eight bearers, all in black suits, dark glasses and bowler hats.

Once everyone was seated, the wreath-covered coffin was carried inside in what could only be described as a regal manner. The moment it entered the church, the door was closed and now it was time to carry the hundreds of wreaths into the churchyard. A space had been set aside for them; for a while, they would swamp the modest graveyard.

And so the funeral service of one of London's major villains got underway as I moved among the parked cars, all black, all polished and all magnificent. I had another chat with the man I'd met at the beginning; his role as the service proceeded was to patrol among the mourners' cars just to ensure their safety. He told me that when it was over, he would move his own vehicle to one side, and the entire procession would re-form for the return journey to London. They would all travel together, just as they had arrived, in procession.

The service and interment took almost an hour. From my vantage point, I saw the mourners leave the church and congregate in the churchyard for the final part of the ceremony, and then it was time to leave. They filed out, spent very little time in conversation, and returned to their vehicles. As they had arrived, the hearse was first to leave, moving slowly away to allow the others time to move into position behind; then the flower cars assembled and finally, once everyone was aboard their own vehicles, the signal was given and the whole gathering began to move. It was done in a very orderly manner as my first contact waved them one by one into the town and along the narrow road which led behind the church and back out towards the A1, some miles away.

Meanwhile all other traffic had been halted and so the funeral party left in a smooth operation. I had no complaints from members of the public about this disruption to the town's routine. Detective Superintendent Radcliffe waved from the window of his car as he joined the motorcade, and finally, as the last car was departing, the man to whom I had first spoken came across and said, 'Thanks, Constable, a nice job. No problems.'

'I did nothing,' I shrugged. 'You had it all organized.'

'That's how we do things,' he grinned. 'No problems. Here, this is for you, a thank you.'

And suddenly he stepped forward and pushed something into the breast pocket of my tunic. It was a wad of notes. Pound notes by the look of them.

'No,' I said. 'I can't . . . I can't accept anything . . . I did nothing anyway . . .'

'Exactly,' he said. 'You did just as we wanted. Everything went very smoothly; Ivor would have been chuffed. And you are honest . . . now that's mighty rare where I come from!'

'But I can't take money for this, not for anything,' I insisted.

'You've a charity back at your nick?'

'Yes, the Police Widows, it's the North Riding Police Widows' Supplementary Pension Fund.'

'Then give it to them, Constable. With our compliments. Ivor would be pleased about that as well. He had a soft spot for widows and old ladies. Now I must go. Thanks for a very pleasant afternoon.'

And he left to catch up with the others and suddenly, the

little town returned to normal. People went back into their shops, offices and homes, traffic began to flow and I was left with memories of a strange afternoon.

Furthermore, I had £200 in my pocket. I was determined not to keep it one minute longer than necessary and, at the first opportunity, I placed it firmly in our collecting box. I would make sure I told the sergeant about it the moment he returned; I felt we should bank it as soon as possible and get a receipt, if only for my own peace of mind. After all, it represented about ten weeks' work for me!

But was the money the proceeds of crime? Or stolen property? Or just something given in gratitude by the family of a loved one? Whatever its source, I would never find out and lots of our police widows would gain some benefit. I felt Ivor Barron, a local lad, would be pleased about that.

# Chapter 3

Police officers working in a popular tourist area inevitably find themselves dealing with masses of lost and found property. People are always finding things which, it is suggested, indicates others are always losing things. I think more property is lost than is reported found. Quite often, people find things in the street and adopt the notion that 'Finder's keepers' and do not report it to the authorities, i.e. the police. 'Finder's keepers' is not a strictly true adage because the finder of an object has a legal obligation to take reasonable steps to trace the owner. To keep a valuable item of found property without taking reasonable steps to trace the loser could open the finder to a charge of theft.

Clearly, the nature of the object and the place it was found – and perhaps the circumstances of the finding – determine what those steps should be. A person who finds a penny in the street has a much reduced obligation than, say, a person who finds a briefcase full of valuable jewellery in a restaurant. The 'reasonable' steps taken to trace the owner must therefore vary greatly and the most simple means of fulfilling that obligation is to report the matter either to the police or to some other responsible authority, like a bus company, owner of the restaurant or proprietor of premises where the object was found.

This was particularly evident to serving police officers in the 1960s when a considerable proportion of their daily work involved the recording of lost and found property. Large registers were maintained and police stations were equipped with a 'Found Property' cupboard or room which housed a bewildering assortment of junk. At times, the shelves of such places looked like second-hand stores or even cheap antique shops and periodically the place would be cleared of unclaimed items which were sold at auction, the income being paid into official funds.

During the height of the tourist season, officers who worked in seaside resorts and other places popular with day-trippers and holiday-makers were swamped with reports of both lost and found property – reports of lost property included the normal quota of wallets, handbags, purses, umbrellas, cameras, binoculars, sweaters, sandals, spectacles and money, either in notes or coins, but in addition people reported the loss of other odd objects. A bus driver once reported to me that he had lost his bus – it hadn't been stolen, he'd just forgotten where he had parked it. Another man reported losing a lamp post – he had bought it an at auction thinking it might enhance his garden, then carried it away over his shoulder. He then parked it outside a café whilst he had lunch inside but had then forgotten it was there and walked off without it. When he realized he'd left it behind, he went back to find it but couldn't recall the route back to the café in question. By the time he located the café, his lamp post had disappeared and it was never found. So was it lost or stolen? Who can say? A similar incident involved a lady pensioner who had left a loaf of bread in a café – it had gone when she returned to retrieve it and she reported the disappearance. A loss? Or a theft? Who knows? If you found a loaf, what reasonable steps would you take to trace the owner? Or if you found a stray lamp post? A very simple response in these cases would be to inform the café proprietor and police respectively.

Not surprisingly, we had to cope with mountains of found property, sometimes of the most amazing kind. When I was a young constable at Strensford, for example, the items reported to me as found property during just one summer season included such diverse objects as a brassière size 34B, a pair of mens' trousers, a set of false teeth, a fresh salmon, a gold-nibbed Waterman's fountain pen, a starting pistol, dozens of cameras, hundreds of wallets and purses, a folding chair and a motor car spare wheel. More surprisingly, not one of those objects was reported lost. How on earth can anyone lose something like their trousers or a starting pistol without making some kind of fuss about it?

In addition to the mundane, however, there was always the exotic – people would find unexploded bombs on the moors or beneath their gardens; they would uncover skeletons of human beings while excavating the foundations of their new home or its extension or they would find, while improving their old house, buried treasure in the form of hidden coins or silver plate. When these incidents came to our notice, most were dealt with in a very professional and acceptable manner and I know the police made great efforts to restore found items to their legal owners.

This kind of supplementary work formed a considerable part of my rural constabulary duties and if one factor emerged from that work, it was that the majority of people are surprisingly honest. Sadly, however, there are always dishonest people around and it is not unknown for a thief to find a wallet or handbag and remove any cash before throwing away the wallet or handbag. A more honest person might then find it and take it to the police station – only to be accused of stealing the contents if the owner was traced. For that reason, and to prevent allegations of dishonesty by the police, the contents of all purses, wallets, handbags, suitcases and other containers are thoroughly checked in front of witnesses. We have to safeguard ourselves as well as the honest finders.

We were not concerned with property lost or found in private places such as hotels or shops, nor did we want to know about things lost or found on buses and trains unless, of course, it was something like a machine-gun, hand grenade or deadly poison, or if it might be the proceeds of crime. There were special procedures for dealing with lost and found objects like guns, explosives, poisons, medicines, cheque books, keys, jemmies, confidential papers and anything of an unusual nature. For example, a wedding album was once found in a bus shelter and we traced the owner through publicity in the local newspaper. There were also procedures for dealing with perishable objects, and clearly the precise action depended upon the nature of the object in question. A found bar of chocolate might not receive the same treatment as a piece of wet fish.

If an ordinary thing was found, say a £1 note, with no indication of the loser's address, we would persuade the finder to retain the money for three months. If it was not claimed within three months, then the finder had a right to it.

One thing that puzzles many members of the public is the distinction between lost and found property. If someone finds something, it is found. If someone loses something, it is lost. That is very simple to understand. One cannot take lost property into a police station. If its lost, it is lost and wouldn't be available to take to the police. Thus the police maintain two registers, one for lost property and the other for found property. We've had countless verbal battles over this simple issue! People will insist upon handing in 'lost' property – if it's being handed in, surely it is found?

And so it was, against this background of lost and found objects, that I received a telephone call from a lady living in Crampton. It was half past nine one fine and dry Thursday morning and I was about to depart, in my Mini-van, on a patrol of my beat in the communities around Aidensfield. Her call was therefore very well timed; she could be my first customer of the day.

Mrs Mary Morton, who lived at No. 5 in a row of terraced houses near Crampton Hall, told me she had found a wedding cake. It was on the wall which ran behind the telephone kiosk in the village.

'A real one?' I asked with some surprise.

'Yes,' she said. 'It's lovely, all covered with white icing and silver horseshoes. There's just the one tier, though, and no candles so it's not a birthday cake.'

'Is it in good condition? What I'm asking is whether it has been thrown away or discarded for some reason.'

'No, it's beautiful,' she said. 'Brand new by the look of it. That's why I thought I'd better report it.'

'Right,' I said. 'I'm about to leave my office on patrol so I'll come straight down to Crampton to see you. Where's the cake now? Did you bring it home?'

'No, it's quite heavy and besides, I thought I'd better leave it where it was in case someone came looking for it.'

'Very sensible,' I said. 'I'll be there in ten minutes.'

As I drove towards Crampton, I tried to recollect whether I'd heard of any forthcoming weddings in the locality but could not recall any, but there were several ladies in the district who made and decorated cakes for weddings, birthdays, christenings and other celebrations. It was possible such a lady had inadvertently left it behind, perhaps when rearranging her car boot after making a telephone call?

Why else would a brand-new wedding cake be left sitting on a stone wall in a quiet Yorkshire village?

On my way to Mary's house I passed the telephone kiosk in Crampton and sure enough, there was the splendid white-iced cake on a low wall which adjoined it. I halted to look at it; standing on a square base covered with silver foil, it was square shaped with sides about fifteen inches long (45cm) and it was about four inches (10 cm) high. It was covered with pure white icing with decorated edges, corners and base, and there was a silver-coloured horseshoe at one side of the upper portion and a silver-coloured bell at the other. In my opinion – and I was no expert on such cakes – it looked very new indeed. The kiosk in Crampton was not directly outside the tiny shop-cum-post office but I decided to ask in case anyone knew the story surrounding this cake. When I went in, the shopkeeper, Stuart Cannon, smiled and said, 'I can guess why you're here, Nick. The cake on the wall.'

'Right,' I said. 'Any ideas? Where's it come from? Who does it belong to?'

'Search me.' He spread his arms in a gesture of bafflement. 'Mary Norton spotted it just after nine and told me, but I've no idea where it's come from. She's left it there in case anybody comes back to collect it.'

'Well, at least the weather's fine; it's not getting rained on or blown off its perch,' I laughed. 'The question is whether I take it into custody for safe-keeping or let it remain there in case someone comes to collect it. It might have been put there especially for a customer to pick up, one of the local cake-makers might have come to that arrangement.'

'It would have been safer inside the kiosk,' he said. 'At least it would be secure from the weather, or any birds that might fancy a peck at it, or better still, it could have been left here for collection. We're open all day; it's the sort of thing we often do; we're often asked to look after things temporarily, like someone's door key.'

'I'll leave it where it is for now,' I told him. 'I'm going to see Mary, she's made an official report of finding it so if it's not claimed in three months, it's hers.'

'Well, seeing she's been married for about thirty years, she won't have much use for it. But I'm sure it will find its owner – somebody must be missing it! Folks don't make wedding cakes unless there's a good reason. Like a wedding.'

Mary was a white-haired lady in her fifties, an affable woman with a ready smile. She invited me into her comfortable home with its blazing fire and, without asking me, produced a cup of tea and a plate of buttered scones. I settled down to enjoy them – at times like this, the work of a village constable was very pleasant indeed.

Mary's husband, Len, worked for Crampton Estate on the maintenance side and their cottage also belonged to the estate; their three children were now grown up and had left home to work in various parts of England and so Mary, who had worked in the big house from time to time as a general maid, now found time to relax at home. She did, however, perform dozens of small tasks for the community. She cleaned the village hall, for example, helped with the flowers for the church, took it upon herself to remove litter from the streets and even swept and cleaned the telephone kiosk That's how she had come to find the cake. Armed with her brush, shovel and duster she had gone to clean the kiosk and had made her remarkable discovery.

I listened to her tale and jotted the salient details in my official notebook, then said, 'Well, Mary, I'm going to treat this as a case of found property. I'm also going to ask you to retain it for three months which means if it's not claimed, it becomes yours.'

'Oh, but that would be dishonest, Mr Rhea; it's not mine, you see.'

'On the contrary, Mary, it's very honest,' I explained. 'You've done the honest thing by reporting it. Stuart in the shop knows about it, word will obviously spread around the village and, if necessary, we could place notes in the shop or even the kiosk to say it's in safe hands. If someone does come looking for it, it'll be better here in the village than down at Ashfordly Police Station. And it will keep for three months, won't it?'

'Oh, yes, I'm sure it will. It's a fruit cake, I had a look underneath, it'll probably improve with keeping anyway.'

'Well, I think it would be better in your care, Mary, that's if you have space to store it. If we leave it outside, it could be attacked by birds or animals, or damaged by the weather, knocked off the wall and smashed into little pieces, or stolen . . .'

'Well, yes, there's plenty of room in my pantry, Mr Rhea, and if the loser comes here I can return it. So yes, I would-n't mind doing that.'

'Thanks. Well, I'll go and pick it up and run it round here in my van. Personal delivery! Then, as I said, if it's not claimed within three months, it's yours.'

'Well, I'm not sure what I can do with such a nice wedding cake, Mr Rhea, but I suppose I could raffle it for charity or donate it to the church or something.'

'Brilliant, yes. Anything like that.'

And so the deed was done. I transported the cake to Mary's house and she assured me it would be safe in her pantry. I said I would have a word with one of the local news-papers to see if they would print an article about the mystery cake in the hope the loser would make an effort to recover it, and I assured her I would also inform Stuart in the shop so that he knew where its temporary home would be. He said he would place a notice in his window asking the loser to contact Mary and so, between us, we did our best to trace the owner of the cake. Mary had contacts with most of the local cake-makers and said she would pass the word around them, just in case one of them, or one of their customers, had mislaid it. I thanked her for her public spiritedness and went on my way.

A couple of days later I managed to have words with a reporter from the *Gazette* who said she would print a tale; she might even persuade a photographer to take a picture of the cake on its original wall and so began our efforts to trace the loser of this lovely piece of confection. The press ran a nice story about it, complete with a photograph of the cake sitting on the wall near the kiosk, and we managed, between us, to mention it to all the known cake-makers in the district.

In spite of the efforts of Mary Morton, Stuart in the shop, various other villagers, the local press and myself, no one came forward to claim the wedding cake – if there had been a wedding, of course, it would have happened long ago. Three months later, therefore, I had the pleasure of returning to Mary's neat little house to formally state that the cake was now hers to do with as she wished. She was most insistent that she did not want it for herself – she felt she had no right to it – but she had not forgotten her earlier vow to offer the cake for a charitable purpose. Clearly in the interim weeks, she had been thinking about the cake's destination because she told me she would consider various options before committing herself to its disposal.

It would be a few weeks later when my wife and I received an invitation to Crampton Hall to celebrate the Diamond Wedding of Jessie and Donald Newton. I had no real connection with either of that couple, although I knew they had formerly worked for Lord and Lady Crampton on the local estate. Now, both in their eighties, the Newtons lived in retirement in one of the Crampton properties and, according to the invitation, we were invited to join Lord and Lady Crampton, the Newtons and friends from the village to celebrate their sixtieth wedding anniversary. The celebration was only for a couple of hours' duration because of the frailty of the old couple – it was from 6 p.m. until 8 p.m. with drinks and light refreshments. I was puzzled as to why we had received this invitation, for I did not associate it with what became known as the Crampton wedding cake.

When Mary and I arrived, it all became evident. Mary Morton told us that the old couple had no family and no one with whom to celebrate their diamond wedding. And so Mary had realized the unwanted cake would make an ideal focus for a celebration; she'd spoken to Lord and Lady Crampton's secretary and put forward the idea of a short party in the Hall, with all the village invited – and it would be complete with wedding cake.

And so the Crampton wedding cake became part of local folklore; almost everyone in the village had a small piece of it. In that respect, it was just like a real wedding. But to this day, no one knows how that cake came to be sitting unwanted on top of a wall near the telephone kiosk.

Another rather bizarre incident involved property which went missing after the sale of some house contents in Elsinby. The former owner was Eric Hinchley, a widower in his early eighties. His wife had died five or six years earlier and following Eric's death, his two sons and one daughter decided to sell the contents of the house, and then the house itself. As they all lived in distant and different parts of England, each being a considerable way from the village, they had no use for their former home and so it, and everything it contained, was offered for sale in two separate lots.

Prior to the sale of the house contents, they removed the various items Eric had left to them individually in his will – family heirlooms and such – and the remainder, much of it rubbish, cheap furniture and gardening equipment if one is honest, was due to be sold one Saturday in March. The day of the sale began with a clear and frosty morning; the lots were made available for viewing both around the exterior and interior of the house and, as always on these occasions, the event attracted considerable interest. Antique dealers were guaranteed to attend in the hope they would find something remarkable – as they often did – but ordinary folks from the surrounding area also came to buy things which caught their fancy. The fact it was a fine, dry and sunny day ensured a good attendance, with many of the viewers making a day of it by having, in advance of the sale, a meal and a few drinks in the local pub, the Hopbind Inn.

It never failed to surprise me how or why people bought second-hand furniture, kitchen utensils and garden tools at prices approaching those they would pay for new goods. Perhaps they thought they were getting a bargain? But these sales always generated a huge amount of interest and lots of good-humoured bidding and buying, along with some extra-mural wheeling and dealing. I was on duty that Saturday and made most of the opportunity to view the goods, but the only things which caught my fancy were six miniature oil paintings by a local artist called George Dowkes. He had died just before the Second World War and I thought his portrayal of remote moorland scenes was wonderful; each of these gems was about six inches long by four inches wide, all with simple wooden matching frames and all signed by the artist. Antiques of the future? Although I knew very little about art, I liked the look of these paintings and considered they could become collectables at some future date. Providing nothing untoward happened, such as an incident which demanded my official presence, I would return for the sale, ostensibly to deal with any traffic problems which might occur on the narrow lane outside but also to make a modest bid for those miniatures. Among the clutter for sale I spotted an ancient woodworm-ridden grandfather clock with a white painted face, date dial and seconds hand, although I had no intention of making a bid chiefly because we had nowhere to place another grandfather clock in our rather cramped police house.

I'd already managed to buy one cheaply a few years earlier at such a sale. At that time, though, grandfather clocks – or long case clocks to give them their formal name – were largely unwanted. They could be bought for £4 or £5 at this kind of house sale and indeed many were left unsold, only to be chopped up for firewood. How things have changed! Some of those old clocks which ended their days as kindling sticks for lighting fires would now be worth several thousand pounds. There were times I wished I had dry, and spacious outbuildings in which to store unwanted longcase clocks!

After my lunch, therefore, I motored down to Eric's former home at Ghyllside Cottage, parked in an adjoining field along with other hopefuls, and made my way to the sale. The auctioneer had established a platform on the patio outside the house with his clerk's desk alongside, plus an army of assistants to identify the lots, move them when sold and generally ensure that the operation was efficient. It was that aspect of sales that intrigued me, particularly in rural areas. I'd attended one or two farm sales and had seen the auctioneer knock down lot after lot to different bidders after nothing more than nods of their heads. Very rarely were names mentioned – the auctioneer and his assistant or clerk seemed to know the identity of most bidders and buyers without anyone having to identify themselves, and although this appeared to be a recipe for confusion when it came to paying and taking possession of one's purchases, the expected problems never arose. From time to time, of course, with strangers attending on occasions, names were mentioned, often with an address of some kind even if it was merely a village name. Like Jacobson, Aidensfield.

At farm sales especially, I had also heard lots knocked down to farmsteads rather than people – I'd seen ploughs and other implements knocked down to something like 'Brock Rigg Farm' or a fine herd of milking Friesans or store pigs being sold to 'Pasture House' rather than the name of the people concerned. Despite all that potential for confusion, people got what they bidded for and the auctioneer received due payment. I am sure the proceedings at auction sales are much more efficient than they appear to an outsider like myself.

The late Eric Hinchley's belongings featured in such a sale. There was the anticipated large crowd, some there merely as spectators, so I established myself close to an exit in case I had to make a hurried departure. Prompt at two, the auction began. All the contents of the house had now been brought outdoors and arranged around the garden in order of their lot number.

Lot No. 1 was a fine chest of drawers in polished mahogany and the attendants held this aloft so that all were reminded of its splendour and appeal. In his booming voice, Rudolph Burley, our local auctioneer, began the sale. He went on to say, 'Lot number one, ladies and gentleman, a fine set of mahogany drawers, late Victorian, five drawers in perfect condition, all with knobs . . . what am I bid? Who will start me at two pounds? Two pounds? All right. One pound seventeen and six . . . one pound seventeen and six . . . thank you, sir, one pound seventeen and six I am bid . . . one pound eighteen . . . one pound eighteen ... one pound eighteen I am bid ... ah, nineteen. One pound nineteen shillings ... one pound nineteen shillings ... two pounds to my left. Two pounds I am bid ... two pounds from the gentleman on my left ... a bargain at the price, ladies and gentleman, a very smart piece of furniture ... two pounds ... two guineas ... two guineas I am bid ...'

And so the proceedings got underway beneath the blue afternoon skies. Midway through the afternoon, the grandfather clock was hoisted high by a pair of sturdy attendants but I did not dare to make a bid. It was sold to someone called Green at Howe Farm for the princely sum of £7 and all I had to hold my attention now was that set of Dowkes miniatures. I stood in my quiet corner as lot after lot was sold and then it was the turn of my set of paintings. I'd once bid for a set of Brontë novels in similar circumstances and surprised myself by buying them. Then things began to happen.

'A fine set of miniatures by a renowned local artist,' boomed Rudolph. 'Six miniatures of the moors, in oil, all signed and all with matching frames. Dowkes is one of our best known local artists who died just before the war. Very collectable. What am I bid?'

No one volunteered a bid. I dare not start the proceedings because I had no idea of their value but then a woman came in with a bid when Rudolph got down to 'Five shillings.'

'Five shillings I am bid, five shillings ... five ... any advance on five. Five and sixpence? Five and sixpence ... thank you, sir. Now six shillings ... six shillings ... sir, yes. The gentleman with the brown trilby ... six shillings ... this is a give-away price ... a paltry six shillings for six fine original oil paintings ... six shillings. Any advance on six shillings?'

I decided I could afford at least ten shillings or even one

pound for this collection but, being relatively inexperi-enced at auctions decided not to join the bidding just yet. I wanted to test whether or not they were worth my ten bob – and the only way was to see whether anyone else was prepared to bid that kind of money. And they did. In fact the bidding went quickly up to ten shillings and so I entered the fray at ten shillings and sixpence. Half a guinea!

'Ah,' smiled Burley. 'Constable Rhea is bidding ten shillings and sixpence . . . ten and six I am bid . . . any advance on ten and six . . . eleven to the gentleman in the brown trilby . . . eleven shillings . . . eleven and six anyone. Yes, PC Rhea. Eleven and sixpence to our village constable. Eleven and six I am bid . . .'

Before I knew it, I was bidding one pound and then one guinea for the paintings and I had to make a rapid mental calculation of the amount of cash in my pocket as the man in the brown trilby pushed the bids ever higher at sixpence a time. I calculated I had a few pence more than thirty shillings in my pocket . . . one pound ten shillings is the equivalent of £1.50 in modern decimalized money and so, in a moment of rashness I decided to make one final bid of thirty shillings. That was £1 10s.0d. It was a lot of money for a village constable with four children to feed. But the man in the brown trilby caught Rudolph's eyes and beat me to that bid; it went to him.

I became aware of Rudolph saying, 'Thirty shillings I am bid . . . thirty shillings for these lovely miniatures . . . thirty shillings to the gentleman in the brown trilby . . . going once . . .'

'One and a half guineas,' I called, simultaneously raising my hand to ensure I was spotted by the auctioneer. 'One pound eleven and sixpence.'

I must have exuded a look of sheer determination because the man in the brown trilby indicated he wished to make no further bids nor did anyone else. I wondered if the uniform had any bearing on the fellow's decision not to compete? I hoped not! Then I heard Rudolph calling, 'One and a half guineas I am bid . . . one and a half guineas from PC Rhea . . . one and a half guineas . . . going once, going twice. . . .' Then bang! Down came the gavel and I found myself the proud owner of a fine set of Dowkes miniatures.

I decided not to wait until the end of the auction; I had achieved my purpose and had shown a uniformed police presence, and I knew also that the customers would not all leave at the same time. There would be no need for me to undertake traffic duty to see them safely off the premises. Unlike their arrival in a steady stream, they would depart one by one as they bought their hearts' desires, either taking their trophies home in their own vehicles, or making arrangements with the firm of auctioneers. I paid cash for my purchase, jokingly said I did not require my acquisitions to be transported home for me, and left. I placed the pictures in the police van and drove home feeling very happy that I had managed to buy the Dowkes miniatures. Mary liked them too, which was a bonus, and so we hung them in our lounge – and we still enjoy them.

It was a few days after the auction that I received a call from Rudolph Burley. He rang me at home just before 9.30 on the Tuesday following.

'Nick,' he said. 'We've a problem. I've got to report it to you for insurance purposes. We've had a longcase clock stolen. It was from that auction you attended, the one where you bought those Dowkes miniatures.'

'Stolen? Not from the auction, surely?'

'No, you might say it was lost in transit. It left here with one of our delivery men and the buyer claims it never arrived at his home. Our delivery man swears he delivered it. It all leaves a nasty taste. I thought I had trustworthy staff.'

'I'll come and see you straight away, Rudolph. Are you at home in Aidensfield or in your office?'

'I'm in the office in Ashfordly, I've a meeting at twelve but will wait for you.'

'I'll be there within the half-hour,' I promised.

By ten o'clock I was sitting in Rudolph's splendid office which was beautifully furnished with antiques, and he arranged for his secretary to provide us with coffee and biscuits. Spread across his spacious desk were the files from Saturday's sale and I could see by the expression of concern on his face that he was seriously worried about the implications of this theft. As the coffee was poured, we chatted about the weather and local news, and then, when we were alone, we settled down to discuss the missing longcase clock.

'It was bought by a chap called Green,' he told me. 'I did not know the man, he's new to the area and he paid cash. This is my clerk's record of the sale . . . Lot a hundred and nineteen. Sold to Mr Green of Howe Farm, Thackerston for seven pounds, paid in cash. To be delivered.'

'I remember the sale,' I told Rudolph. 'I had an eye on that clock too!'

'They're becoming more popular these days,' he smiled. 'It wouldn't surprise me if those old longcase clocks become very collectable in the future. Anyway, Mr Green paid his money and asked us to deliver his clock. We charged him an extra pound for the delivery, which he paid in cash, and we told him the clock would be delivered sometime during Saturday evening. That's perfectly normal, we provide a delivery service for the larger stuff and like to get it off our premises as soon as possible, as we don't want it hanging around during the weekend. Our man says he delivered it, Green says he didn't. That's it, in a nutshell.'

'You've been to discuss it with him?'

'Yes, I went on Monday. He didn't raise a fuss until Monday – we were shut on Sunday, of course. He reckons he waited in all Saturday evening after the sale, and all day Sunday. But his clock never arrived. He rang me on Monday morning, yesterday that was, and I said I'd make enquiries and call him back. I went out to see him, to look around his outbuildings and other likely places where it might have been left, but there was no sign of it. It has still not arrived, Nick, so I said I would call the police.'

'You've spoken to the delivery man?'

'Yes. We used a firm of furniture removers: they have a small van for this job, the big one's a bit on the large side for some of our country lanes. There were two men, a driver and his mate, and I went to see them yesterday afternoon. They swear they left the clock in an outbuilding because there was no one in at the farm, but Green says he was in all evening.'

'Well, a grandfather clock can't just vanish into thin air, Rudolph. Have you had previous problems with these delivery men?'

'No, never. I've used them for years, Nick; there's never been any hint of trouble with them. And all the other stuff was delivered, some of it more valuable than that old clock.'

'And what about Green? Is he up to some kind of fiddle?'

'I don't know him. He's new to the area but he seems straight enough to me. He paid cash and I can't see how he could benefit by claiming the clock had not been delivered.'

'Has he asked for compensation?' I asked.

'Not yet, nor has he made any kind of insurance claim. He just wants to know what happened to his clock. And so do I, Nick!'

'Are we saying it was stolen from Green's premises after it

was delivered, after it was left in an outbuilding?'

'That seems the only logical answer,' he said. 'I can't believe our delivery men would steal it, and I don't think Green is making up the whole story.'

'I'll have to speak to the delivery men, Rudolph, and Mr Green.'

'I've already warned them to expect you,' he said.

I took down full details in my pocket book, along with a comprehensive description of the longcase clock – it was made by J.J. Jessop of Batley in the West Riding in 1799 – and told Rudolph I would treat the report as a crime, unless I was able to trace the clock. My next call was at Mr Green's home, Howe Farm, above Thackerston. Although this had been a former farmstead, it was now a private house, the land having been sold and the house modernized to create a very handsome and comfortable home. As I drove into the yard and parked the van near the back door, a small fair-haired man appeared. I guessed he was in his early sixties, balding slightly, but dressed expensively and rather nattily. I did not know him, nor did I recognize him from the sale, but I had not seen his face as he'd been bidding for the clock. He'd been hidden among the crowd of other bidders.

'Ah, the policeman who bid for those miniatures!' he smiled, as I removed my cap. 'I think you got a good buy, Mr Rhea.'

'I was delighted,' I told him as he led me indoors. 'I had more luck than you, it seems!'

'Mr Burley said you would be calling, but there's not much I can add to what I told him. Anyway, if I know my wife, the coffee will be on. Come in and hear my tale of woe!'

Over yet another coffee therefore, I listened to Mr Green's story. He said his name was Alan Green and he had sold a thriving business in Leeds. He had supplied the hotel trade with kitchen equipment and had decided to sell the business and his private house in Leeds to buy a property in the country and enjoy a different lifestyle. He was spending money on modernizing this former farmhouse but had decided to furnish it with antiques – hence his purchase of the Jessop longcase clock.

'I couldn't fetch it home in my car,' he said, 'so I agreed to let the auctioneer deliver it. I even paid him a pound to do so, but it never arrived, Mr Rhea. The delivery men have apparently told Mr Burley they left it in one of the outhouses because there was no one here when they called, but we've been here all the time, Mr Rhea. No one has been to deliver that clock. I can swear that on the Bible if necessary.'

'But you have outbuildings?'

'Yes, lots of them. Do you want a look around?'

'I'd better, just to satisfy my own curiosity, and to convince my sergeant that I've done a proper job.'

And so, after enjoying the coffee and a chat with Alan Green, he led me around the exterior of the former farm. There were lots of stone outbuildings, ranging from small ones which had formerly been implement sheds to larger ones which had served as cow byres or lambing sheds. There was no sign of a longcase clock, and he even gave me a guided tour of his house, just to emphasize the fact it was nowhere on the premises. There was no grandfather clock at all, although if there had been one, I would have known whether or not it was the one I sought. After all, I had seen it at the auction.

I told Mr Green that my next port of call was Coverdales, the firm of furniture removers commissioned by Rudolph to deliver the sold goods. Their depot was in Brantsford, about twenty minutes' drive away and when I arrived, I was met by the proprietor, Maurice Coverdale. I knew him by sight for he was a familiar figure in the town, but had not previously spoken to him. He was a stocky man in his late forties who had built up this business from a one-van outfit to one which now operated ten pantechnicons and more than a dozen smaller vans throughout the north of England. 'Coverdales Cover the Dales' was his slogan.

'Rudolph rang me, Mr Rhea,' he said. 'He said you'd be calling, so I didn't put those lads on the roads this morning, I kept 'em in the depot. Washing vans. It's given 'em something useful to do while waiting. I've never had such a clean fleet! I've had words with 'em, by the way, and they swear they left that clock in an outbuilding. They're good lads, Mr Rhea, reliable and honest, otherwise they wouldn't be working here. I believe 'em. In our job, we're in and out of other folks' homes all day, we're trusted to handle all sorts of belongings; valuables and not-so-valuable, so I can't afford to employ dishonest staff.'

On his desk were the papers relevant to the delivery of the missing clock, but I didn't study them at this stage. At my request he first summoned the two young men into his office and introduced me. One was a tall strong fellow in his late twenties; with a bull-like face and short cropped hair, he looked like a bouncer in a night club and said he was called Gordon Bailey. His mate was smaller and slightly younger, although built like an all-in wrestler beneath a mop of long and untidy fair hair. He was Tom Bradley.

'You know why I'm here,' I said to them, as they stood before me, both looking slightly apprehensive about this rather awkward turn of events. 'But I'm not here to accuse you of anything. All I want to do is to establish the facts.'

Bailey acted as spokesman. 'There's nowt we can say, Mr Rhea, apart from what we told the boss. We had a vanful of stuff after the sale on Saturday and the idea was to get it all delivered that day, so we just did the rounds and unloaded the stuff. We've done it before for Burley's Auctioneers, we know the routine.'

'And the longcase clock, or grandfather as most people would call it? How did you deliver that?'

'There was nobody in at the farm so we left it in an outbuilding, Mr Rhea. It had a door on it, the outbuilding, and it was dry and clean. We stood the clock in a corner, checked at the house again just in case they hadn't heard us first time and when we got no reply, we left. We thought the chap would find it easily enough, he'd be expecting it.'

'So what time did you get to Thackerston? Was it early in that delivery run or towards the end?' I asked.

'Thackerston?' frowned Bailey. 'We had no drops in Thackerston, Mr Rhea.'

'But you said you called at the farm with the grandfather clock and left it in an outhouse.'

'Aye, but that wasn't at Thackerston, Mr Rhea, it was at Slemmington.'

'Slemmington?' I was baffled now. 'But Howe Farm is at Thackerston.'

'No, it wasn't Howe Farm, Mr Rhea. It was Greenhowe Farm, and I know Greenhowe Farm is at Slemmington. I used to play there as a lad most weekends; I know it like the back of my hand. I don't know the folks there now, though. Anyway, that's where we took the clock, just like it said on our delivery note.'

'The clock was for a Mr Green at Howe Farm, not Greenhowe Farm,' I laughed. 'You left it at the wrong place!'

'You daft bats!' snapped Coverdale. 'You'd better get yourselves up there right away, the pair of you, and get that clock back . . . and then take it to the right place! I reckon you ought to go with 'em, Mr Rhea, to smooth things out . . . I mean, there's a chap at this Greenhowe Farm with a clock that isn't his and it seems to me he's said nowt about it, not that he'd have any idea where it had come from. . . .'

61

I did not know Greenhowe Farm or its occupant because it was several miles away from my Aidensfield beat and had never had any reason to pay a visit, but I decided it was a good idea to accompany the removal men, if only to smooth things out as Coverdale had suggested.

Meanwhile, I thought I'd better look at the copy of delivery note, so that I was fully aware of all the facts. Coverdale found it for me, and I must admit it was not very clear. It was a poor quality carbon copy – the second copy as it transpired – of a record made by the auctioneer's clerk in a rather scrawly handwriting and bore the lot number in addition to a part that could have borne the words 'Greenhowe Farm' or 'Green Howe Farm'. The first copy of that auctioneer's note was attached to the goods – a brief reminder for the crew of the vehicle. Coverdale explained that the pad carried in the cab by the driver would state the location of Greenhowe Farm or Howe Farm, but these lads, knowing the area so well, simply operated from the information carried on the abbreviated tags. They knew – or thought they knew – where each delivery had to be made.

Having seen how the mistake had been made, I assured the pair that there was no question of them being suspected of any kind of crime or wrong-doing, and so we all sallied forth towards Greenhowe Farm in Slemmington. It was a rambling type of farmstead with clusters of brick buildings seemingly spread over a large area and it did not appear to be kept in very good order. There was no live-stock, I noted. I parked beside Coverdale's van and followed Bailey and Bradley towards one of the outbuild-ings, a brick structure with a strong wooden door and a large window.

'I hope it's still here, Mr Rhea,' Gordon Bailey had a look of concern on his face. 'This is where we put it.'

And it was still there, standing proud in its corner, still

bearing its copy of the record which contained its lot number complete with the address of either Green Howe Farm or Greenhowe Farm in bad handwriting, and a red scrawl which said, 'Paid'.

'You start to put it in your van,' I said. 'I'll go and see if I can find anyone around the place. Then I suggest you take it straight over to Mr Green at Howe Farm. Then I'll go and tell Mr Burley what's happened.'

'Yes, we will, thank you, Mr Rhea, I hope Mr Burley's not too upset.'

As they went about their business, I rattled the brass door-knocker on the kitchen door and after what seemed an eternity, an elderly woman opened it. I reckoned she must be heading towards ninety. Rather stooped and with most of her grey hair hidden beneath a coloured scarf, she peered at me short-sightedly and said, 'Yes?'

'I'm PC Rhea from Aidensfield,' I introduced myself. 'I'm here because there has been a mistake with a grandfather clock—'

'I haven't got a grandfather clock.' She screwed up her nose and eyes and I wondered if she ever wore spectacles. 'What would I want with one of those things? I can't do with all that winding up.'

'Er, no, but one was inadvertently left in one of your outbuildings; the men are here to remove it . . . it was a mistake.'

'Here to move my grandfather clock? How can they when I haven't got one?' Now she cupped her ear with her right hand. 'You'll have to speak up, young man.'

'It wasn't your clock . . .' I raised my voice a few decibels.

'I know that, my hearing's not as good as it was, you know but there's no need to shout. I know it wasn't my clock, I haven't got one, you know, not a grandfather. Why would I want a grandfather clock?'

'You don't, it was left here in error . . .'

'What sort of terror?'

'Error. The grandfather clock was an error.'

'But I haven't got one, Constable, and I don't want one, and they don't terrify me, you know.'

I decided it was best simply to remove the clock without any further attempt at an explanation and raised my voice a little more to say, 'Someone left a clock here by mistake and these men have come to take it away.'

'Well, it must have been a mistake because I don't want one and I hope they know I haven't one and don't want another. They'd better take it away.'

'Right, well, thank you, er, Mrs . . .'

'Green,' she smiled.

# Chapter 4

The opening of a new pub was a considerable rarity in the countryside around Aidensfield. Indeed, many old inns, both rural and urban, had closed since the end of the Second World War and survivors were not finding it easy to earn a decent living solely from the sale of intoxicants. Many licensees and/or their wives or husbands had secondary jobs and some pubs opened only for limited periods. The changes brought about by various licensing laws in the early years of the twentieth century had resulted in reduced opening hours (or permitted hours, as they were known) and this, combined many years later with the effects of the breathalyser, meant that existing pubs had to change if they were to survive. The battle to prosper entirely from the sale of intoxicants was almost over; it was increasingly evident that pubs had to sell other products. Some began to serve food at the bar, such as pickled eggs or sandwiches, but many did not take this modest step and closed their doors for ever. It was abundantly clear that if the traditional English pub was going to survive in rural areas, some dramatic changes were necessary – this realization came at a time when people were beginning to travel overseas for cheap holidays and invariably they compared the relaxed liquor laws of continental Europe with our very restrictive system. But things did change even before the breathalyser legislation became effective. In 1964 the English liquor licensing laws were updated. This long awaited improvement came with the Licensing Act of that year which consolidated other legislation, but also allowed pubs to apply for either a restaurant licence, a residential licence or a combined residential and restaurant licence.

This meant that village inns could, in effect, operate like small hotels complete with a dining-room and sleeping accommodation. To qualify for a restaurant licence they had to have premises which were structurely built or adapted and genuinely used for the habitual provision of the main midday meal and/or the main evening meal. (The words lunch and dinner were not used in the legislation because they have different meanings across the county.) To qualify for a *residential* licence, the premises had to be genuinely used for habitually providing for reward board and lodging, including breakfast and at least one of the other customary main meals. The so-called combined licence could be obtained by providing the requirements of both these new licences.

With some drive and enthusiasm from the owners or managers, and some changes to their structure, therefore, country pubs could derive much benefit from these relaxations. Residents in hotels (and their bona fide friends) had, of course, enjoyed the freedom to drink outside the normal licensing hours – this could now apply to residents in pubs which in turn meant they could host events like weddings and birthday parties with the staff and residents not having to worry about closing time. I'm sure the notion of boozing late in a country pub continued to exercise some appeal, even to those who could legally do so! It has long been said that beer, spirits and wine drunk after permitted hours always tastes better than that sold within the law!

This was welcome progress, albeit not yet quite so relaxed and easy as buying intoxicating liquor on the continent of

Europe, but there is no doubt it helped many village inns to survive, even when the breathalyser came along a few years later in 1967. The main point was that village inns needed no longer to function merely as drinking houses. They could become fashionable eating places, even to the point of women entering them unaccompanied for a meal or a drink. Although many licensees did their best to maintain the traditional bar which was patronized by local people who did not necessarily want to have a full meal on the premises, it was soon evident that a new clientele had been created. People were beginning to travel from the towns into our countryside for a nice meal and a relaxing drink beside a log fire, or overlooking an expansive moorland view. Quite suddenly, it was fashionable and enjoyable to eat out at smart rural inns, the appeal of many being their rustic appearance, ancient beams, inglenooks, log fires, fascinating history, quality of their meals and, of course, their location in a beautiful place. Remote inns on lofty hilltops, or tucked away at the end of long country lanes suddenly became the focus of interest for an entire new generation of pub-goers.

It was not altogether surprising therefore that the news soon broke that a new inn was to be opened in Crampton, a charming village on my rural beat. Within living memory, there had never been an inn in Crampton although research by local historians had revealed that there had been one during the seventeenth, eighteenth and nineteenth centuries. It had been called The Royal Oak and had served the village faithfully for many, many years. It was a traditional village inn patronized by men and serving ale, probably with the licensee working for the estate while his wife looked after the pub as a part-time chore alongside her normal domestic duties.

No one knew why The Royal Oak had closed because records ended around 1875 when the former inn had reverted to a private house. The building was owned by Crampton Estate and some people with long memories thought the closure might have resulted from the whim of a former Lord Crampton who did not drink alcohol and who, therefore, thought others should not do so. Whatever the reason for its demise, however, the building had thereafter functioned as a normal rented cottage, albeit a large one. Then, in late 1960s, the estate began to sell off a lot of its unwanted properties. Like so many other rural businesses, modernization meant that fewer staff were needed which in turn meant that fewer tied cottages were required to house them. From a purely financial aspect, empty houses were expensive to maintain; the notion of holiday cottages had not yet made a full impact in some areas – Crampton did not regard itself as a tourist village – and apart from that, these estate cottages would require modernization and supervision if they were used by holidaymakers. The simple answer was to sell them in whatever state they happened to be. Thus Crampton Estate began its policy of selling unwanted properties, most of which were small, charming cottages in need of improvement.

One of those houses, however, was the former Royal Oak inn, and its history was publicized in the sale material. Eventually, it was bought by an enterprising young couple who had managed a very smart restaurant just off Oxford Street in London, and the first thing they did upon arrival was to strip away the 1930s interior and decor to reveal a fascinating stone-walled house with ancient oak beams, a huge inglenook fireplace, a stone floor and even a room which had been boarded up for some unknown reason. During this work, various artefacts were discovered such as old beer bottles, horseshoes, coins, keys and clay pipes and these were kept for future display. At that early stage of its refurbishment, of course, there was no hint it would became an inn; the young owners never spoke of their intentions, leaving everyone to believe they were merely turning it into a very fashionable, attractive and spacious country cottage. Within a few months, though, the news leaked out. When the village heard that the incoming pair were planning to turn it into a modern pub with an upmarket restaurant and *en suite* accommodation, there was the predictable mixed reaction: some villagers were in favour while others vigorously opposed the idea.

The opponents forecast excess noise, unruly behaviour in the streets, car doors banging late at night, litter dumped in the village, unsavoury people being attracted to the village and young people becoming intoxicated on a regular basis. They painted a vivid picture of anticipated debauchery and wild living. Those in favour realized the pub would bring much-needed trade into the village, thus benefiting the shop and post office and even new enterprises – already there was talk of a garden centre being established and an artist was contemplating a studio and gallery in Crampton. The National Park authority also supported all these new ventures.

In addition, the pub would generate jobs at the inn and it would provide a new centre for village activities and meetings – one of its rooms could host groups or small conferences up to thirty people in number. In planning their new inn, the owners – Jennie and Andrew Gilpin – were aware of the arguments both for and against their project, and they had had the wisdom to meet the villagers socially before making their plans known. They were a very likeable couple, they were responsible too, and they had the talent and experience to make a great success of their bold idea.

Their careful cultivation of the villagers in the weeks preceeding their application won them many supporters. Prior to opening the pub, they would have to apply to the licensing magistrates for the necessary Justice's Licence as a prelude to making application for the required excise licence, both being required before they could legally sell intoxicants on their premises. They made their intentions known to the police; consequently, I was aware that they intended applying for a full licence, i.e. one which allowed the sale by retail of all kinds of alcoholic drink for consumption both on or off the premises, along with what became known as a Part IV licence, i.e. a combined residential and restaurant licence. It was known as a Part IV licence because its provisions were specified in Part IV of the Licensing Act, 1964.

The police role in the run-up to the application for the licences was to advise the magistrates on the merits or otherwise of having a new pub in Crampton and so it was that I found myself having to compile a short report covering both the positive and negative sides. I tried to be impartial and honest in my assesssment. I referred to the spacious car-park behind the premises which would remove vehicles from the streets; I touched upon the need for some kind of focal point for social activities in Crampton, other than the facilities offered at the Hall by Lord Crampton. I did admit there would be a certain amount of noise which would be particularly evident around closing time each night and there would be a corresponding increase in vehicular traffic within the village. I mentioned the benefits, too, such as job opportunities and the possible impact on helping further new businesses to flourish in the vicinity and added a final sentence saying that the Gilpins were a responsible couple with no criminal record and that I saw no reason for the licence to be refused. And so, after all the preliminaries, the necessary licence was granted. The magistrates at Eltering issued the vital Justices' Licence and so the new Royal Oak at Crampton was set to become a reality.

The fact it was a restaurant with boarding accommodation and bar facilities rapidly attracted interest across a wide area; there was the usual advance publicity about an opening date, specimen menus were published in local newspapers ahead of the opening date, and then came the time of the official opening, a royal occasion as it was billed. Shortly before the official opening, I popped into the Royal Oak one Monday morning during my routine patrol and found Andrew, the owner, busy with a paint-brush. He was smartening an area which had been overlooked in a corner behind the bar counter. He was a stocky individual with a thinning head of fair hair, and I guessed he would be in his mid-forties. He spoke with a southern accent and appeared to be warm, confident and likeable.

'I'm just breaking off for a coffee, Nick,' he said. 'Fancy joining me? I'm glad you popped in, there's something I need to talk to you about.'

'I'd love to,' I said. I was always careful not to be seen as accepting a bribe, but a coffee during professional discussions would not jeopardize my career! Minutes later we were sitting in the new dining-room after he had shown me around the premises, now fully carpeted and furnished and looking very smart indeed. Everything was new and up-to-date, and the kitchen was especially impressive.

'I wanted a brief word about our opening ceremony,' he said. 'I hope you can join us off duty so you can enjoy yourself – I think we can cope with the expected crowd and traffic, I wouldn't want you to work late on our account! It will be on Wednesday, 5th June and I will appoint a couple of attendants just to make sure the street outside doesn't become clogged or obstructed. I intend inviting all the neighbours! That should prevent them complaining about the noise.'

'Will it be an all-invitation event, or can anyone join in?' I asked.

'We will be issuing invitations to key guests,' he said. 'Our suppliers are included, as are our advisers on decor and furnishings. The people living close to us will also get one, as will Lord and Lady Crampton, their estate agents, our bank manager, some local business contacts, representatives from the National Park authority and so on. In addition, we're hoping the public will come, there'll be free tickets for drinks and a buffet but the restaurant won't open for dinner. Some cars might have to park in the street but I'll ensure there is no obstruction and I trust that if the neighbours are all at the party, we'll not upset anyone!'

'It all sounds very straightforward to me,' I said. 'I can't see any problem.'

'There is just one other thing I should mention,' and his eyes contained more than a hint of mischief. 'I can't see that it will present any real problems but you never know how people are going to react . . .'

'You're not having a giant bonfire with fireworks and nude dancers, are you?' I laughed.

'Well, with free drinks all night anything can happen!' he chuckled. 'But seriously, we won't let things get out of control. Because we're the *Royal* Oak we thought we would make it a royal occasion, so we're going to have a small ceremonial opening of the main door. Princess Margaret will formally cut a ribbon to declare the inn open. That will be at half past seven.'

'Princess Margaret?' I gasped. 'But how on earth have you managed that? I didn't think top grade members of the Royal Family would agree to open a village inn, and besides, our security people should have been told. There are lots of things to consider before a royal visit,' I began to lecture him. 'Months of planning go into making the arrangements; the palace authorities and Central Office of Information take over the event because there's the protocol side of things, with certain people being invited, the Lord Lieutenant being involved, local dignitaries, district and county council officials. I hope you've done all the necessary pre-planning . . .'

'That's why I wanted a word with you,' he chuckled. 'It's not really Princess Margaret, she's a look-alike. I don't want you to reveal that! It's a secret, but I felt you should know in advance because the police are involved in genuine royal visits.'

I was speechless for a few moments and then laughed at his audacity. 'A look-alike? Yes, all right, Andrew, I like your cheek! Your secret is safe with me. So what prompted this idea?'

'Her name is Matilda Hyatt; she's from London and was a regular at the restaurant where I worked. She gets lots of work in the south, opening fêtes, unveiling plaques, cutting ribbons on the entrance to new housing estates, that sort of thing, always dressed up to look like Princess Margaret. She even speaks like her and has cultivated Margaret's royal mannerisms and deportment, even down to smoking a ciga-rette in a holder. She can make a very nice speech too! You'd honestly believe it really is Margaret, even when you're close to her. I asked her to come and open our pub and she's agreed to do it as Margaret. So there we are, I thought you'd better know. Once word gets around, it could attract a crowd – and, I hope, a lot of interest, not only from the Press. We can all use a bit of free publicity.'

'But if you advertise the event as being opened by Princess Margaret, won't some people feel tricked when they find it's only a look-alike?' I commented.

On a previous occasion, I had attended the opening of a new shop in Ashfordly which had been supposedly opened by the Duke of Kent; this had also been a look-alike charac-ter and some toffee-nosed ladies had not been at all pleased at the deception. They'd come hoping to shake hands with the genuine duke only to find it was an actor doing a wonderful job of impersonating him.

'We won't advertise it in Princess Margaret's name,' he grinned with more than a hint of further mischievousness in

those eyes. 'We'll advertise the fact that our official guest at
the opening ceremony will be 'Matilda Hyatt' with her
name in quotation marks, adding that she is a long-time
friend of Jennie and Andrew Gilpin, and alongside her
name we shall place a photograph of Matilda in her Princess
Margaret guise.'

'They'll still fall for it, won't they?' I laughed. 'If she's as
convincing as you say, they'll think it's the princess using a
pseudonym, trying to hide her real identity so she can do a
small favour for some friends . . .'

'That's their problem, Nick. I should add she's not known
here in the north so I think folks will fall for the trick. I
doubt if she's done her Margaret act north of Watford Gap!
I'll just tell the truth but it could draw in a crowd – which is
what I want to do. As I said, I'm going to make it an all-ticket
affair – tickets will be free, but once they've gone, that's it,
I'll print no more. No one can be admitted without a ticket
– there's just not the space, so that'll control things on the
night!'

I thought the notion of admission tickets was a good idea
and after discussing some of the finer points of his ploy, I
could see nothing wrong with it from a criminal law point of
view. If there was a deception of any kind it was the sort associated with a good April Fool's Day type of joke and I
thanked Andrew for letting me know in advance. It would
prompt a lot of enquiries and speculation once the news
spread, not only in Crampton but also elsewhere. But I
made a resolution to keep Andrew's secret.

As the Royal Oak's publicity got underway, so interest in
the opening ceremony began to increase and the people of
Crampton scrambled to apply for one of Andrew's free tickets. He gave one to me and Mary and, as I patrolled my beat
in those warm summer days, I realized that his trick had
worked, at least on some of the people. As I moved among
the local populace, not only in Crampton but also in

Aidensfield, Elsinby and elsewhere, I learned that the rumour had got around that HRH The Princess Margaret was coming to open the Royal Oak. The rumour was strengthened by the tale that HRH had expressed her desire that it should be a low-key affair with the minimum of publicity, hence she was coming under a false name. The rumour also suggested that only the local people were aware of this and so lots of them tried desperately to keep the secret while simultaneously dropping hints that 'Matilda Hyatt' was none other than Princess Margaret. As an example of creative public relations, it was a wonderful idea. In fact, those who had realized this was merely a clever joke tried to educate the others, but the more it was stressed the woman was not really the princess, the more they disbelieved it. And so it was that a high proportion of local people were absolutely sure the princess was coming to their village in heavy disguise to perform a nice gesture for a long-time friend from London. And they wanted to be there to see her and even, God willing, talk to her. Rumours are such a wonderful means of communication – the more one denies a rumour, the more strength it seems to gain. And so it was with the rumour of Princess Margaret's forthcoming visit to Crampton.

One consequence was that Andrew Gilpin rapidly exhausted his supply of tickets long before the event and so he was guaranteed a full house for his opening ceremony, but it quickly became evident that arrangements would have to be made to cater for a substantial overflow of spectators. Andrew and I kept in close contact during the final days before the formal opening and it was abundantly clear, from the number of people who said they would turn up even if they could not get inside for a drink, that he would have to find some means of coping with them. They would have to be allowed to view the opening ceremony if nothing else, and I knew he'd want to ensure they got a drink and something to eat, even if it meant paying. It was going to be a busy night. He said he would speak to people living at either side and opposite the inn to see if they would allow visitors on the sloping grass lawns outside their premises. They provided an elevated vantage point off the road from which the front door and its regal ribbon could be seen. I felt sure these people would agree. And then Inspector Breckon rang from Eltering Police. Eltering was the headquarters of our Sub-Division which meant that Inspector Breckon was in charge of Ashfordly Section, and thus our sergeant's senior officer. Our boss, in other words, the officer in charge immediately below the superintendent at Divisional Headquarters.

'Ah, PC Rhea,' he said. Breckon was a nice man, a genuine sort of person who was both liked and respected by police and public alike. 'Do you, as the local constable, know anything about an impending private visit of Her Royal Highness, The Princess Margaret to Crampton?'

'Yes, sir,' I said, proud of my local knowledge. 'But it's not really the princess. It's a look-alike, a woman called Matilda Hyatt. She's coming to open the new pub, the Royal Oak, in June. It's a publicity stunt, sir.'

'That's not what I have heard, PC Rhea. I understand the woman really is Princess Margaret masquerading as Matilda Hyatt for one of her secret outings to visit friends. She does this, you know, from time to time; she likes to get away from the strictures of royal protocol, and shake off the reins of royal life and pop up in all sorts of unexpected places under a variety of false names.'

'Not on this occasion, sir,' I said, with as much confidence as I could muster. 'It's a look-alike.'

'Don't be too sure about that, PC Rhea. I understand Her Royal Highness was a regular patron of the restaurant in London where the Gilpins used to work, and she became friendly with them. I have it, on good authority, that she is also staying overnight at Pattington Manor. She is insisting that the story is put around that the 'royal' visitor is a look-alike whereas it is not; it's the real thing, PC Rhea. And you know what that means, even for a private visit.'

'Formalties, sir? Special Branch? The Security Service? And all that?'

'All that indeed, PC Rhea. And more! Lots of involve-ment by us, from a security and personal safety aspect, not to mention crowd control and traffic regulation. So I want you to go back to your licensee of the Royal Oak to ask him just what is going on. If this really is Her Royal Highness, then we've got to move fast to set up some kind of police containment operation.'

'I'm sure we don't need all that for a private visit, sir, even if it is the Princess.'

'We do, PC Rhea; we are responsible for her safety while she is in our county. We can't have royal princesses wander-ing as they please around our sub-division and especially in our remote villages even if they are opening pubs for friends. So get yourself down to Crampton again and ask that licensee just what is going on. Then get back to me as soon as you can.'

When I returned to the Royal Oak, Andrew, this time with Jennie at his side, shook his head. 'No, Nick, it's not the real princess. I know what the rumours are saying, it happens every time, but this is merely a look-alike. She's a good one, in fact she's the very best, and I doubt if even the Queen could distinguish her from Princess Margaret, but tell your Inspector Breckon he has no need to worry. Matilda is used to this sort of thing and we'll cope.'

'He's heard she's staying at Pattington Manor,' I added. 'That's added more strength to the rumour. I believe members of the Royal Family have stayed with Sir Edmund and Lady Carpenter on previous occasions.'

'I don't know them, being fairly new to this area,' said

Andrew. 'But yes, Matilda is staying there, she knows the Carpenters. They spend a lot of time in London. They'll bring her here in one of their cars, I've given them guest tickets too.'

'The inspector also told me that Princess Margaret patronized your restaurant in London?'

'We never discuss our clients, Nick. We're a bit like priests and confession, doctor and patient, solicitors and client. Hairdressers, even!'

'So if this really was Princess Margaret, you would never admit it, would you? You couldn't. You'd be sworn to secrecy!'

'Absolutely right, Nick I'm telling you this is Matilda Hyatt who happens to be the double of Princess Margaret,' and he smiled one of those mischievous smiles.

'I'll relay that to my inspector,' I laughed. 'I'm looking forward to this!'

'So am I,' he grinned.

When I passed this information back to the inspector he said, 'Well, yes, that's what he would say, wouldn't he? All right, PC Rhea, you go ahead with whatever arrangements you have agreed and I will organize some coverage and a discreet police presence in and around Crampton that evening. Just to be on the safe side.'

The neighbours of the Royal Oak were very helpful in allowing uninvited guests to make use of their lawns which abutted the street and even their gardens and so the great day dawned. I was working a nine-to-five shift that day because of my commitment in the evening and, having spoken to Andrew and Jennie that afternoon, went away feeling that everything would be fine, there'd be no problems. The day was fine and warm and I felt sure the entire event would pass safely into Crampton's history. I had discussed with him the precise time and route for the arrival of 'Matilda Hyatt' and in many respects, it had developed into a miniature copy of a genuine royal visit. A parking space was allocated for the Carpenters' limousine in which she would arrive, there would be a spare bedroom in the inn should she wish to powder her nose prior to the ribbon cutting, or to rest with perhaps a glass of champagne afterwards and a formal presentation list had been prepared.

It had all the trimmings of a visit by one of the minor members of the royal family. Even the Press had expressed an interest and three photographers and three reporters were expected. 'Matilda Hyatt' was going to perform a wonderful piece of publicity for the Royal Oak inn.

As invited guests, Mary and I had positions close to the front door, and, well before 7.30, we took our positions and had a good view of the purple ribbon which was stretched across the entrance. There was a good deal of chatter and excitement in the minutes prior to the formal opening and among the crowd of several hundred, I saw a few plain clothes police officers. Two uniformed constables also arrived to control traffic and then, prompt at 7.28, a gleaming black Humber Snipe purred smoothly into the village through cheering crowds and eased to a halt outside the pub. Andrew and Jennie in smart dark business suits stood outside their ribboned door as the chauffeur leapt out and opened the rear door of the limousine. To the cheers of the crowd, a figure emerged, smiled and shook the hands of both Jennie and Andrew. Was it Princess Margaret? Or her double? Andrew presented her with a pair of silver scissors and with a great deal of deference, guided her to the purple ribbon. As she went about this short ceremony, the big black car moved forward and reversed into the car-park behind the inn.

In Margaret's voice, she said, 'I have great pleasure in declaring open this new Royal Oak Inn' and expertly snipped the ribbon which fell aside in two parts. Then she opened the door and stepped inside to loud applause and cheers, followed by Jennie and Andrew. As they went inside, doubtless upstairs to a rest room, so the guests pressed forward clutching their tickets. But the guest had not gone upstairs – she had simply walked through the building and, with Andrew's guidance, out of the rear door and into the waiting Humber. Within seconds, as the crowds were pressing forward, she was whisked away along the route maintained by the police. And that was it.

Jennie and Andrew had a wonderful evening, it was a fine party with lots of happiness and good wishes, and even those people who could not get into the inn due to a lack of space were given drinks and food from the buffet. They enjoyed it out of doors on a warm summer night in what became almost a carnival atmosphere. It was a very memorable and happy occasion which featured in several local newspapers, and it started Jennie and Andrew upon their very successful career as rural restaurateurs.

But was the official visitor Princess Margaret or not? I couldn't possibly say.

As the national park authorities and other tourist organizations worked hard to attract more visitors to the moors, so the inns of the region began to flourish with their new restaurant-type meals, and a spin-off was that an increasing number of people with spare rooms in their private houses realized they could earn a useful extra income by accepting visitors for bed and breakfast. Some of these advertised their services in local newspapers and shops while others relied almost entirely upon the oldest and possibly the best publicity system – WOM (word of mouth). Personal recommendation was, and still is, by far the best form of publicity.

A high proportion of farmers on the moors realized they could offer wonderful and spacious facilities for bed and breakfast; some of their buildings dated to the sixteenth and seventeeth centuries and had retained a marvellously historic atmosphere, but in the cases where farmers offered accommodation to visitors, there was an added attraction – the livestock. Enterprising farmers came to realize that visitors from cities and towns rarely, if ever, came into contact with farm animals or birds, consequently some offered bed and breakfast facilities with the added attraction that, dependent upon the season, visitors could feed the hens or ducks and collect the eggs, help to milk the cows or feed the calves, assist with lambing time and shepherding, exercise the dogs and horses or even help with mucking out the pigs! Some farmers even went further by opening their premises to visitors, rather like small domestic zoos. Visitors could explore the premises and observe the livestock at rest or at play, with children being allowed to feed young animals like lambs, calves, foals, puppies and kittens. Since those early days, of course, this kind of attraction has been subjected to rules and regulations about safety and hygiene, but when I was the constable at Aidensfield, they remained very informal and highly popular throughout the year, whether they offered merely bed and breakfast or simply allowed visitors to mingle with their animals without any human residential facilities.

Such a farm was Scar Head in the heights of Craydale. Owned by George and Elsie Heaton, a man and wife team, the stout, dark-grey, stone-built farmhouse stood proud on the edge of Craydale Scar and commanded expansive views across the surrounding moors.

The house was surrounded by a clutch of stone outbuildings which formed a protective barrier around it, sheltering it from the weather and ever-present winds. They comprised cow byres, pig sties, stables, barns, stores and implement sheds, some of which had fallen into disuse. Being well-known pig farmers, however, the sties were well used and spread across a large area of surrounding land, with the pigs being contained by effective electric fencing.

In spite of the shield of stone around it, the house appeared lofty, bleak and exposed. As it stood beside the route of a public footpath, however, it attracted regular callers such as ramblers who were either lost or wanted to use a toilet, or in some cases so hungry they would plead for a snack of some kind. And Elsie would always oblige, either making the unexpected guest a cup of tea and a sandwich, or even providing the strangers with a helping from their personal dinner, tea or supper. And they never charged a penny, thus adding to the legendary generosity of moorland farmers.

In time, however, it dawned on George and Elsie that they could make a useful income from these regular passers-by. As the 1960s progressed with people having an increasing amount of leisure time, so lots of them joined rambling clubs and walking groups and set about exploring the hidden corners of England. Farms along the routes of the longer walks began to open their doors by creating delight-ful tea-rooms or refreshment bars with scrumptious home-made food, and some also offered bed and breakfast. As the numbers of ramblers increased, it prompted George and Elsie to make good financial use of some of their outbuild-ings.

They had a row of stone-built sheds, now unused, which would make a lovely single-storey accommodation block complete with bathroom, showers, toilets and drying room – and it boasted superb views across the moors. In addition, they had a large spare sitting-room in the main house which could become a tea-room or cafeteria. Furthermore, muddy boots and wet clothing should present no problems to this remote and weathered establishment.

George and Elsie invested a considerable sum in convert-ing the outbuildings into eight very fashionable and comfortable single-bedded rooms. They were not *en suite*, but at the end of the corridor was a bathroom with a toilet, another room containing half a dozen washbasins, a small block with more toilets, and a shower complex. They upgraded their kitchen to cope with unannounced arrivals and made the spare sitting-room into a serviceable cafeteria with a stone floor (easily cleaned) and another set of magnificent views. Snacks, hot and cold, could be available in there, almost on a self-service basis. One corner of the cafeteria had been furnished with easy chairs and sofas so that hikers could relax in something comfortable and there was even an open fire which burned for most of the year. Elsie and George reckoned that Elsie could cope with sudden arrivals who wanted feeding, whereas those using their accommodation block would have their breakfasts and evening meals at pre-arranged times. If things developed to such a point that they had a regular flow of customers, then the appointment of some kind of domestic help would be considered. Elsie and George were ready for their first paying customers, and there would be lots of pork, ham and bacon on offer.

In spite of its undoubted appeal and handsome, rugged appearance, Scar Head could also appear rather daunting and forbidding, particularly when the weather was at its worst. On its exposed site, the wind could whistle through the buildings to create eerie noises which always sounded terrifying at night; loose pieces of rope or felt would flap; objects could get blown over to fall with a crash; owls hooted and flew among the outbuildings; bats skimmed the roof tops, and foxes were known to prowl among the poultry sheds, sometimes with vixens screaming in the darkness, while in the black distance, pigs would grunt and cows would low. In spite of the friendliness of the couple who owned it, Scar Head could appear terrifying to those of a nervous disposition, especially on a dark, cold night with a strong breeze and more than a hint of a storm brewing on the horizon. It was to this rather awesome site, therefore, that Libby and Steven Cole made their way early one April, by which time Scar Head had been successfully operating its bed and breakfast scheme for about a year.

Newly married and with both of them keen country lovers, hikers and bird-watchers, Libby and Steven were having a walking honeymoon on the moors. They were hoping to complete a circuit of a large area within the National Park, using well-established footpaths and sleeping in bed and breakfast houses *en route*. They had not reserved any accommodation prior to starting their trek believing they would have no trouble finding rooms, as the busy tourist season had not yet begun. The route they had planned took in several villages and market towns and so it was, on the Wednesday, midway through their one-week hike, they reached Scar Head.

Libby was feeling rather tired and so, even though it was only around five o'clock in the evening, they decided to remain there overnight. Elsie Heaton made them most welcome, showed them their rooms – two singles because she had no doubles – and took their orders for an evening meal, strongly recommending her pork chops, and in the meantime they could relax near the fire. They were the only people sleeping overnight and, being both tired and newly wed, adjourned to their rooms – or perhaps just one of the rooms – quite early. All the rooms had individual locking doors, although the door of the corridor outside, leading into the farm complex, did not lock. That was deliberately done so that people could come and go at any time of the day or night; the outer door was fastened only by a spring roller type of latch so that it could be pushed open quite easily.

Libby did not sleep very well and at one stage, in the early hours, thought she heard someone walking past their room; there was what seemed to be heavy breathing in the corridor outside their door. A late arrival perhaps? Some time later Libby needed to go to the toilet and so, noting the time was then 3.30 a.m. on her watch, crept out of bed, took a torch, made sure the corridor was deserted and made her way along to the bathroom which, she knew, also contained a toilet. It was the nearest one, hence her decision to use it.

Without switching on any lights either in her room or in the corridor beyond, she made her way by torchlight, but when she reached the bathroom, she noted the door was standing slightly ajar and noises were coming from within.

It sounded like deep breathing noises, very similar to those she'd heard earlier passing along the corridor. Now she began to experience fear; there was no light showing in the bathroom but the door had a frosted glass window with a net curtain behind. In the darkness, she could not discern any kind of figure within but deduced that someone was inside even if she could not see them. It seemed that she and Steven were not the only residents of this block, although she was sure Mr and Mrs Heaton lived in the big house. It was hardly feasible they'd use this bathroom toilet during the night and so, with a cold shiver of fear, she ran to one of the other toilets while checking behind with her torch to make sure she wasn't being followed.

When she emerged with the beam of her torch again lighting her way, she crept towards the bathroom. The door was still ajar and, as she tiptoed past, she could hear the deep sonorous breathing sounds still emanating from inside and ran terrified back to her room. There *had* been somebody out there ... Steven, who'd managed to share their single bed, stirred as she hurriedly relocked their door and slipped gratefully back between the sheets.

'All right?' he muttered in his heavy drowsiness.

'There was somebody in the bathroom with the light switched off and the door half open,' she whispered hoarsely. 'I could hear them breathing, I was frightened.'

'It must be another hiker or guest of some sort,' he

murmured. 'Mebbe the bulb's blown or the light's fused or something,' and he cuddled her to him as they settled down for the rest of the night. It took a long time for her to slip back into dreamland but at least she had Steven with her and their door was locked.

Steven awoke around 7.30 the following morning and although he had no intention of having a bath – he preferred a shower – he recalled Libby's nervous chatter during the night when she'd indicated someone had been in the bathroom with the light out. As he pottered towards the bathroom in the bright light of that new morning, therefore, he noted the door was standing ajar and decided to look inside. But, as he reached it, he could hear the sound of heavy breathing from within and, through the frosted glass with its net curtain, could just distinguish the pink figure lying very still in the bath but breathing heavily. As the door was standing slightly open, he was tempted to poke his head around it, just to check whether or not the person needed help. Thinking carefully before he acted, however, he realized this could be someone lying naked and, if so, he would be intruding and could even be accused of being a peeping tom, so he decided against it. If someone wanted to lie in the bath with the door half open, it was their privilege! And so he passed by and went elsewhere for his shave and shower.

On his return, the situation had not changed and so he told Libby of his findings, saying he felt sure she would be safe in hurrying for a shower in daylight but said he would accompany her to the door of the ladies' units. As they tiptoed past the bathroom, the snoring sounds continued, but they did not peep inside and so, half an hour later when they were washed, dressed and packed, they left their room and went across to the main house for breakfast.

Mrs Heaton was in the cafeteria and proffered a handwritten menu which included porridge, grapefruit chunks or cereals, followed by home-made pork sausages, home-cured bacon, farm fresh eggs, black pudding, beans on toast, scrambled egg, tomatoes, mushrooms or even fried sliced potatoes, along with coffee and toast, or tea or fresh fruit drinks. A traditional English breakfast, as it was described.

Mrs Heaton fussed over her young charges, asking if they had slept comfortably to which they said they had been slightly restless while politely adding they thought it was due to the newness of the beds, and then Steven asked, 'Are we the only guests here at the moment, Mrs Heaton?'

'You are,' she confirmed. 'But I'm sure it will get busier as summer approaches.'

'It's just that we thought we heard someone passing along our corridor during the night, and I think there's someone in the bathroom, or there was when we left our room a few minutes ago.'

'Oh, that'll be Susie,' smiled Mrs Heaton. 'She's taken to sleeping in that bath; she started last summer, when it was so hot. She wanted somewhere cool and found her way in there; don't ask me how she found it, or how she gets past the electric fence, but now she goes in every night.'

'Susie?' asked Libby. 'Who is Susie?'

'Our sow. A large white, she is. Wonderful animal, Mrs Cole, she's had litter after litter with no trouble at all; she's more like a pet than a farm animal.'

'A pig? You mean it was a pig in that bath?' laughed Steven.

'Oh yes, Mr Cole, she loves that new bath. She gets there about midnight and she's usually out by six, long before our clients want to use it. She must have been tired and over-slept this morning.'

When the Coles checked the bathroom as they collected their belongings prior to leaving, it was empty, but the bath showed definite signs of being occupied. It would be cleaned when Mrs Heaton came to do her chores upon the Coles' departure.

*Nicholas Rhea*

I learned of this yarn later that day. I was strolling down Elsinby main street in my uniform, undertaking one of my routine patrols when Steven Cole approached me.

'Excuse me, Constable,' he said. 'I'm not sure whether this is a matter for the police, but is there any law against a pig sleeping in a bath in bed and breakfast accommodation?'

'Anyone who keeps a boarding establishment for dogs and cats must have a local authority licence,' I smiled. 'And they must maintain a register showing the date of arrival and departure, as well as a description of the animal, but I don't know of any similar regulations for pigs. I've come across people who keep their coal in the bath, and I knew another man who kept his bicycle spare parts and motor car spare parts in the bath, but this is the first time I've heard of a pig liking a bath.'

And at that point, I was told the whole story of the pig in the bath. I had to admit I knew of no law against it.

# Chapter 5

If there is one thing that distinguishes tourists from local residents in a national park, it is the fact that so many visitors think it sensible to feed wild creatures or even farm livestock with titbits and scraps from the table or picnic hamper. Among those at the receiving end of this thoughtless 'generosity' are seagulls and moorland sheep, neither of which should be fed in this way. Some of the food offered to them is totally unsuitable and even dangerous to their health; even cows and horses are offered food as they peer longingly over hedges and walls. After all, a nice apple may be harmless to a pony, and who could resist letting a little woolly lamb lick a lollipop? But in spite of this, they shouldn't be fed.

There was one instance in Strensford, a busy seaside resort, when a small girl was attacked by a herring gull. It was a Sunday and she was enjoying a day at the seaside with her parents and two sisters. As always on a fine Sunday in spring, the town was busy with day-trippers and this family, called Pickard, were strolling along the harbourside and enjoying the picturesque scene before them. The tide was high, the harbour was full, and boats of every kind were bobbing and rocking on the calm water. There were fishing boats, rowing boats, cabin cruisers, a small yacht or two, a couple of larger timber-carrying vessels and even an inflatable dinghy. Some men and lads were standing at the rails with their fishing rods; harbour workers were busy doing whatever harbour workers do each day; day-trippers were standing at the harbour rails simply watching the passing show or else taking photographs and among it all, the townspeople were going quietly about their daily routine.

Along the harbourside were the colourful and at times noisy amusement arcades and bingo halls, shellfish stalls, cafés, fish-and-chip shops and the inevitable Lifeboat House with its doors open and a lifeboat inside, hoping for donations. It is one of those amazing facts of national life that our lifeboat service is funded entirely by charitable donations. More astonishing is the fact it manages to survive. In all, therefore, it was a busy and happy scene.

Susie Pickard, aged eight, had noticed an ice-cream kiosk near the bandstand on the harbourside and, as children do, had expressed great interest in sampling a cornet and so Dad, whose name was Chris, volunteered to get one for each member of the family. Off he went, joined a small queue, made his purchases and eventually returned to the family. During his brief absence, a small cabin cruiser had arrived and was berthing directly below the Pickards. Fascinated, they all leant over the rails to watch, Susie included. Dad handed out the cornets which were accepted almost without a word as the children were concentrating on the scene directly below them; not many children from inland Leeds have the chance to see a small boat berthing and its occupants preparing to climb the ladders onto the harbourside.

The problem hereabouts was that the seagulls of Strensford, a clamorous mixture of herring gulls, black-headed gulls, kittiwakes and a few great black-backed gulls, knew that when lots of people flocked to the harbourside, it was inevitable they would toss scraps into the air to watch the amazing aerial antics of the noisy birds as they swooped to take the offerings in mid-air.

In this way, the gulls were tempted with unwanted fish-and-chips, ice-cream cornets, half-eaten sandwiches, all manner of cakes and biscuits, candy floss, toffees and that bewildering range of edibles that people consume in the streets while on holiday. None of this is food which the birds would consume in their natural habitat, but birds are stupid creatures and will take and eat almost anything if it is presented to them. It is easier than foraging. The end result is that flocks of squawking seagulls of all kinds gather in the skies above crowds of tourists in the hope that some titbits will come their way, as indeed they usually do. Residents dislike this intensely because seagulls cannot distinguish between them and tourists; they think all creatures that walk on two legs are going to toss food for them to enjoy and so, when ladies are hanging out their washing, or when men are cleaning their cars, or when people are doing ordinary tasks out of doors in seaside places, they are often plagued with noisy gulls seeking food and releasing their large and juicy droppings on to precious things below, like freshly washed clothes and clean cars.

And so it was, as Susie Pickard stood against those railings and leaned over to observe the boat below, a flock of hungry gulls appeared and began to dive and swoop only inches above the heads of the people along the harbourside, screaming and calling and demanding food as, quite literally, they dive-bombed unsuspecting people in their search for food. As Susie clutched her cornet in both hands while watching the boat, so a massive herring gull spotted it; for the bird, this was food and if that human did not cast it into the air for the bird to catch, then the bird would snatch it from her grasp. It was quite practised in such skills.

In concentrating on the scene below, neither Susie nor her parents realized the child's ice-cream cornet was being targeted by that very determined gull. In such cases, herring gulls display no fear of humans; the fact they have been fed so often and so well by their human friends means they will always seek more food from them and so, as Susie held her ice cream away from her body, the mighty bird dived like a falling stone to seize it. But Susie moved her ice cream at that critical moment, not intentionally nor even to avoid the bird's attention; quite simply, she moved it closer to her mouth for another taste and this momentarily disorientated the gull. It had to make some last-minute adjustments to the flight-path of its ferocious dive and so, when it arrived before Susie to snatch her ice cream, its body and wings collided with her head and face. These are very large and heavy birds with enormously powerful wings and in those few moments there were screams from both Susie and the gull, shouts from Chris as he tried to beat off the thrashing bird and squawks from all the other gulls at the sight of a piece of food. Susie was knocked over by the ferocity of the bird's attack and her ice cream fell into the harbour to be followed into the water by hordes of screaming gulls, while the sudden shock of it all made her burst into tears. She was bruised about the face, and there were some scratches to her skin too, but otherwise she was unharmed. She was more frightened than hurt.

It was at that moment, as the bird made its lunge for the ice cream, that I happened to walk into the scene. I was patrolling Strensford for the day and the din produced by the birds told me something was happening not far away. I rounded the bulk of the bandstand to notice some kind of mayhem. Being an inquisitive copper, therefore, I went to have a closer look and suddenly found myself running to help the child. There was little I could do. Her parents picked her up and tried to calm her, but she cried a lot from the shock of that moment. I made a brief First Aid type of examination of her face and head and found a few scratches and red marks which would eventually turn into bruises but otherwise she seemed unharmed. I told her parents that if they were unhappy, she could either be taken to the hospital for a check-up or perhaps visit the First Aid post which adjoined the Lifeboat House. Susie declined both suggestions and her parents did not force her. Children are very resilient and, within minutes, little Susie was laughing at her ordeal and her dad offered to buy her another ice cream. Not surprisingly, she declined.

Although this incident was traumatic for the child and her family, such things were fairly common in Strensford and other seaside resorts. Generations of seabirds have come to learn that human beings are daft enough to throw them scraps, and the outcome is that they harass visitors and residents alike if they think food is available. People who live permanently in those places can all tell stories of daring seagulls making off with trophies such as sandwiches, ice creams and fish-and chips, often snatching them from the hands of their unsuspecting victims. In most cases, the humans are not hurt by these muggings, the only loss being their food, although I know one man who lost his toupé when a diving seagull knocked it into the harbour and then tried to eat it, and in more recent times a man had his gold credit card snatched by a seagull, doubtless thinking it was some kind of biscuit.

I might add that I have also been mugged by a seagull. I was sitting on the beach at Jersey in the Channel Isles, about to munch a nice lettuce and tomato sandwich, when I was hit on the back of my head with what felt like a bag of wet sand. It was a herring gull and it had its beady eyes on my sandwich – but for some reason, it misjudged its assault and failed to relieve me of my lunch. It sat and watched me for a few minutes before flying off – probably to try its skills with some other unsuspecting holidaymaker.

If seagulls have learned that tourists can provide them with food, then so have moorland sheep which live in tourist areas. On the North York Moors, black-faced sheep roam free. There are no fences or fields to contain them, and they live on the exposed heights among the heather, sharing their domain with the grouse. Each farmer identifies his own animals by colouring their wool with dye, say a red splotch on the shoulder, or a blue one on the rump, or a green one in the middle of its back. In return, the sheep know their own patch of moorland; generations of them have been born and reared there and so they instinctively know which part of the moor is their home. In Yorkshire dialect terms, this is known as heeaft – a heeaft yow (hefted ewe) is one which recognizes her own patch of moor and, when her lambs are born, this knowledge will pass to them.

Nonetheless, when bad weather threatens, or even when the moorland is too dry to produce the grass they need, the sheep will make their way along well-defined sheep 'trods' into the villages. There they will munch the grass in the village centres and along the verges of the roads until it is as smooth as the finest lawn. Wonderful examples of this can be seen in villages like Goathland, Glaisdale, and Danby, or along the roadsides across the moors. The smooth green grass presents a lovely picture of tidiness and care – all done by the sheep. As these villages attract tourists who come by bus, car, train, bike and on foot, it follows there is often a curious mixture of bemused day-trippers and sheep, the sheep taking absolutely no notice whatever of the tourists who regard the sheep as curiosities and so take photographs of them.

But over the years, those sheep have learned that if they wander into the villages when the visitors are around, they will get fed. Just like daft tourists who feed seagulls, so equally daft ones feed moorland sheep with all manner of unsuitable items, many of which are distinctly unhealthy for the animals. This is done in spite of notices on village greens which say 'Do Not Feed the Sheep'. The result of all this free food is that when a motorist halts his car in some of those moorland villages, it will attract the sheep who potter towards it in the expectation of some titbit or other. Many tourists have found their cars surrounded by a flock of twenty or thirty horned black-faced sheep, and even if the sheep are harmless, the hapless townies probably don't know that.

It was this kind of situation which prompted an alarm call to Ashfordly Police Station because a couple of elderly visitors from Birmingham, who had booked bed and breakfast accommodation in Briggsby, had not returned after their day on the moors. They had told their landlady they would return by six that evening because they were going out to a nice hotel for dinner; it was unlike them to be so late.

I took that call during my spell of duty in Ashfordly. 'So where were they going?' I asked.

'They said something about heading over the moors, through Rosedale and across by Hamer House towards the Esk Valley,' said Mrs Ripley, the landlady. 'They wanted to see Rosedale, Chimney Bank, the old railway line and the remains of the abbey, then they were going up to Hamer and over the moors into Eskdale, Lealholm and Glaisdale, they said. They hoped to find a nice pub somewhere for lunch, but they took a flask of coffee each, and some apples and bars of chocolate.'

By gentle questioning, I learned they were Frederick and Amy Bielby, both in their late sixties, and I was provided with a vague description of the couple. They drove a black Hillman Minx whose registration number had been recorded in Mrs Ripley's register of guests – that was the easiest of clues from my point of view. I told her we had not received any information of accidents or incidents involving that car, but said I would check hospitals and surgeries to see whether either had been treated or admitted in any kind of emergency. If that failed, I would circulate a description of them and their car in the hope that our officers on patrol would come across it. It was about 7.30 when she rang me; they were only an hour and a half overdue which was no real reason for major concern. Their car could have broken down; they could have had a puncture; they could have got lost, or they might even have met friends . . . but I assured Mrs Ripley we would do our best to locate them and she promised to ring me if they returned.

Because it is impossible for a solitary constable to search the entire area of the North York Moors, there was no point of setting off alone but I could visit the areas supposedly on the Bielby's itinerary for the day, and I could alert my colleagues who were also on patrol in different parts of the moors. I stressed the fact there seemed to be no justifiable cause for alarm for the old folks weren't worryingly overdue and so, armed with their car registration number, a small army of police officers on routine patrol maintained a watching brief as they moved around the heathery acres. I left Ashfordly police station after a brief explanation of my plans to the duty constable in Eltering Sub-Divisional Police Station. As the sergeant was on leave and there was no other constable on duty in Ashfordly, I switched the telephone through to him; if Mrs Ripley rang during my absence, he would take the call at Eltering and contact me by radio. It was mid-May and there were two or three hours of sunlight to aid our search before darkness descended.

Having been born and reared on the moors, and having explored them on foot, by cycle and by car, I knew them very well indeed and decided to search those parts mentioned by Mrs Ripley. Although the Bielbys' intended route was not part of my beat, it laid within our sub-division and we were expected to patrol that greater area. The days of constables patrolling their patches on pedal cycles was over; with our radio-equipped motor vehicles we could cover much greater areas than hitherto and this modest expedition was one example. I warmed to my task.

Within twenty-five minutes of leaving Ashfordly, there-fore, I was descending the 1-in-3 (33%) gradient of Chimney Bank at Rosedale with its endless views of the surrounding moorland and dale, having not found the couple *en route*. I toured the village, drove up the steep slope leading to Egton Bridge, Glaisdale and Hamer House and had a most enjoyable drive across some of England's most spectacular scenery with Fylingdales Ballistic Missile Early Warning Station's three white balls sitting like a clutch of eggs on the far horizon to the east and the blue North Sea off Whitby to the north-east. I passed through Glaisdale and Lealholm without finding the car and without hearing any like news from my colleagues via my official radio, then headed up the Esk Valley to Danby and Castleton before turning back across the lofty spine of Castleton Rigg with even more extensive views on all sides. I passed Young Ralph, otherwise known as Ralph Cross, dropped into Hutton-le-Hole and made my way back to Ashfordly via Brantsford. It was a tour of the moors so beloved of visitors and tourists, but for me it was a duty trip – but with no sign of the missing couple. By now this stage, of course, time was passing and darkness was nigh. I tried to visualize the route that might have been taken from Eskdale on the return trip to Briggsby but, in a landscape laced with minor roads and quiet lanes, they could have taken one of several roads. I parked at the roadside for a few minutes to study my map in the hope it might provide some inspiration – and it did. Lying slightly off the beaten track between the peaks of the moor above Castleton and the comparatively low-lying area around Ashfordly was the remote and very charming village of Gelderslack.

It was renowned for its Surprise View, a vantage point on the top of a steep hill literally at the end of the village. You can drive along the village without realizing this view is awaiting; the road suddenly dips to the left at the top of a cliff and there, directly below, is a drop of several hundred feet with staggering views beyond. Lots of tourists make their way to admire that breathtaking vista – it was quite feasible that the Bielbys had done so because it involved only a slight detour from their route back to Briggsby. I hoped they hadn't lost their nerve and driven over the edge of the cliff, but realized that if that had been their fate, I would have known about it. As I crested the rise towards the famous viewing point, there was no sign of them or their car and I felt slightly dismayed – then, about a hundred yards away on the village green with its tall stone cross near the centre, I saw a grey-haired man and woman sitting on folding chairs behind their parked car. The boot lid was up; clearly, they were having a picnic even though it was almost dark. I drove slowly towards them – the car was a black Hillman Minx and, as I approached, I could read its front number plate even though the car and the couple were surrounded by dozens of black-faced moorland sheep, all lying peacefully on the grass. It was the Bielby's car. I had found them, safe and sound, I brought my car to a halt on the road nearby. I left the car and walked across to them, weaving between the sheep, some of which rose to their feet and moved away at my approach, and some of which did not budge an inch. After all, this was their heft, their home patch, and with night falling fast, they were preparing for sleep. And I had no real wish to disturb them.

'Mr and Mrs Bielby?' I called as I strode towards the couple.

'Oh, thank heaven you've come, constable . . . we've been sitting here for hours . . . it's so cold and we daren't move, not with all those dangerous animals surrounding us,' called Mr Bielby in his distinctive Birmingham accent.

'Dangerous animals?' I looked around in mild surprise; it hadn't occured to me they were talking about the sheep.

'What dangerous animals?'

'Them there, with those horns, those sheep, they came and surrounded us when we got our picnic out. I thought we were going to get butted or worse . . . then more came and we couldn't get away from them, they just stood there looking at us with those horns . . . really menacing . . . all standing with their heads down. We thought they would charge at us if we moved, they've got us surrounded like wolves or lions waiting for the kill. Very nasty, Constable . . . and nobody's come past, nobody's been to help us . . . so can you do something?'

'You mean you've been sat here all this time, frightened to move because of some stupid sheep?'

'Well, yes, we couldn't move, could we, not until they'd all gone? They're just sitting and waiting for us to do something silly. I mean, what could we do? What if they all charged at us, we'd stand no chance. Me and Rosie would have been injured or worse . . . it's been dreadful, Constable, really dreadful.'

'They're harmless,' I said, trying not to laugh at the notion of them sitting here terrified like this. 'Look, I've walked among them without any trouble.'

'Harmless?' he almost shrieked in disbelief. 'How can things with horns like that be harmless?'

Their dilemma reminded me of a similar incident in Craydale when a team of electricians had been marooned up a pylon when it was encircled by a herd of cows.

'They are quite harmless,' I tried to reassure the old couple. 'If they came when you produced your food from the hamper, they'd be expecting titbits; visitors feed them and its a stupid thing to do. If you didn't give them anything, they'd just wait hopefully, standing around or even lying down. And now, with it getting dark, they're preparing for bed: this is probably where they sleep every night. But they're completely harmless. If you'd driven away, they've have moved to let your car through; they're not daft enough to let themselves get run over, and if you'd walked through them, they'd not touch you.'

'Oh, no, Constable, I can't believe that, not with those horns . . .they're vicious. If we'd tried to move, they'd have got us.'

I explained that even though the sheep bore horns, they were females and quite harmless and I stood near one, seized one of its horns with my right hand and hauled it to its feet. 'Go on,' I shouted. 'Get out of it . . .' and then I slapped its rump. It moved with some reluctance and so I adopted another trick – I whistled. When someone whistles, the sheep often think it's a shepherd or farmer whistling instructions to his dog and they start to move or even run. And this worked. Several rose to their feet and so I clapped my hands and shouted as I walked among them, shooing them away from the path of the car and hauling some by their horns.

They were very loath to move, having practically settled down for the night, but after some shouting, whistling, pushing and shoving, I cleared a route to the car for the Bielbys, and made a route off the green for their car. Following my daring and brave 'rescue', they hurriedly packed their picnic utensils, leapt into their car while keeping their terrified eyes on the sheep which now stood and stared back at them, and then, without a word of thanks, roared away into the thickening gloom. The style in which their car accelerated away made me wonder if they thought all the hounds in hell were chasing them.

I radioed Eltering Police Station to say that the missing couple had been traced safe and sound and were now heading back to their lodgings. PC Rogers, the duty constable, said he would issue a cancellation message and offered to ring Mrs Ripley at Briggsby to inform her that her lodgers were safe and sound, and on their way back. I heard no more from the Bielbys but wondered what sort of story they would tell their friends about the dangerous animals which lurked on the wild moors of Yorkshire looking for vulnerable prey in the form of elderly motorists. On the other hand, if they were very wise, they'd say absolutely nothing about it.

In another similar incident, I was patrolling Aidensfield village green one fine August bank holiday Monday when a distraught young woman ran across to me.

'Oh thank God you're here,' she panted. 'In my car . . . can you come quickly?'

'What's happened?' I asked, wondering if it had caught fire or run away without a driver.

'A sheep's climbed into it and won't get out,' she said. 'I don't know what do do.'

'Oh, right,' I smiled. 'No problem. But what on earth is a sheep doing in your car?'

'Well, my little girl was sitting in the front passenger seat as we'd parked on the green and were having ice-creams. I was outside the car, on that seat over there, with my two other children,' and she indicated the seat in question. 'Julie stayed inside the car, but the driver's door was open to keep it cool . . . then this sheep just jumped in. I think it wanted Julie's ice-cream but she opened her door and jumped out before it could grab it. Now it's laid down across the two front seats and won't get out.'

'Have you tried buying it an ice-cream?' I laughed. 'The trouble is that visitors feed the sheep with stupid things like ice-creams and now, if the sheep see one, they'll try and grab it! So maybe an ice-cream will tempt it out?'

'You're joking!'

'It might work if brute force doesn't,' I laughed, and strode towards the little car with the sheep on the front seat. It was one of the native black-faced ewes and at my

101

approach, her eyes seemed to suggest she intended staying here until someone produced an ice-cream. But I did not think feeding ice-creams to sheep was a good idea, even to tempt them out of private cars and so I did the only thing possible – I leaned into the car from the passenger side, grabbed one of the ewe's horns, whistled like a shepherd, and in a moment she was leaping from the car.

I slammed both doors and was pleased the animal had not caused any dirt or damage. I explained to the young lady that these animals would often try to get into cars if they spotted people eating inside with the doors open. I'm not sure she believed me; she expressed the view that the sheep might have been someone's pet lamb and I had to admit it was possible.

'Maybe it belongs to Bo Peep?' I suggested.

# Chapter 6

One of my continuing duties as a village constable was to protect unoccupied property. Much of this entailed visits to private houses when the owners or occupiers were away for a lengthy period, although some would ask us to keep an eye on their homes even if they were absent for just a few days. Most town police stations maintained an 'Unoccupied Property Register' which listed such houses both in the town in question and in the surrounding villages. As the village constable at Aidensfield, of course, I maintained my own very localized record and made sure I checked all the unoccupied houses as often as possible.

Each register contained the dates of absence of the householders as well as a name for the keyholder or a family member upon whom we could call for assistance if there were problems. These could include almost anything from vandalism to leaking water pipes, although the real reason behind this scheme was to deter thieves, burglars and housebreakers. Part of our on-going crime prevention advice was to suggest that householders notified us if they expected to be absent for any length of time. The scheme began almost with the formation of the police service when wealthy or important residents requested this service from their local constabulary. In time it expanded to include ordinary mortals, particularly those with homes in isolated places. People living in streets or among other houses could generally rely upon friends to care for their homes during any absence, long or short, but country dwellers and people in large detached houses tended to rely on the police who patrolled the locality regularly.

From our point of view, it was a simple but effective system. Bobbies on patrol would study the Unoccupied Property Register at the start of their tour of duty, particularly when on night shift, and would make a point of visiting each of the empty houses to check they were secure. In our notebooks, we maintained a personal list of the houses we checked, along with the dates and times of our visits and a note that the house was secure. Those visits were then entered in the register. If such a house was broken into, or property stolen from the garden (which, unfortunately, did sometimes happen) we could then point to the time it was last known to be secure and so get some idea of the time the villain had paid his visit. It was widely considered that our uniformed visits had the effect of deterring would-be raiders because they never knew when we would be arriving to carry out our checks although detractors claimed our visits advertised the fact the house was temporarily unoccupied and therefore vulnerable. Whatever its merits, it was a service we offered to the public and it was quite free of charge; many people, at that time, took advantage of our willingness to undertake this modest chore.

From time to time, however, the Unoccupied Property Register required updating because long-term entries tended to get forgotten and overlooked as new ones were included. The idea was to put a red line through each entry which was no longer active, i.e. to cancel it because the householder had returned and everything was in order. As current entries filled new pages, however, so the older ones could easily be removed from sight and therefore pushed out of mind. The system was by no means infallible.

Every so often, therefore, the sergeant would unearth this hefty volume from its resting place, plonk it on the desk before the constable who was performing office duty and instruct him to bring forward and update any older entries. The sergeant would then make sure the patrolling bobbies checked the houses listed on those old entries; it meant, of course, that the system depended heavily upon human efficiency – but in spite of such care, mistakes were sometimes made.

During one quiet spell when I was performing a four-hour period of office duty, Sergeant Craddock asked me to check the Unoccupied Property Register at Ashfordly Police Station. He wanted me to start at the beginning to check that there were no long-term unoccupied properties which had been overlooked; if so, he said, I should bring them forward and place their details among those currently active. In that way, he said, our patrols would ensure the houses were checked. There were quite a few whose dates had expired and which had not been cancelled – possibly because they had, in fact, been overlooked. I found only one long-term entry which, according to our records, was still listing an unoccupied house which required our supervision. It was a very old entry; indeed, I'd never been to check the house during my time at Aidensfield. On checking the date, I found it had been logged eight years earlier. Eight years!

'You mean there's just the one?' beamed Sergeant Craddock when I told him I could find only one apparently active record. 'Then we are not as inefficient as I thought, PC Rhea. But as you discovered the entry, you can have the privilege of checking it, just to ensure our records are accurate. Where is it?'

'It's at Shelvingby, Sergeant.' I read out the details. 'Blue

105

Rock House, Shelvingby. The entry is eight years old and there's no date to indicate when it was expected to be reoccupied. The owners are shown as Shelvingby Estate, who registered it with us. According to this, it must still be empty, but it seems it hasn't been checked for years.'

'Is it within our Division, PC Rhea? Isn't the divisional boundary somewhere in that area?'

'I'll check the map,' I told him. 'Shelvingby is certainly in our division, but if that house is a long way out of the village, up on the moors somewhere, it could lie in another division. If so, it should be their responsibility, not ours.'

The framed one-inch Ordnance Survey map depicting the boundaries of Ashfordly Section, some of which were also the boundaries of the Division in which Ashfordly lay, hung on the wall of the sergeant's office and so we trooped through to examine it. I found Shelvingby without any problem, but then had to search the upland regions all around it in the hope of finding Blue Rock House. Such maps depicted single farms and houses which were in isolated locations and then I found it. Blue Rock House was a remote farm or house near the source of Blue Rock Beck, a moorland gill which flowed from the higher parts of the moors. According to the map, the house was about a thousand feet above sea-level with no surfaced road leading to it. The map showed what appeared to be an unfenced track leading to Blue Rock; that route led from an unclassified road which served Shelvingby and it passed close to another farm, Moorgate, before heading out to Blue Rock.

'It's in our Division, Sergeant, and therefore in our Section, but only just! It couldn't be any nearer the border; it's almost standing on it.'

'So it is our responsibility,' said Craddock. 'At least we know there is a house there. Why not ring the estate? They'll tell you if anyone's living there and whether we need to keep it on our Unoccupied Register.'

When I rang Shelvingby Estate Office, I was told that Blue Rock House had been sold by them some six years ago. The tenant farmer had died and the estate considered the farm to be uneconomic due to its remoteness. The fields around it had been absorbed by a neighbouring property which also belonged to the estate, and the unwanted house had been put on the open market.

'It was bought by a man called Kenneth Ian Midgely,' the estate secretary told me. 'I remember his name because we often get calls about the house, from people like the council, or even people wanting to buy it; ramblers often pass that way and get an urge to buy a house in the country, but all we can do is pass the owner's name to them. I have no other address for Mr Midgely; we refer all enquiries to Blue Rock House,' she added. 'Sorry I can't be more helpful.'

Next, I checked the telephone directory to see if Midgely was listed, but he wasn't and so Craddock said, 'You could check the electoral register to see if he or anyone else is living there, or you could call the local council offices to see if it's listed in their ratepayers' register. On the other hand, it might still be unoccupied, of course.'

All my attempts were fruitless. None of the official lists showed an occupant of Blue Rock House and the council said they'd collected no rates for it in recent years. According to their lists, it was deserted and might even be in a ruinous state.

'There's only one way to settle this.' Sergeant Craddock smiled at me. 'That means a trip out there, PC Rhea. Go and have a look at the house. Don't make a special journey, it's not all that important, but if you are in Shelvingby for any reason, make time to pay it a visit. Then we can get our records up to date.'

And so it was, about two weeks later on a cool but sunny

107

April afternoon, I found myself in Shelvingby on a routine patrol. I was checking stock movement licences on several farms, that being one of my regular tasks, and decided to drive out to Blue Rock House. I had researched the somewhat odd name for the place and had found the lofty hill behind the site was called Blue Rock Hill, and there was also Blue Rock Beck flowing from it and heading down towards the river. I knew the colour of the exposed granite rocks on those moors could, in some natural lights, appear to be a dark slate blue and I wondered if that was the origin of the name. Another alternative was that the name could have come from a bird – the so-called blue rock. In some areas, this was the local name for the stock dove which could be confusing because there is also a bird called a rock dove. However, blue rock was definitely the alternative name for the stock dove, although, to confuse things a little, it was sometimes called a ring dove by the local people! This is a bird which loves cliffs, parkland and farms surrounded by old trees and if comparison is needed, it is smaller than its cousin, the wood pigeon and is a blue-grey colour. Many of the domestic pigeons one finds in parks and gardens are very similar to the wild stock dove in both size and colour, and it is thought many of them are descended from wild stock doves.

Whatever the source of its name, however, the house occupied an extremely remote location in the midst of rugged and inhospitable moorland. In my Mini-van, I struggled along a rough lane from Shelvingby and when I went past Moorgate Farm I found myself upon a very uneven, unsurfaced and rocky track which ran between high banks of thick heather and bracken. It was so bad I decided to leave my van and walk the rest of the way. With huge rocks protruding from the bed and sides of the track, I was fearful for the exhaust pipe and underparts of the little van, as well as the sides. It was a ten-minute walk.

I placed my uniform cap on my head so that I would appear to be a police officer as I approached – just in case I was observed with suspicion! As I ascended the increasingly steep track, I could see the dramatic house directly ahead. It was huge and solid, being three storeys high and built of dark blue-grey blocks of granite with a blue tiled roof. It looked most formidable, almost like something out of a Brontë novel, and it boasted several chimney stacks plus a cluster of outbuildings which surrounded it like chicks sheltering near a mother hen. As I approached, I began to discern very clear signs of dereliction – a gate hanging off its hinges, various agricultural implements rusting in the yard, tiles missing from both the house and outbuildings, rosebay willowherb, weeds and nettles growing in abundance, some of them up to chest height in places around the house with yet more sprouting from walls and window openings. There was even a small sapling, a mountain ash I thought, sprouting from one of the gutters on the roof. Doors of several outbuildings and the kitchen door of the house were standing wide open and in some cases hanging off their hinges, and there were several broken panes of glass in the windows of all storeys. The wind was sighing through the old house and outbuildings to give it a rather unsettling atmosphere – I could imagine how terrifying it might be at night with a strong wind blowing and owls flitting about the premises. Trying to be practical and efficient in my work, I noticed an old grey tractor and a trailer, both rusted and useless; there was even an old car with flat tyres and rusted paintwork in one of the doorless outhouses. I could see cobwebbed bottles of cattle medicine on window ledges in one of the outbuildings, but saw no sign of closed curtains, lights or other indications of habitation. Quite clearly, no one lived here. Did they?

I walked through the remains of the farm gate and into

the yard. It was flagged with York stone slabs now with weeds pushing their way between the gaps and their presence confirmed that the place must be deserted. If anyone had walked among those weeds, there would be signs of them being trampled, but they were flourishing in a completely wild and unhampered state. I strode towards the kitchen door for it was open and hanging from its hinges, all the time looking for signs of human presence but saw nothing. I reached the door and shouted.

'Hello,' I called, and my voice echoed in the empty depths. 'Hello, is anyone there?'

There was no reply.

In some ways I felt like a trespasser and I felt more than a tremor of apprehension as I tried to make up my mind whether or not to enter the house. If it was occupied, I would be an intruder invading the privacy of the people who lived here, but if it was empty and deserted, then my actions could not be considered intrusive. Indeed, it could even be argued that it was my duty to ensure that whoever was living here was not in need of help, and the fact the house was on our list of unoccupied property was a further reason for checking its current state of affairs. Shouting to warn anyone of my presence, I stepped inside. The thought that I might be in any sort of danger never occurred to me – I didn't consider there might be some unstable or terrified person waiting inside with a loaded shotgun, or with a savage dog waiting to be unleashed – all the indications were that the place was deserted, and had been for a long, long time. Nonetheless, I must admit to some trepidation, some unknown fear which made me perspire slightly, at the thought that I had no idea what I would find.

But the moment I entered the kitchen and my eyes adjusted in the gloom after the brilliance of the sunshine, I could see the place truly was deserted even if the kitchen bore signs of use. There was a table with some food wrappers and empty soup tins upon it, the dusty shelves held mugs and pans all smothered with grime and cobwebs. I recalled that Blue Rock House lay close to the route of a moorland track used by ramblers and thought some must have come here to rest and shelter and to eat their rations for there was no cooker or kettle.

'Hello,' I called again, my voice echoing in the vast hall beyond the kitchen, and without getting a reply, I decided to explore this solid old house. For all its exposed location and the neglect it had endured, it was surprisingly dry inside and so I went from room to room, shouting in advance, stirring up clouds of dust when I opened cupboard doors or disturbed the furniture. None of the walls bore wallpaper, all were plastered and emulsioned. It was only partly furnished: a small lounge contained a dusty and rather smelly three-piece suite and an old radio set, along with more empty baked-bean tins and paper wrappings; there were wonderful antique chairs in the hall along with a grandfather clock which had stopped at eighteen minutes past three, but the other rooms downstairs – all four of them – were empty with no rugs, carpets or floor covering. I found a cellar too, full of old furniture and beer bottles but no sign of recent use. There was no indoor toilet downstairs. I guessed it would be outside, in one of the outbuildings – and used by ramblers.

I climbed the stairs, noting there was no carpet and that the banister and stairwell were smothered with dust and cobwebs. If ramblers were in the habit of popping in here for rest or shelter, it seemed they did not climb the stairs. The dust had not been disturbed for years. I found myself on a large landing with a cobwebbed window overlooking the route of the beck and offering spectacular views; ahead of me was a choice of six solid wooden doors, all closed. The walls of the landing were plastered too, just like those in the

111

rest of the house, and they were coloured a dull cream, now grimy and dusty. A solitary light bulb, without a shade, dangled from the ceiling.

I decided I should check the bedrooms. The first three were totally unfurnished, with bare floorboards, and nothing on their bare, plastered walls. The fourth door led into an old-fashioned bathroom with a huge iron bath standing on high legs, and a washbasin occupying the wall beneath a window, while next to it was a tiny room containing a toilet, also very ancient but a water closet nonetheless. That was the fifth door.

The sixth door gave me a dreadful shock.

When I opened it expecting to find an empty room, I was shocked to see an occupied bed complete with covers. Within those same seconds, I saw the curtains were open, a wardrobe door was also standing open and mens' clothes were hanging inside, old and dusty, while a dressing-table contained some personal bits and pieces. A wallet, some keys, a comb . . . all smothered in dust and webs. Then I realized the occupant of the bed was a corpse, a very dead one. A human corpse. Male. White hair but little else showing from the covers. Skeletal with all the flesh gone and nothing but the brown bony skull remaining beneath those wisps of white hair.

Momentarily, I did not know what to do. 'This is not an emergency,' I told myself after regaining my breath. 'This person has been dead for months or even years so there's no need to go rushing back to the van and calling the ambulance or the emergency services . . . this person's not going to go anywhere.'

Carefully, I moved closer to the bed, noting the absence of the smell of death or of putrefying flesh, and eased back the covers. The body was fully dressed in male clothing. As the curtains were open, I wondered if he had felt ill and had come to lie down for a while – and never got up again. I went over to the wallet and opened it, blowing off the dust, but it contained only a few pounds in notes and cash. I thought it might have contained some means of identification, like a driving licence or library ticket, but there was none. I decided not to search the room at this stage – I would have to inform my sergeant and perhaps get the Scenes of Crime team to examine the remains of the man and the entire house to determine if the death was suspicious. There would also have to be a post-mortem examination of the remains in an attempt to determine the cause of death. A lot of work lay ahead.

I left everything else exactly where it was, closed the door and left, hurrying down the stairs and out to my van to radio Ashfordly Control with my unexpected news. What had been the simple checking of an Unoccupied Property Register had now developed into an inquiry into the mysterious death of an unknown person.

'Delta Alpha Two Four to Control,' I said into my handset. 'Are you receiving?'

'Receiving, Delta Alpha Two Four,' returned the distinctive voice of PC Alf Ventress. 'Go ahead.'

I told Alf about my discovery, stressing the lack of need to regard it as any kind of emergency, but suggesting Sergeant Craddock and the Scenes of Crime team come to examine the house and the remains. He advised me to remain where I was until support arrived and so I did, not returning to the house but waiting near my van.

Thus began a protracted enquiry to establish the identity of the dead man and to determine precisely what had happened in that house. The outcome was that we never knew. The post-mortem examination on the remains was inconclusive due to the skeletal state of the body, but there were no signs of injury such as broken bones or bullet wounds, and tests of the bones failed to find any traces of toxic substances. As the corpse was fully dressed, and the curtains left open, we could only speculate the fellow had been taken ill and had died alone. His clothing was not that of a hiker although it was a countryman's attire – corduroy trousers and a working shirt, with a pair of heavy shoes tucked under the bed.

His name was never known. Nothing in the house bore any name or address and in spite of our nationwide search for Kenneth Ian Midgley, the man who had bought Blue Rock House from the estate, he was never traced. We had no idea who had furnished the house, however sparsely, and we never found anyone who claimed the deceased was a friend or relation. The fellow might have been a passerby who chanced to find the house when he was feeling ill; he could have been a friend of Mr Midgley, or he could have been Mr Midgley himself. We never knew. His remains were quietly buried in Shelvingby churchyard, the funeral being paid for by Shelvingby Estate and there they lie today in an unmarked grave.

In the absence of anyone claiming ownership of Blue Rock House, the estate said they would assume responsibility and they began by repairing the roof, fixing the doors and windows, and boarding-up the premises until a decision could be made as to its future.

With no one ever claiming it, and with the estate not really interested in spending large sums on renovating such a remote house, it gradually started to suffer from a second period of neglect. Time, weather and vandals all did their best to destroy the house and today it is a ruin, a battered shell of beautiful dark-blue stone with the wind howling through the rafters and the creatures of the moor making their homes among deserted rooms. Ramblers continue to make their way past the old house and some find shelter behind its remaining walls, sitting there out of the wind to enjoy their flasks and sandwiches. Few, I suspect, know the story I have just related.

There are times I still ponder that mystery, but I wonder how many ramblers realize they may have rested, eaten and even slept there with a corpse lying upstairs. Or perhaps they came to eat, drink and be merry while the poor man was desperately in need of help? With none going to his aid. Or perhaps some of them had explored the empty house and found the body in the bedroom, but had been too afraid to notify anyone. We shall never know. The secret of Blue Rock House remains a secret.

A similar story is told about another house on the outskirts of a village but in this case, the yarn has been part of the district's folklore for centuries. The premises, owned by a family called Stewart, are a farm, not on the heights of the moor but standing beside one of the minor roads which wends its way through the lower reaches of one of the dales within the park's boundaries.

The house is not part of the village but lies midway between Thackerston and Elsinby; its address, however, is Thornton Hall, Thackerston and it is a large, successful farmstead which, when I was the Aidensfield village constable, hosted a herd of pedigree Friesian dairy cows, some magnificent Cleveland Bay horses and other livestock such as sheep, pigs, geese, ducks and hens. It also grew potatoes, wheat and hay and supported a small workforce of two men in addition to the Stewarts – Mr and Mrs Alan Stewart and two sons, Robert and Clive.

As a matter of interest, the suffix 'ton' indicates a farm or settlement of centuries past and the prefix 'thorn', rather than being the name of its original occupant as occurs in some instances, could possibly relate to the wealth of hawthorns which continue to flourish around these premises. There are many villages which bear the name Thornton, either on its own or with either a prefix or suffix, and which may refer to a former homestead surrounded by a thorn enclosure. At its early beginnings, probably around the time of the Roman occupation or even earlier, the premises would have been farmed by a single family and, as time progressed the family would have increased and the farmstead would have expanded to accommodate them and their descendents. Many of these farmsteads developed into thriving villages with an input of new blood and extra accommodation while others, like Thornton Hall, continued to flourish as large and successful family farms.

The precise age of Thornton Hall is unknown, although there is evidence that a house or settlement of some kind has occupied the site for more than a thousand years, with some existing stonework dating from the tenth and eleventh centuries. Some local historians claimed that Thornton Hall had portions of stonework and new buildings which had been added during every century since 1066. Not surprisingly, therefore, some said the place was haunted. Down the centuries, local folklore reminded each new generation that Thornton Hall had a ghost. And equally, in every century, lots of people claimed to have seen her, with the recorded descriptions being surprisingly similar. The apparition was described as a young woman, even a girl perhaps of around twelve to fourteen years of age, with long blonde hair and dressed in a long white gown with a blue sash around her waist, and always with tears flowing down her cheeks. The similarities of the sightings were remarkable because they had been observed by people who could not have known the earlier witnesses and few written accounts were available. Certainly, some of the witnesses claimed not to have known the place was haunted, nor had they read any literature about the homestead.

To my knowledge, none of the sightings had occurred within the premises. The current occupiers, whose Stewart

116

descendants have lived there for more than 450 years, claimed never to have seen their own personal ghost. All the sightings had been in one of the fields bordering the road; over the years, the Lady in White, as she had become known, had been seen by people on horseback with the horses shying or refusing to continue; she had been seen by walkers and cyclists, car drivers and even a bus driver. Some said their dogs would never pass that point at certain times of the year.

All the witnesses told very similar stories – they had seen the figure of the weeping girl in her long white gown as she stood obviously in some distress just inside the hawthorn hedge on a piece of rising ground. Many of the local people refused to walk past Thornton Hall at night, although they would bravely ride past in cars or on motor bikes, sometimes at full moon, in the hope of seeing this local spectre. As happens in such cases, those who deliberately set out to find her never did so; those who did see her always did so by sheer chance usually when their minds were on other things, and there did not seem to be any particular date or time for her appearances. With such a powerful story, it is not suprising it persisted right into modern times – or, to be precise, until the time I assumed my duties at Aidensfield.

On my appointment as the village constable, I was told about the ghost and one of the earliest pieces of advice I received from the local people was not to patrol on foot near the piece of rising ground in case the Lady in White made an appearance and caused my hair to stand on end. I was intrigued by this tale and knew there must be some event, probably dating back centuries, which had given rise to the story and, I should add, the thought of a ghostly apparition did not frighten me. When going to live in a new area, it is always my practice to learn as much as I can about the district, including its history, topography, folklore, personalities and attractions and so the story of the Lady in White was one which I decided to examine in my spare time. Oddly enough, I never heard any of the Stewarts mention the ghost, even though I was a regular caller at the farm.

Reading the general history of the locality, however, I found nothing which would explain the ghost story and certainly there was nothing in the records of Thornton Hall which would explain it. During its long history, Thornton Hall had never been a fortified home, a manor, a castle, or part of a monastery, all these being structures which seemed to attract ghost stories. It has always been a farm and family home, not some politically sensitive thing to be fought over by brigands, destroyed by warring tribes, or demolished by religious strife. I knew, of course, that ghosts had a tendency to appear in many other kinds of places such as the bedrooms or lounges of private houses, at lonely crossroads, near river-banks, in dense woodlands, on cliff tops and among ancient ruins of many kinds or even along the route of former roads, but this one, according to the yarns, always appeared on a piece of rising ground just inside one of the fields of Thornton Hall. The field bordered the road and I began to wonder whether, in ancient times, some fatal tragedy had occurred near there, but, according to the stories, the girl did not look like the rider of a horse or someone who was dressed for out-of-doors. And, so far as I could tell, none of the young female members of the resident family had met with a fatal accident or unnatural death. The Lady in White wore a long white dress with a blue sash – a nightdress perhaps? Or something which formed part of a religious service? A first communion gown? A type of shroud even? But why was she crying?

During my first months at Aidensfield, I never found a satisfactory answer to the riddle. Then a man, walking home in the early hours of the morning after watching nightjars in a local wood, announced he had seen the apparition. Few believed his story – they never do believe accounts from people who claim to have seen ghosts – and I think that not many believed he had been watching nightjars, a species of bird, in the nearby woodland.

And then things changed.

The bell of my office door at the Aidensfield police house rang about ten o'clock one April morning and when I responded, I found a casually dressed man outside. In his late thirties, in jeans, walking boots and a rather ragged sweater, and sporting a large brown beard and long hair to match, he smiled when I opened the door. It was a warm smile and I noticed a small dirty Mini parked outside the house and a young woman in the passenger seat.

'Ah!' he said. 'Good morning, Constable. You are PC Rhea, I believe?'

'I am,' I nodded. 'So how can I help you?'

I wondered if he was lost or perhaps looking for holiday accommodation in the village, or perhaps he had something to report like witnessing a crime or even being the victim of a crime, or involved in a traffic accident. In opening one's police office door to strangers, one never knew what would follow – that's why the work of a rural police officer was so interesting and varied, and so full of surprises. And this man was carrying a briefcase.

'Jeremy Winstanley,' he introduced himself in a pleasing Northumbrian accent. 'I'm an archaeologist. I'd like to have a short chat with you if you can spare the time. Sorry I didn't make an appointment, but I was in the area, at Thornton Hall in fact, and thought I'd pop in on the off-chance I'd catch you.'

'No problem,' I assured him. 'Not very many of my callers do make appointments, they usually arrive as the result of some kind of emergency. But come in,' I invited, adding, 'you've someone in the car? Does she want to come in, too?'

'I'm sure she'd rather do that than sit outside; it's not everyone who has the chance of seeing the inside of a rural police station!'

'It's not really a police station,' I laughed. 'It's my private house which happens to have a police office attached. It's like a study really, where I write my reports and attend to visitors. We don't have cells here!'

'It's Rene, my wife,' he said, and went to bring her in.

I called through to my own wife, Mary, who was in the kitchen, that I had visitors who might enjoy a cup of coffee as they were not here in any kind of emergency, and she put the kettle on. Rene, a short, rather plump young woman whose attire matched that of her husband, smiled and followed him into my small office. I found enough chairs for us all and settled them down at the opposite side of my place at the desk.

On cue, Mary appeared and asked, 'Coffee anyone? Tea?'

'Wonderful,' beamed Jeremy. 'Coffee please, black. No sugar.'

'Me too,' smiled his wife. 'I never expected to be given coffee at a police station.'

'It's not a police station,' Jeremy corrected her with his newly acquired knowledge. 'It's a police house with this office attached.'

'All right,' she beamed at me. 'I never expected to be given coffee at a police house with an office attached!'

'I can't function without my morning coffee,' I told them. 'And you happened to arrive at just the right time. So, how can I help you?'

'As I said' – Jeremy settled down and lifted his briefcase on to the desk to open it – 'we're archaeologists, free-lancers. Both Rene and me. We're working at Thornton Hall and we are about to start excavations there. We shall be leading a team of about twenty who will be arriving in the next few days. There will be vehicles, tents, equipment, quite a lot of activity of one sort or another and it will continue for quite a long time, certainly several months. Our numbers on site at any one time will vary from two to twenty-two and some days there maybe no one there at all, but we felt you should know what we're doing and who we are.'

'Thanks, that's very considerate of you. I'll pop down there whenever I can, just to make sure no one interferes with the excavations when you're not around. So where will you be working? I had no idea there was anything of archaeological interest at Thornton Hall.'

'I'm sure the house and its outbuildings are all of great interest, it's a very old site, Mr Rhea, but we'll be working in one of the fields. You know the farm?'

'I do,' I nodded. 'It's one of my regular calling places. I know the Stewarts and I drive past quite frequently.'

Then Mary appeared with a tray of coffee and biscuits which she placed on my desk.

I introduced her to the couple and they shook hands, the Winstanleys thanking her profusely, after which I said, 'Mr and Mrs Winstanley are archaeologists, Mary; they're going to be working at Thornton Hall.'

'Where the Lady in White appears?' she smiled, having often heard me talk about her.

'The Lady in White?' asked Rene. 'You mean the place is said to be haunted?'

She raised the question out of interest, not fear, and so, after inviting Mary to join us for coffee, I told them about the legend of the Lady in White, explaining that it was something the resident Stewarts never seemed to discuss. The couple listened intently and I noticed that some knowing glances were exchanged between them, but they did not interrupt, neither did they pour scorn on the yarn.

When I had finished, Jeremy said, 'Now I'll explain our

121

presence. One of our members is a keen amateur pilot and a few months ago, he flew over Thornton Hall's land. It was a chance flight, he just happened to be taking that route without any previous planning, but he's a very alert character and saw what appeared to be the outline of a former settlement between the house and the lane which passes by. It covers a substantial area. The outlines of former buildings and excavations can often be seen from the air while being virtually invisible at ground level. He was very excited about this and so we – that's the pilot, Jim Newton and ourselves, approached the owners of Thornton Hall, the Stewarts, to see whether they would allow us to conduct a preliminary excavation, just to ascertain whether there is a former structure of some kind under their field.'

'They're a friendly family,' I spoke from personal knowledge. 'And so they didn't object?'

'Not at all, they seemed to welcome the idea. Our preliminary search shows that there is definitely some kind of settlement or building under that field We think it might even date to Roman times and so, with their blessing, we're going to excavate it. I wanted you to know because our presence will generate queries and there will be quite of a lot of coming and going from the site; and, of course, when we're not there, there will be the question of security even though the site is on private property. I know you cannot spend time there on our behalf, it's our responsibility, but I'm sure you'll keep an eye on the place whenever you are passing. And if you can't, the Lady in White might be our best protector!'

'I'm sure she'll keep an eye on things and, of course, I will too,' I told them. 'I'll be most interested to know what you uncover.'

'Then feel free to pop in for a chat while we're there; we might even run to a coffee if you're lucky!'

'Will you be camping on site?' I asked.

'No, there will be tents but they'll be to protect some of the areas we uncover. Rene and I have been invited to use a cottage in the grounds of Thornton Hall; it's a former labourer's cottage which they let for holidays and when it's not booked, we can use it. We'll do that from time to time, although most days we'll travel out from York where we live. We're being funded by a consortium led by Leeds University, by the way.'

He produced a business card bearing his address and telephone number should I need to contact him. We chatted for a while with him showing me large-scale maps of the farm with several targeted areas marked in red, and after about half an hour they left to go about their business while I prepared for my daily patrol of Aidensfield beat.

When work started, news of the project excited the local people and many went down to see what was going on, albeit not during the night when the ghost of the Lady in White might be around, and, as the weeks and months passed, evidence of primitive stone and turf walls was bared, stone floors discovered, pieces of pottery and bone found along with some metal tools while black marks were also located on some stones where fires had been lit. Clearly, the site was that of a former settlement although, at the time of this initial search, the precise age or period had not been accurately determined, albeit with the earliest parts probably dating to the Iron Age, roughly some 500 years before Christ. Some of the artefacts could have come from later inhabitants, however – there was a lot of work and research to be completed for it appeared to have been a fairly long-term settlement which had spanned several centuries. Just like the current Thornton Hall in fact.

And then came drama.

My telephone rang one lunch time and I answered it to learn that the caller was Alan Stewart of Thornton Hall.

'Good afternoon, Nick.' His deep voice was easily recognizable. 'I've got Jerry Winstanley here, he wants to talk to you.'

When Jeremy Winstanley spoke he sounded breathless and excited. 'Er, hello PC Rhea, er, this is a bit awkward but we've found a body, well, a skeleton to be precise, during our dig . . . I think it's very old but I'm sure it's human and it's in a very ancient part of the site . . . I know I have to report such things to you, so that the coroner is aware of it, maybe for an inquest, but I'm sure the remains are thousands of years old.'

'Right,' I said. 'I'll come straight down and have a look.'

I rang Ashfordly Police Station to tell PC Alf Ventress that human remains had been found on the site at Thornton Hall and that it seemed they were very old, but I had to examine the scene and then set in motion the formal proceedings which were necessary to deal with the discovery. There would have to be a post-mortem. examination of the remains, clearly done with a view to establishing their gender, age and, if possible, the cause of death and there might have to be an inquest – that would depend upon what was revealed by the examination of the remains.

When I was shown the remains by Jeremy, they were in what appeared to be a stone coffin, although the bones were not laid out as if they had been subjected to a normal burial. They were curled up almost in a foetal position and appeared to be a small person, a child perhaps.

'Have you any opinion on this?' I asked Jeremy.

'It's an occupational hazard,' he smiled ruefully. 'Almost every time we begin an excavation on a very ancient site we think we might find human remains – and so we do from time to time. I think these bones are very old indeed.'

'It's a strange sort of tomb,' I ventured, looking at what appeared to be two stone walls side by side with a narrow gap separating them, and with a stone floor beneath.

'It's not a grave,' he said, 'it's the foundations of a wall. I'm guessing this was done in pagan times, when it was the custom to wall up a virgin inside a new building in the belief it would give strength to the structure. Chieftains anxious to build the finest and most secure castles would even wall up their own daughters . . . I think this is a girl from a distant pagan time. She must have died a horrible death after being sealed into this wall.'

'A murder from a long, long time ago,' I whispered.

'And far too ancient for you to do anything about it, except perhaps to give these bones a decent burial. We don't touch that area until your forensic experts and pathologists have examined it. We can work in another part of the site; it won't unduly delay our efforts.'

And so I set in motion the necessary procedures. The post-mortem on the bones, performed by a forensic pathologist who specialized in ancient remains, determined the bones were that of a girl aged about twelve to fourteen. There were no signs of brutality on the bones, e.g. no broken ribs, skull, limbs, neck, fingers or vertebrae and his conclusions echoed those of Jeremy Winstanley. In his opinion, she had been walled up within that building and left to die, probably around 500 BC.

The coroner held an inquest which delivered an open verdict, so the bones could be buried; later, there was a modest funeral in Elsinby churchyard which was attended by the archaeological team, myself and Mary, a few villagers, a Catholic priest, an Anglican vicar and a gentleman who knew the procedures at pagan burials. Thus she was given a fitting, albeit late, send-off to whatever heaven in which she believed.

It was Father Brendan O'Malley, the Catholic priest from the Church of St Francis of Assisi in Elsinby who spoke to me after the simple but rather moving burial service and said, 'Nick, I think we know why that unfortunate Lady in White haunted that area. The poor, poor girl, what a dreadful way to die. I shall pray for her. I'm sure it's never too late for that in the eternal scheme of things, and I hope she will now rest in peace. I think we'll not be troubled with any more hauntings.'

And to my knowledge, there has been no reported sighting of the Lady in White since that time.

# Chapter 7

When the North York Moors National Park became a reality in 1952, as the only one on the eastern side of England, there arose the question of an emblem or logo. It would have to be something suitable for use on a variety of arte-facts such as publicity material, official vehicles, stationery and popular merchandise like T-shirts, key rings and ball-point pens. In addition, it would have to capture the unique flavour of the area in a simple but highly visible manner.

Although I was not present at those discussions, it is not difficult to imagine the range of themes that might have been suggested – a moorland scene with an expanse of the famous heather, one of its equally famous and instantly recognizable structures such as Rievaulx Abbey or Beggar's Bridge, the Roman road at Wheeldale, a river or coastal scene, Lake Gormire near Sutton Bank, one of the area's thatched cottages, some of the park's renowned wild plants such as daffodils from Farndale or sundews from the moors, a forest or woodland scene with bluebells, or merely some representative wild creature, a salmon perhaps, a badger or maybe a bird. But if a bird was chosen, then surely it would have to be the red grouse; this is not found outside the British Isles and it is an essential and historic part of the North Yorkshire moorland scene. The grouse cannot survive without the heather, and the grouse management system with its shooting parties and heather burning maintains the heather in splendid condition. Wild though it may look, the heather is a valuable crop, carefully managed and nurtured: the heather needs the grouse and the grouse needs the heather. Each is vital to the other.

However, if the North York Moors are famous for having the largest open area of heather in England and the highest woodland cover of any English national park, as well as the indigenous red grouse, or even the astonishing coastline with its fishing villages like Robin Hood's Bay and Staithes, they are equally noted for having the highest sea-cliff on the east coast (Boulby Head near Staithes – 660 feet, 201 metres) and England's deepest mine shaft (3,750 feet, 1,143 metres deep) at Boulby Potash Mine. The moorland is also known for being the scene of the first enemy aircraft to be shot down in World War II near Sleights by Group Captain Peter Townsend. That is marked by a small obelisk on the roadside verge at Sleights Lane End at the junction of the A169 and A171 near Whitby. In addition, the moors are also the scene of the world's first ever flight by a manned aircraft. This was the work of Sir George Cayley from Brompton near Scarborough who, as early as 1809, produced a glider large enough to lift off the ground anyone who tried to hold on to it while it was in flight. By 1853, however, he had improved his glider so much that he took it into Brompton Dale, sat his coachman on board and launched him across the valley. The unhappy man flew about fifty yards but, unware of his place in aviation history, he shouted, 'I wish to give notice! I was hired to drive, not to fly.' The Wright brothers flew their famous *Kitty Hawk* some fifty-one years later – but it had an engine. Sir George Cayley's machine was a glider and lacked mechanical power but, nonetheless, it was the first manned flight.

It follows that those who tried to conjure up a suitable emblem or logo for the North York Moors National Park had a huge and very difficult of choice of subjects – too many perhaps – and then the famous moorland crosses were mentioned.

There are some 1,300 crosses on the North Yorks moors, some now little more than a stone base lost among the undergrowth, some shaped not in the least like a cross, but several still standing like sentinels just as they have for hundreds of years. Lilla Cross, almost in the shadow of Fylingdales Ballistic Missile Early Warning Station is perhaps the oldest Christian relic in England, being erected around AD 626. When the monks travelled the moors between their great abbeys, they marked their routes with stone crosses. Perhaps the most famous, and certainly the most prominent is Ralph Cross, erroneously known as Ralph's Cross but more correctly known as Young Ralph.

There are two Ralph Crosses – Old Ralph, a small chap at only five feet high, stands about 200 yards from the more famous Young Ralph; Young Ralph is about nine feet tall with a slim shape topped by the famous cross shape. Both stand close to the road which leads from Hutton-le-Hole to Castleton. Young Ralph occupies one of the highest points of the moors with astonishing long distance views for almost 360 degrees. The age of the original Young Ralph is unknown, but the present cross, which has been subjected to several repairs, is thought to be an eighteenth-century replica. Its purpose was probably that of a way marker or even a place at which the monks halted to celebrate mass or to fulfil their religious offices during long journeys.

It is just one of many moorland crosses which bear personal names – I can add a few such as Percy Cross, Jack Cross, Mauley Cross, John Cross, Cooper Cross, Tom Smith's Cross, Donna Cross, Jenny Bradley, Anna Ain Howe Cross, Hudson's Cross, Redman Cross, Robinson Cross and, at Whitby Abbey (just outside the park's boundaries) there is the more modern Caedmon Cross, erected in 1898 to the memory of the cowherd Caedmon who became England's first poet.

But it was the distinctive outline of Young Ralph on its lofty and lonely setting, along with its part in the history of life on these moors, which was chosen as the National Park's emblem and logo. It won favour ahead of any prominent landmark, even though it was a man-made object, and it was felt more suitable than any wild bird or animal. There was a suggestion that if a grouse had been selected, it would have led to comments like 'The park is Yorkshire's biggest grouse. . . .' grouse being widely used as a word meaning to grumble or complain! After much discussion, therefore, Young Ralph became the emblem of the new national park – and I believe it was a wise decision. It is a very apt image which is readily identifiable.

I knew Young Ralph from my childhood days for I used to cycle past on my regular excursions into the moors, and I was also very aware of an ancient custom associated with the cross. On the top of the upright shaft was a small hollow which had been carved out of the stone, and into this small depression the generous wayfarers of old would place their small spare coins as an act of charity. The less fortunate who happened to be travelling that same route would examine the hollow in the top of the cross to see whether any money had been left, and if there was, they would help themselves. That was the long accepted custom. I found it quite touching to discover that it continued well into the twentieth century.

It remained a delightful display of honesty, trust and charity for although most of us living in the area knew of this ancient custom, none would remove any of the small sums which accumulated there. They were for charity, not for local children. Many is the time I have cycled to Ralph Cross as a child, parked my bike against it and stood on the crossbar or saddle to reach into the hollow on top. And if there was money – usually pennies, threepenny bits or perhaps an odd sixpence or two – I would leave it, sometimes even adding a small donation of my own. It was always interesting to see just how much cash had been deposited but whenever I checked, it was rarely more than two or three shillings (10–15p). That was a useful sum to a hungry tramp – it would buy him food and drink.

I have no idea who, in modern times, would help themselves to that small cache of coins for I doubt if anyone really needs such a tiny amount of money. To my knowledge, it rarely totalled more than two or three shillings but it meant that even in the twentieth century, the mutual aid society of ancient times was alive and functioning high on the North York Moors.

One problem associated with this custom was the height of Young Ralph, some nine feet (2.75 metres or so). A person on horseback, for example, could easily place money into the hollow on top or remove it; if two people were present, they could give one another a helping lift or leg-up, but one person, without a horse or cycle to elevate them, would not find it easy to deposit coins or remove them. A disaster occurred in 1961 when a man attempted to climb the cross to retrieve money from the top and in so doing, broke the slender shaft into three pieces. It was skilfully repaired but only a few weeks later, a severe gale caused it to tilt alarmingly and so further repairs were required. And then in 1985 (many years after I had ended my spell as the constable of Aidensfield), some vandalizing idiots equipped with a powerful vehicle and a strong chain actually succeeded in toppling the cross to the ground and smashing it. It took a long time for new parts to be crafted and for the cross to be re-erected, and no one knows who caused the damage or why they went to such lengths to carry out such an unnecessary act of completely mindless vandalism. It was a drastic means of inspecting the hollow on top!

During my service as the constable of Aidensfield, my

routine patrols rarely went within striking distance of Young Ralph, although in later years as our beats expanded due to modernization, I found myself paying the occasional visit. Our divisional boundaries now passed very close to the site and we were instructed to pay regular attention to the outermost regions of our expanding patch. With strong childhood memories of my earlier trips, I found it quite odd to be sitting at the same place in my police vehicle but still gazing across to the North Sea on one side and the expanse of the heather on the other.

In spite of the passage of time, I'd heard that people were still placing their small change in the hollow on top, a fact which indicated that, in spite of the welfare service, others less fortunate came to take advantage of it. Now, of course, being an adult, I was not tempted to try an ascent of the cross to check whether or not this was true – for that, I relied on word of mouth from local people who had tested the truth of the custom. They assured me that people continued to place coins on Young Ralph and that others continued to collect them.

It was this practice which intrigued Inspector Harry Breckon when I told him about it during a supervisory visit to me one morning in May. He was the officer in charge of Eltering Sub Division in whose area my beat was situated; my beat, Aidensfield, was part of Ashfordly Section which in turn lay within the larger Eltering Sub-Division. Thus Inspector Breckon was my boss, and senior to my local sergeant too. On that day in May, therefore, he radioed me when I was on patrol and suggested a rendezvous at Ralph's Cross, as he called it. I didn't like to correct him! It was a routine part of his supervisory duties to arrange such meetings, for they gave him a chance to update his subordinates about matters of duty, and them to express any concerns or worries they might have, both professional or personal. And, I suspect, it also allowed him to visit some beautiful parts of the countryside, ostensibly in the furtherance of his police duties. He suggested eleven o'clock that morning for our meeting, adding that we might pop into the remote Lion Inn on its lofty moorland site, not for a social drink but on an official visit.

The landlord had applied for an occasional licence for a customer's 21st birthday party in a local village hall and the inspector wanted to clarify a few points. A large part of our rural duties entailed visiting pubs during the times they were open but also when they were closed (or supposed to be closed!), to ensure the law was being upheld. However, there were lots of ancilliary aspects to the liquor licensing laws which had to be considered. This type of application was one of them.

At eleven o'clock, therefore, I parked my Mini-van on the wide grass verge, shorn bowls-green smooth by the constant nibbling of the ever-present moorland sheep, and awaited my inspector in his small black official car, a Ford Anglia. He arrived on time, parked near my van and climbed out; I did likewise, greeted him with a 'Good morning, sir', saluted him, because we were both in uniform, and awaited his next remark. He was a charming man, very capable but never officious and always considerate to the young constables in his charge.

'Everything all right, Rhea?' he asked. 'No problems?'

'No problems, sir, nothing outstanding,' I assured him.

'You'll be finding things quiet after your spell as acting sergeant?'

'I enjoyed it, sir, but there's always something to do on a rural beat,' I replied diplomatically.

'That's the way to success,' he smiled. 'Never let yourself be idle; keep yourself active; be creative. So now it's a case of waiting for a vacancy in the post of sergeant's rank, eh?'

'Yes, sir, but I'm quite happy at Aidensfield, doing this kind of work.'

'I can see that, but don't fall into the trap of staying too long in one place, however much you enjoy the work. Think of the future; you do have a young family to consider, remember, and a flourishing career will help them.'

'I'll remember that, sir, thank you.'

'Good. All comes to those who wait, never forget that! Well, this is a fine place, isn't it? You know, I often bring Mrs Breckon up here for an outing on my day off. We walk across the moors, We love the wind in our hair and the springiness of the turf beneath our feet . . . a wonderful place.'

'I love it too, sir,' I told him, and then mentioned my childhood cycle trips to this very place.

'You know the history of this old cross, do you?' he asked, with a twinkle in his eye. He'd done this sort of thing before, asking whether I knew the history or background of well-known locations.

'Yes, sir,' I said, and promptly launched into my brief knowledge of Young Ralph Cross, Old Ralph Cross and Fat Betty, the name of another stone not far away. Fat Betty cannot be missed because she is painted white and is rather squat in shape. I told him the famous legend of the crosses, i.e. that if Young Ralph and Fat Betty ever meet, they'll get married. Then there is the tale that if three kings ever meet at Young Ralph Cross, the world will come to an end. And, as a grand finale to my educative piece, I told him about the age-old custom of placing coins in the hollow on Young Ralph.

'Is that true?' he asked, with signs of disbelief on his face. 'Is it still done?'

'Oh yes, sir,' I assured him, with all the confidence I could muster. 'It's been the custom for centuries and it was certainly carried on when I was a child. I'm fairly sure it's still done.'

'You mean people actually place money on top of that

cross so that others can help themselves to it?' He sounded highly sceptical. Here was a suspicious police mind at work . . . why would any sane person want to give money away?

'That was the original idea,' I confirmed. 'It was a means for people with money to help those without any, to obtain food and drink I believe, especially during long journeys in remote areas.'

'And you are trying to convince me it is still done? In the twentieth century?'

'Yes, sir. In fact you can see the repair marks on the cross now, it was broken when a man tried to climb up to take some money, and that was as recently as 1961.'

'I wasn't stationed in this part of the world at that time,' he said. 'I was at Leyburn in the Dales and missed that story. Well, blow me. So are you saying there's money up there now? Just waiting for someone to collect it?'

'Well, I can't guarantee there'll be any there now, sir, it might have been collected very recently, that's if there was any.'

'Well, young Rhea, I think we should put the story to the test. So reverse your van as close as you can to the cross, stand on the floor of the rear compartment and see if you can reach up there. But whatever you do, make sure you don't harm the cross! We don't want to be responsible for more damage!'

Orders from a senior officer are orders even if they seem rather odd and so, as Inspector Breckon watched with a smile on his face, I manoeuvred my van into a suitable position. As I prepared to climb on to the edge of the rear compartment so that I might reach on to the top of Young Ralph, he came to watch and was clearly amused by this performance. I wondered what any members of the public might think if they happened to see us in action but the road was quiet and we were operating unseen – fortunately, in my opinion.

By standing in the rear of my van, just above the back bumper which was only a foot or so from the shaft of the cross, I could turn around so that I was facing the stonework, support myself by lightly holding the shaft or even one of the open van doors and then reach up to the hollow. It was slightly damp, I noted, as my fingers dipped into it but I was not high enough to see into the saucer-like hollow. It would be rainwater, I guessed, for we'd had some heavy showers over the past few days. But as my fingers explored, I found several coins but could not guess their denominations. Gingerly, I scraped them towards the edge and scooped them out, one by one. There were several – as I placed them one by one on the roof of the van, I noted four sixpences, eight threepenny bits, fifteen pennies and eighteen halfpennies, and even a couple of farthings, now obsolete. And as I scraped the damp bowl to ensure everything was recovered, I found another coin. I scooped it out, saw it was different from any of the others but couldn't decide what it was. I placed it with the others as Inspector Breckon was counting our total.

'Six shillings and a ha'penny, Rhea, reckoning without that last one. That's counting the farthings even if they've been demonetized. That's amazing . . .'

'I'm not sure what this other one is, sir,' and I handed it to him. 'Do you think it's some kind of foreign coin?'

'Good grief, Rhea!' he almost shouted, after he had closely examined my final trophy. 'Don't you know what this is?'

'No, sir,' I admitted, climbing down from my uncomfortable perch.

'Well, it's not a foreign coin, you should know that. This is a James I sixpence, Rhea, see? Minted in 1604? And that coat of arms below the date . . . good grief, lad, this is amazing! It won't have been up there all that time, will it?'

'No, sir,' I smiled. 'I'm sure the pot is emptied regularly.

Besides, the cross was knocked down in 1961, we know that.'

'Well, this is a turn-up! We can't put this one back for all and sundry to help themselves to, can we?'

'Is it valuable, sir?' I knew very little about our ancient coinage but it was evident he knew something about the subject.

'It depends on its condition and rarity value, but I'd say this could fetch about twenty pounds in a coin-dealer's shop. It could bring more at auction if a collector really wanted to get hold of it.'

'Twenty pounds?' I almost shouted. That was about two weeks' wages for me!

'Well you found it,' he said, and then added, 'But you are a police officer and I doubt if you'd want to keep it.'

'But who would put it up there, sir?' I was as puzzled as he.

'Search me, Rhea. It might be somebody who thought it was a foreign coin and wanted rid of it. People do that, don't they? It's like putting foreign coins into church collection plates, or hoping shopkeepers won't notice them if you hand them over among a lot of other small stuff, or even hoping fruit machines will accept them. That's probably why those farthings are there, nobody wants them these days as they can't be spent! But back to the James I sixpence. No one who knows what this really is would have left it up there for the good of someone else's soul, Rhea, you can be sure about that. So yes, this is a true find. So, can I ask what you are going to do with it?'

'I think it should go to a museum,' I heard myself say.

'You don't think it's stolen property then?' was his next question. 'Someone anxious to get rid of incriminating evidence?'

'I doubt if they'd place stolen property somewhere like this, sir, knowing it could be found and perhaps identified. If this is a valuable coin, its loss must have been reported,

137

but I've not heard of any raids on coin collections or museums or coin dealers' premises. I favour the theory it was placed there because the donor had no idea what it was and wanted rid of it because he couldn't spend it. Like those farthings.'

'I agree with that; it might even be the same person, thinking he's got rid of farthings and a foreign coin! So you don't think we should inform the coroner? On the grounds the old coin might be treasure trove? It is silver, you know.'

'Treasure trove is property which has been concealed, sir, hidden quite deliberately. Like buried treasure. If this was put up there, sir, it must have been done by someone who knew of the old custom in which case he wanted it to be found by a needy person. That suggests it has not been hidden or concealed. The farthings don't qualify as treasure trove of course, being neither silver nor gold.'

'Fair enough. I think your idea of donating it to a museum is the best. So replace that six shillings, Rhea, and don't include those two farthings. You can't spend farthings now, their worthwhile life ended in 1960, so I think they could go to a museum as well. They'll be collectors' items one day. Then make a note in your pocket book of this unexpected event and I shall countersign it to show your actions are genuine.'

And so we did that. I replaced all the other small change, made a note about my interesting find and then we adjourned to the Lion Inn to discuss the licensee's application for an occasional licence. A few days later, I donated the farthings and the James I sixpence to the newly founded folk museum in the village of Grandstone, but didn't say where any had been found. I didn't want the curiosity of visitors and locals alike to compel them to go hunting ancient silver coins or out-of-date farthings on the top of Young Ralph!

Even today, however, I have no idea how that fascinating

old coin came to be placed on the top of that old cross, nor do I know who put it there. And who put the farthings there? We may never know.

The story of the ancient coin on Ralph Cross is just one example of the very strange things which, from time to time, happen in the countryside. Another example occurred when a young woman hurried into the office attached to my police house at Aidensfield.

Fortunately, I was there, attending to some paperwork before going out on patrol. The woman was in her early thirties, a pretty person with dark hair and a face with rosy cheeks and a pair of beautiful dark eyes. But she was panting heavily and clearly in some distress. It was about 9.15 in the morning, I noted, and I recognized her as a resident of Aidensfield, even if I did not know her name. I'd seen her around the village.

'Oh thank God you're here!' she panted, as she arrived at the counter. 'I must tell somebody . . .'

'Well, take your time,' I said. 'Get your breath back . . . another few minutes won't hurt.'

She stood before me as she took several long and very deep breaths and clearly she was determined to tell me her story in a cool and calm manner. After a few minutes, and after taking a few more shallow breaths, she gasped, 'I've found a body . . .'

'A body?' I asked, trying to remain as calm as possible. 'Human?'

'Yes,' she nodded. 'Human. It's in Elsinby Woods, near the river-bank not far from the path . . . do you know the woods?'

'Reasonably well,' I nodded.

'It's about half a mile into the woods from the Elsinby side, under a pile of leaves and undergrowth, near the rock everyone calls the Wishing Stone,' she assured me. 'One of the legs is sticking out, that's how I found it. Well, my dog found it ... she's a labrador. It's awful, Constable, truly awful ... so I came straight here.'

'You did exactly the right thing.' I felt she ought to be reassured about her actions. 'Can you take me there now?'

'Yes, yes, of course. I have time. . . .'

And so it was that I informed Eltering Sub-Division that I was going to investigate a report of a found human body and that I would be absent from my office for at least an hour. I added I would provide a situation report as soon as possible. In such cases, the local constable is often first on the scene and it is his preliminary duty to assess the situation, bearing in mind that the corpse could be the result of a suicide, a natural death, or even murder. In some cases, the answer is obvious but in cases of doubt the death is always treated as suspicious and the CID, along with the Scenes of Crime Department, are then called to the scene. A great deal of responsibility, particularly in the preservation of evidence, therefore falls upon the shoulders of the rural constable if he is the first police officer to visit the scene. And in most cases, he is first on the scene.

His prime task is to make a swift but thoroughly professional assessment of the situation. He must consider immediate matters like preservation of the scene and any evidence, plus the speedy tracing of reliable witnesses. If the case proves to be murder, his actions during those first moments can be vital. A careless approach can immediately destroy valuable evidence and the guilty person may evade justice. For these reasons, I was aware of my responsibilities as I headed for the wood with the lady witness.

The young woman in question was Shirley Hanson, married with two children who were attending Aidensfield Primary School. She had escorted the children to school that morning and had then taken her dog for a walk, a thing she did each school-day morning. Her husband, Ron,

CONSTABLE AROUND THE PARK

worked in Ashfordly in a bakery – I knew him by sight. As I followed in my police van, Shirley drove her car back to Elsinby; she parked at the entrance to the woodland path and so we began our trek into the woods. I knew the walk sufficiently well to appreciate it would take about twenty minutes to reach the point to which she had referred.

She was clearly in a state of high excitement as she led me along the woodland path while her dog, Bess, following off the lead, was snuffling and foraging among the vegetation beside the path. She was clearly revelling in her second walk of that morning. As Shirley forged ahead in her determined and speedy manner, I found myself trailing behind and panting in my efforts to keep pace with her. It was clear she considered herself to be on a mission of some kind. During that hectic walk I questioned her about the discovery, learning there had been no one else at the scene when she had arrived, that the body seemed to have been there for some time because most of it was buried under leaves and undergrowth, and that she had not touched anything. Immediately upon spotting the remains, she had hurried to inform the police before telling anyone else.

Luckily, in the circumstances, I was on duty and at home in my office.

After about fifteen minutes of fast walking, she halted and pointed into the woodland to the right of the pathway. I could see what appeared to be a large pile of vegetable rubbish comprising leaves, cut undergrowth, chopped-off branches and some stumps of dead trees. It was, I thought, a pile of discarded bits and pieces of the sort foresters and wood-cutters would make, which would eventually rot down and become compost for the benefit of the woodland in time to come. It had probably been there for generations and might even become a bonfire when it was sufficiently dry, but that was not the case at that time. Now, it was just a pile of woodland rejects – but, as Shirley pointed out to me rather excitedly, protuding from the base on the side furthest from the path was the unmistakable shape of a human leg. The rest of the body was hidden.

From a distance, I could see the limb was covered with what looked like a dark-green trouser leg but the top, above the knee, was concealed beneath the pile of leaves and wood; a bare foot was showing at the exposed end. No other part of the body could be seen. Her dog was romping around among the trees and paid no attention to the remains; Shirley called Bess to heel and she obeyed, tail wagging as if some treat was to follow. I must admit I was surprised the dog did not pay any attention to the discovery – I would have thought the smell would have attracted her but she was a very obedient animal and sat at Shirley's heel while I decided what to do next.

'When you first saw it, did you approach it?' I asked.

If this did develop into a murder enquiry, the investigating team would want to know who had approached it and from what direction so that traces of the finder's presence along a particular route could be eliminated from suspicion.

'No, I saw Bess sniffing at it and realized what it was straight away, that bare foot . . . so I called her to heel then came back straight away to find you. I didn't go near it.'

I must now cross those few yards to determine just how much of the body was there, whether it was male or female, whether it had been there for some time and whether it bore injuries which would indicate a violent death. My Sub-Divisional commander would require as much initial information as I could provide, for that would help in determining the subsequent action. Having established as much as I could about Shirley's movements at the scene, it was now my turn to approach the remains.

I decided upon a wide approach, not the direct one from the path just in case someone had dragged or carried the body from the path; if it was murder, of course, the victim could have been killed anywhere in these woods and hidden here or, of course, the crime could have happened at some distance beyond the wood's boundaries, and the remains brought here for concealment. I thought that was unlikely – transporting a corpse along a woodland path would not be very easy! All kinds of probabilities began to flood into my mind as I made my way carefully through a tangled mass of briars, bracken and undergrowth. Shirley, with Bess still sitting patiently at her heel, stood on the path to watch my progress.

When I was within some six feet of the leg, I halted to view it from that angle. I could see that the green trouser leg came down to the ankle and that the top of the leg, from the knee upwards, remained concealed but there was something odd about the sight. I'd have thought some other part of the body would now be revealed, especially from the angle at which I was approaching but I could not see any sign of another leg or the base of a torso. Had the body been dismembered? Had it been cut into portable portions for disposal in this woodland? All I could discern was a leg protruding from a pile of natural waste. The dark-green trouser leg made it somewhat difficult to distinguish the leg from its surroundings although the unclad foot was prominent enough, and I guessed Shirley had spotted it due to her dog's behaviour. Most people walking past would never have noticed it, even if the foot was visible and so it was quite a good hiding place – or had been until Shirley's dog had begun to nose around.

Puzzled, I walked closer, my eyes seeking other portions of the body among the greenery and composted rubbish but found none. Then I reached the leg. I stood near the bare foot – and then realized what it was. It was an artificial leg! I bent down to touch it and saw Shirley's hands go to her face in horror at my action.

143

But this was a plastic foot! It was smooth and cool and as pink as a baby's bottom and it was hinged. I moved it slightly and then tugged. The entire leg came away easily from its resting place among the rubbish and I looked at Shirley, seeing the horror on her face as I was apparently treating this human body part with some irreverence.

'It's an artificial leg!' I called to her. By then, I could see that it was the type which fitted on to the stump of a thigh; it was a right leg – the foot told me that. Whoever had disposed of it had covered it with the leg of an old pair of trousers in an attempt to disguise it. Mightily relieved, I placed it on the ground and then searched for any similar trophies, but found none.

Shirley was still watching me with her hands covering her face and for a moment I thought she still believed it was a genuine human leg, but then I realized she was now smothering her laughter. Bess, now sensing that things had changed, resumed her romping among the undergrowth.

'You must think I'm stupid!' She now looked very embarrassed. 'Calling you out to a false leg . . .'

'Not at all, I'm pleased it was a false one. But it looked real enough from a distance, so you did the right thing, Shirley. The problem is what to do with it now!'

'Why would anyone leave a false leg there?' she asked.

'That's a very good question,' I laughed. 'So, do we remove it and take it to the police station as found property? You found it, so if it's not claimed within three months, it could become yours . . .'

'I don't want a false leg!' she retorted.

'I think we should leave it here,' I decided. 'After all, this wood belongs to the estate which makes it private property, and that leg might have an owner. Someone might come back for it; it might have been placed here deliberately. After all, it's not likely someone would actually lose 'or misplace a false leg, is it? So we'll leave it.'

144

When I rang Sub-Divisional Headquarters with my situation report, I said the report had been made in good faith, but that the alleged body part was merely an artificial leg. There were no queries from Sub-Division and that was the end of the matter, except that when I went for a walk through the wood some four or five weeks later, the leg had disappeared. I wondered if the owner had come back for it – but that raised even more curious questions.

# Chapter 8

One of the skills required in a rural police officer was, and perhaps still is, to acquire a deep personal knowledge of the people who live in the village under his care. This can be expanded to include those living in nearby communities. The acquisition of such very localized information can take a long, long time and it has to be gained without appearing to be nosy or probing people's innermost personal secrets! This in-depth understanding of a community and its people is vital if the constable is to efficiently perform his or her duties. It is a very fine path to tread, but it has always been said that a good village constable, or indeed any good police officer of whatever rank, can function at his or her best only when he or she has amassed a wealth of very detailed local knowledge. One never knows when it can be useful in solving crime, dealing with emergencies or even life-saving.

So what sort of knowledge should a constable seek to acquire? The answer is that it can be almost anything. It is virtually impossible to quantify it, but it might include everyday things like the times of local buses or trains or the names of people who work daily in the community like the postman, milkman, dustman, doctor, district nurses, veterinary surgeon and others. At a more important level, especially in the countryside, is the knowledge of where to find emergency help in the shortest possible time – for example, it's useful to know the location of fire-fighting equipment in the moorland forests, the nearest water mains, all the surgeries (doctors' and vets'), the source of heavy lifting equipment, and garages with specialist cutting gear.

Likewise, it's vital to know personnel with special rescue skills, say, underwater, or from cliff faces; it's useful knowing interpreters too. . . . To be frank, it is impossible to list every piece of information that a local constable must carry within his head, and it is vital that he or she responds instantly, positively and with confidence in any given situation or emergency.

Personal knowledge stored in one's brain is infinitely more valuable than dusty files located in offices which are miles from the scene of an emergency. Even in the twenty-first century, files maintained in computers are rarely more efficient than those in the brain of a dedicated police officer. In the 1960s, a capable constable was, quite literally, a walking encyclodaedia who, in addition to all those practical skills, had to possess a working knowledge of criminal law and police procedure. He or she had to know how to react correctly in any situation, as it could, in the future, cause lawyers to amass huge fees as they debated whether or not he had acted legally in making a spilt-second decision; he or she may also expect the courts to later ponder his actions in their typically laborious way. It meant – and the public expected – that a lowly constable on patrol must cope, at a moment's notice, with any kind of incident, large or small, dangerous or humorous and legal or illegal.

In addition, to all this, the constable must also know the people on his beat; this was vital. He must be aware of their peculiarities, their weak spots, their strengths, their vulnerability, their relationships with others, their honesty and reliability, their family background, work and hobbies, their skills and anything else which might aid him in the performance of his duty.

In short, he should take no one at face value; everyone's life has its own private areas in addition to those which appear to the public. A smile on a woman's face might conceal a tormented mind within; a confident swagger in a man might likewise conceal a mass of insecurities or secrets. A man, woman or child walking down the village street offered untold secrets to uncover, some for public consumption, others for little more than gratuitous curiosity.

Such complex thoughts crossed my mind when I became aware of Mrs Charmain Cotterell of High Howe House in Aidensfield. She was an extremely haughty woman in her late fifties whose husband Joseph was a very successful solicitor in Ashfordly. She had no real friends outside her home and never took part in village events, preferring to spend her time either in the house or working in her extensive garden. She employed a home help, a lady who did the shopping and other chores and who undertook a range of internal domestic duties at High Howe House, everything from making the bed and cooking the meals to cleaning and dusting. Mrs Cotterell's helper was called Mrs Jennie Busby, a widow in her sixties who lived in a cottage next door to High Howe House. Although it was a mistress and servant relationship, the pair were in fact good friends. Indeed, Jennie was probably the only real friend that Mrs Cotterell had, and she was a down-to-earth Yorkshire woman whose husband had been a forester. Most of us believed that she could tell Mrs Cotterell that she was being silly or stupid, or that she should behave in a different manner towards the villagers, but it seemed that Mrs Cotterell took absolutely no notice of her working-class friend.

In spite of the difference in their backgrounds, Mrs Cotterell rarely went out of doors without Jennie Busby and, from time to time, they could be seen walking together along the village street, perhaps to visit someone or perhaps to attend the Anglican parish church on a Sunday morning.

Some people claimed the pair were inseparable; some even wondered if there was some other kind of relationship which was deliberately kept from the public eye. What the public saw was two women who were always together. Was that natural, they asked? Did it matter that both were somewhat mature? Eyebrows were raised and unasked questions implied.

In the appearance she presented to the public, however, Mrs Cotterell much resembled the stereotype Victorian lady of quality. She was quite tall with an almost regal bearing, being about five feet ten inches or so and well built to match her height, being neither slim nor overweight. Always beautifully dressed and exquisitely groomed, she wore expensive clothing which often included a fur wrap, a fur coat or a fur stole. Her range of hats was of the kind one might expect at Ascot or Henley Regatta on the heads of duchesses or similar ladies of quality and her overcoats were always expensively tailored to complement her vast range of impressive millinery and shoes. She never appeared in public without gloves. Thus she presented a rather stately demeanour as she strode along the street with her head tilted backwards as if to avoid eye contact with anyone. That air of superiority was enhanced because she rarely spoke to anyone.

If someone said, 'Good morning, Mrs Cotterell', then she might deign to reply with a half-smile and perhaps a measured and clipped 'Good morning' or 'Good afternoon' depending upon the time of day, but that was about all. She would never stop for a chat, not in the street. It had been known, however, for her to bow her head ever so slightly when a person passed by, and to ask discreetly of Mrs Busby, 'Who was that?' Her dear friend and helper would respond accordingly; clearly, Mrs Cotterell had no wish to involve herself with the ordinary mortals of Aidensfield.

From the time I arrived in the village, I had never had any reason to talk to or to visit Mr or Mrs Cotterell in their fine detached house. Mr Cotterell, it seems, was a more outgoing character who ran a thriving solicitor's practice which specialized in business and industrial matters, both within this country and overseas. Had he accepted work within the world of criminal law either for the defence or prosecution, then I might have had more contact with him, but in addition to a very busy professional life in this country, he was often away from home on business trips. He visited places like London, Manchester and Birmingham and even went to overseas cities like New York, Athens, Rome and Paris; he was probably one of the most successful businessmen within the Ashfordly–Aidensfield district. His wife, however, did not travel overseas with him even when he offered her first class accommodation with a guarantee of privacy. He was a nice man, tall, distinguished and friendly, and he was much more affable and sociable than his wife.

He would often walk down to the pub for a drink, chatting to all and sundry *en route* through Aidensfield and apparently loving the chatter, laughter and general *bonhomie* that a village pub can engender. Mrs Cotterell, on the other hand, had never been seen in the pub and very rarely in the shop or post office. She never attended concerts or plays in the village hall and had even (God forbid) rejected the invitation to become President of the Womens' Institute in Aidensfield and worse still, had rejected another invitation to be patron of the Aidensfield and District Flower Club.

Such snobbish behaviour had not pleased the village ladies, serving merely to increase the feeling among the community that Mrs Cotterell considered herself too high and mighty to mix with ordinary mortals. For example, she always left church without pausing for a chat with the other members of the congregation as they departed, although she would wish 'Good day' to the vicar if he managed to present himself to her before she left the premises.

It was this kind of aloofness which set her apart and the result was that, with the passage of time, few villagers tried to cultivate her or befriend her; certainly, she was not invited to village events, dinner parties, socials or any of the village functions. Had she been more sociable, for example, she might have been asked to present the prizes at such important events as the village dog show or to judge the beautiful baby competition, but such was her haughtiness and distanced behaviour, that she isolated herself from the village and its people. People commented on her lack of willingness to socialize and everyone blamed the woman herself. In their view, it was entirely her fault, they reasoned, not theirs; she had quite deliberately distanced herself from them, not them from her!

As the village constable, I knew of Mrs Cotterell and, in time, came to know about her snobbishness. I must admit I did not understand why she behaved in such an aloof manner although I must also admit I never tried to fathom a reason. Everyone, including me, ascribed it to her personality – it was quite simple: she thought she was better than anyone else. That's why she never spoke to anyone in the street, that's why she didn't socialize with the villagers, and that's why she wore big hats and lots of fur. She regarded herself as superior. And that's how I came to regard her.

Then one afternoon in late May, around three o'clock, I received a telephone call from Mrs Cotterell. I was extremely surprised for she had never ever telephoned me on any previous occasion, nor had she made any effort to contact me about any matter whatsoever. I'd have thought that if she'd had a need to contact the police, she would have rung the chief constable himself at Force Headquarters. But no, she was ringing me! My immediate instinct was that she had a complaint of some kind. But no.

'Mrs Cotterell here, Mr Rhea,' she announced, her voice sounding surprisingly normal. There was even a hint of a Yorkshire accent and it did not sound in the least haughty or snobbish. 'You may know my house, High Howe, on the road to Elsinby.'

'Yes, I know it,' I responded with slight suspicion. 'So how can I help you?'

'I hope I am not being a nuisance, PC Rhea, calling you in the middle of the afternoon.'

'Not at all, I'm on duty, and I'm in my office at the moment catching up with some paperwork, but I can break off what I'm doing. There's no problem from my point of view, so please go ahead.'

'Well, it might be nothing, but I believe a spring has broken the surface of the ground in Mr and Mrs Henfield's garden, and water is flowing from it. It might even be a burst water main of course. The Henfields are away, Mr Rhea, so Mrs Busby has told me, and I am worried it might develop into a flood and get into the house.'

'Right,' I said, knowing the house in question. 'I'll go and have a look, Mrs Cotterell. I'll make an assessment of what's happening and then decide what to do about it. It might mean ringing the council or the water authorities if it's a burst pipe. I'll go immediately.'

'Thank you, Mr Rhea, it would put my mind at rest.'

'Will you be at home later if I call to tell you what I've done?'

'Yes, yes of course. I do hope you don't think I'm a nuisance . . .'

'If this is a burst water main or even a small spring, then lots of people will be grateful to you, Mrs Cotterell. You are certainly not a nuisance!'

I pulled on my tunic, gathered my uniform cap from the stand in the office, told Mary where I was heading and within minutes was on the road towards the Henfields' house.

It was only a few minutes' drive and I was soon easing to a halt in their driveway. Although Mrs Cotterell had said they were away, I rang the door bell to announce my arrival and when I was sure they were not at home, I began to explore the garden. I opened the large double gates which admitted me to the rear of the house and into their spacious garden, beautifully tended with smooth lawns, rose beds, a shrubbery and a vegetable garden. I walked rapidly around it seeking any sign of surplus water, a flowing spring or a burst pipe but found nothing, not even the tinest patch of dampness. From the garden, I could see Mrs Cotterell's house looming in the distance over the beech hedge; she had a clear view of these premises from her upper floor but I wondered if she had made a mistake about the garden. I peered over walls and through hedges into the neighbours' gardens but found no sign of a water burst and not even a goldfish pond. Before I left, I knocked on the neighbours' doors to explain my concern, but none had any such problem on their premises. I began to think Mrs Cotterell had been mistaken and so I decided to call on her and ask her to show me the scene from her vantage point.

When I arrived, I rang the bell and she responded instantly with a large smile; she looked infinitely more homely than she did when promenading along Aidensfield High Street in her finery. But, I reasoned, she was at home now. She could relax there.

'I've been into the Henfield's garden,' I explained. 'There's no sign of a leak of any kind, Mrs Cotterell, there's not even a damp patch or a goldfish pond. I went to the neighbouring houses too, but there's nothing there either.'

'Oh dear . . . have I been very silly? Sending you on a wild goose chase?'

'Not at all, clearly there was something which troubled you and I'd like to find out what it was. Where were you when you noticed the water?'

'Upstairs, actually, on the landing. I saw it from the landing window.'

'What time?' I wondered if there'd been a long time lapse before reporting this.

'Just before I called you,' she said. 'Three o'clock or so.'

'Can you show me? It's easy to mis-calculate distance and location from a lofty vantage point.' I tried to reassure her and wanted her to know that I believed she was telling the truth.

'Yes, yes, of course, come this way.'

She led me into the hall of her home and up the wide oak staircase to the landing. At that point, a large window overlooked the adjoining properties and provided a clear view into several neighbouring gardens on all sides.

'That house with the blue slate roof belongs to Mr and Mrs Henfield,' she said with confidence. 'I saw the water in their garden, Mr Rhea, I know I did.'

'Can you see it now?' I asked.

'No, I can't, it's gone, there's no sign of it but it was there ... I'd have asked my husband to look at it but he's in Leeds today and Mrs Busby is having her day off . . .'

'I'll ask around the village,' I assured her, knowing the area was prone to springs appearing in odd places. 'If there is a problem with springs or burst pipes, someone will know. I doubt if a pipe would produce a spout of water in fits and starts, but a spring might; a burst pipe under pressure would be continuous.'

'I don't think it was spouting out, Mr Rhea, it looked like a pool.'

'So it could be a spring and if there's one producing any kind of flow, it needs to be dealt with, we don't want any flooding!'

'Thank you for being so understanding and so quick to respond,' she said with surprising humility.

'If you see it again, ring me straight away,' I told her. 'It is important that we get to the root of this.'

'Yes, yes, of course.'

And so I left her somewhat deflated and feeling that perhaps she had been rather silly, whereas I was confident she had seen something which had troubled her. In my quest to determine the truth, I visited several houses in the village then spoke to a number of local people including the plumber and postman, but none could offer any explanation for this sight of a pool or flood of water. To their knowledge, there had been no reports of burst pipes or new springs, not for several months.

The following day was my rest day and I decided to spend it at home tending the garden; the lawn needed cutting, weeds galore were sprouting from all manner of unexpected places in the borders and there was a loose slab on one of the flights of steps in the garden. I had to fix that before someone tripped over it. I was busy working on the matter when Mary hurried out to me. As it was three o'clock, I thought she was coming to announce tea and biscuits were ready! But she wasn't.

'It was Mrs Cotterell on the phone,' Mary said. 'She can see the water again, she says, and would you come. I said you would. I know you're not on duty. . . .'

'I'll go straight away,' I said.

In my gardening gear, I drove my private car down into the village but this time went directly to her house, not to the Henfields. I arrived within a couple of minutes. After I rang the bell, she came to the door but said, 'Oh, I was expecting the policeman . . .'

'I am the policeman. It's PC Rhea,' I told her. 'I'm not in uniform, Mrs Cotterell, it's my day off, I was gardening, but I've come about the water you've sighted.'

'Oh, yes, sorry I didn't recognize you, Mr Rhea, silly of me . . . but it's not all that urgent, to get you here on your day off . . . but yes, I could see it when I called you.'

'I've got some binoculars in the car,' I said. 'The family uses them when we drive into the country, they could be useful. I'll bring them.'

After I'd collected my binoculars, she led me up to the landing window and pointed towards the Henfields' house. 'There, you see?'

I followed the line of her finger and saw the glistening sight, apparently quivering in the light of the afternoon sun. I must admit it did look like water but I knew it wasn't; it was the sun reflecting from some shiny surface so I took my binoculars and focused them on the spot. It was one of Mr Henfield's cloches; the sun was shining on the glass surface and a tree was moving ever so slightly in the breeze, casting shadows on to the glass to provide a remarkable rippling effect.

'It's the sun shining on to a glass surface,' I told her. 'Have a look through these.'

I showed her how to focus the binoculars to suit her eyes; one eyepiece could be focused quite separately from the other, and soon, under my direction, she found herself gazing at the sparkling cloche.

'Good heavens,' she exclaimed. 'How clear everything is . . . I would never have believed it, Mr Rhea . . . you can see so much. I must get some binoculars, really I must . . . but thank you, you've put my mind at rest now. It did look like water flowing from somewhere, gathering in a pool. It was silly of me really, I suppose . . .'

'No it wasn't,' I tried to reassure her. 'You thought you had identified a problem and you reacted quickly, and you are to be commended for that. If it had been a burst water main, then I'm sure it would have caused a lot of damage, not only to the Henfields' garden or house but to other properties. So thank you. And don't be afraid to call me again if this sort of thing happens.'

I explained that the illusion would only occur for a very short time, a few minutes at the most while the sun shone upon that reflective surface. The movement of the earth would quickly carry the cloche out of the direct line of the sun and very soon the image would vanish – but on these two days, it had occurred twice at around the same time. It might occur around three o'clock tomorrow if conditions were right, I told her, but as the summer days progressed, so the sun's rays would not continue to produce that effect; they would move away and not shine on to the cloche. I was pleased I had ascertained the cause of the mirage and quite forgot about it until, about three or four months later, I got another call from Mrs Cotterell. It was about six o'clock in the evening.

'Hello, Mr Rhea, it's Charmain Cotterell. I'm sorry to bother you again but I think I am being watched by a man. Joseph is away on business in New York, and Mrs Busby has gone to visit her sister so I cannot call them to help me.'

'A man? Do you know who it is?' was my first question.

'No, I have no idea, except he's got very ginger hair.'

'Where does he watch you from?'

'Those allotments on the hillside behind our house; he's peering over a fence at me . . . he was there yesterday too. It is very worrying, Mr Rhea. At first I thought it was my imagination and now he's back, bobbing up and down and ducking out of sight when he thinks I'm looking at him . . . can you come?'

'Yes, of course.' The nights were now drawing in and, as I was still on duty, due to finish at six, I went down to see her. I could see she was very nervous at the thought of being watched by the ginger-headed man and asked from where she had noticed him. This time it had been from her back garden; she had been tending some of her outdoor plants when she'd looked up to see the ginger head and face peering at her from behind a fence of rustic panels. I asked her to lead me outside and so she did.

'There!' she said, her finger pointing up the slope to the allotments. 'There, on the hillside, behind that fence, it is a fence isn't it? Oh, he's gone! He must have seen you, Mr Rhea, he's ducked down . . . but I definitely saw him!'

'Wait here,' I said, having not seen the peeper but having noticed the long high fence. 'I'll go and see what's going

157

on! You stay here, remain in his sights, try to keep his attention upon you. I'll sneak up and surprise him!'

There was plenty of cover on the hillside of hawthorns, shrubs and other vegetation, and the allotments were near the top, some distance from the village below. With a bit of luck, I could sneak up the hillside under cover of the vegetation and catch this character in the act. But when I arrived, all I found was an unkempt bunch of bronze-coloured chrysanthemums. They had grown tall enough to show their heads above the rustic fence and were waving about in the wind, disappearing and reappearing as the strong wind moved them backwards and forwards. There was no sign of anyone standing or moving among the vegetation; none of the greenery had been trampled down and I was sure no one had stood here to watch Mrs Cotterell. In fact, the allotment was very neglected and certainly no one seemed to be caring for the flowers and there was no sign of anyone having tended the patch for months past. Even though they were neglected, the chrysanthemums were flourishing and they were a very handsome bunch indeed. I picked the head off one; I wanted Mrs Cotterell to see the colour.

'I saw you,' she smiled when I returned. 'He ducked down just before you got there . . . did you see who it was?'

'Was his hair this colour?' I asked, showing the flower head.

'Yes, it was. A redhead, Mr Rhea . . .' and then her voice trailed away. 'Oh dear, I've done it again, haven't I? Called you out on a wild goose chase!'

'With good intent!' I said. 'There was no one up there, and the allotment is very neglected; there's no sign of anyone being near that fence, Mrs Cotterell. What you saw was flowers swaying in the wind.'

'Oh dear, this is dreadful, I feel such a fool . . .'

Now, having talked to her and visited her, I felt I knew the reason for her supposed aloofness and her failure to acknowledge people in the street.

'Mrs Cotterell, can I be very personal and perhaps rather rude?'

'Rude to me? Well, I've been a nuisance to you, I suppose I can tolerate a modicum of rudeness!' and she laughed happily. I began to think she was quite a nice person, not at all like the image she portrayed in public.

'I think you need glasses,' I said. 'You didn't recognize me out of uniform and I think you don't recognize people in the street, which is why you don't feel confident in venturing out . . . forgive me if I am wrong but I am saying this with the best possible motives. You mistook those flowers for a man's head, then the previous time we met, when you looked through the binoculars, you were amazed at the clarity of the scene.'

'But I can read, Mr Rhea, I have no trouble with newspapers and books, although I must admit the television is rather blurred. I can't imagine myself with spectacles, Mr Rhea, they would not suit me.'

'It seems you need something to help your long distance sight. There are some very fashionable frames on offer these days. Lots of famous ladies and film stars wear spectacles to remarkable effect.'

'Do they really?'

'They realize the benefits and, on top of that, I think you'd look very smart in spectacles. They can be very fetching, and you would recognize people in the street, or at events . . . you'd see as clearly as you did through my binoculars.'

'And flowers!' she laughed. 'I'd recognize flowers! Even a long way off?'

'Yes, you would!' I was quite amazed at the way in which she responded to my criticism of her, but then I wondered whether she had long been wanting someone to give her just the slightest of nudges towards taking an eye-test. Perhaps she had never thought to mention her failing eyesight to her husband. Perhaps, when she was around the house, he had never realized the extent of her problem? And perhaps she'd been all alone in the dilemma of her deteriorating eyesight.

'I will get Joseph to take me to the optician,' she said. 'Without fail! He's always so busy, Mr Rhea, and I seldom go out with him. I'm sure he's not noticed my short-sightedness, or perhaps it is my fault, trying to pretend everything is normal. I must admit the idea of recognizing people in the street does appeal to me!'

It was several weeks later when I saw her walking down Aidensfield High Street sporting a pair of very fashionable new spectacles. And this time she was beaming at people and greeting them, and she even went into the shop on her own and then the post office. An entire new world had presented itself to Mrs Cotterell; she could see the people who were approaching her and, better still, recognize them and acknowledge them. Not many weeks later, I heard she had accepted the newly vacated post of President of the Women's Institute.

Now, she could see who she was talking to around a table or in a meeting, and if she attended a function in the village hall, she would be able to see what was happening on stage. Thanks to her new specs, Mrs Cotterell could enjoy an entire new world and there was no doubt she had arrived on the social scene of Aidensfield. Of course, she retained that superior air. But, after all, one had come to expect that of Mrs Cotterell. That she was presidential material was never in doubt. I did hear that approaches were being made to her to become the new patron of Aidensfield and District Flower Club – I hoped with all the sincerity in my heart, that if she accepted, she could distinguish a chrysanthemum from a red-haired gentleman of doubtful morals who was prone to peeping over garden fences.

One might question the merit in a village constable knowing that a certain person was short-sighted who didn't correct it by wearing spectacles, but if such a person was the driver of a motor vehicle then such a defect was most significant. It might explain why a driver was involved in an accident; likewise, any evidence provided as the witness to a crime or accident could be regarded with some suspicion – and so, knowing about Mrs Cotterell's eyesight problem was a good example of a useful piece of local knowledge. With luck, I would never have to draw upon that knowledge, but it was there, safely logged into my memory.

If Mrs Cotterell and her problem eyesight presented a slight diversion from my usual duties, then so did Mabel Lofthouse.

She was another lady of the village whose secret I did not know or even suspect – rather like Charmain Cotterell but infinitely more fascinating. Mabel was a lady in her seventies, a spinster who had earned her living as a seamstress. She had proved extremely capable with a needle and thread, and latterly with a sewing machine. She could make ladies' dresses, children's clothes, gentlemen's suits, covers for three-piece suits and chairs, curtains for houses and offices, cushion covers galore and anything else that might be requested. She had always been a freelance worker, living in a small cottage left to her by her parents many, many years earlier. She had no rent or mortgage repayments to find and could therefore maintain herself, although not in a wealthy manner. As a self-employed person in the 1960s, she had once suffered some venom from two teenage sons of a local trades union official. She was just one of millions of ordinary people who were trying to support themselves by their own skills, but those youngsters, probably emulating their father, called her a Fascist and bloated capitalist because she owned her own house and supported herself without a 'proper' job. I had to warn the lads about their behaviour – which promptly branded me a Nazi and right-wing sympathizer! Nonetheless, my warning did the trick – they left her alone afterwards.

Mabel's needs were simple and everything she required was available in the village. She had no wish to live in a town and her only such trip was a journey to Ashfordly by bus each Friday where she attended the market and purchased her rather basic necessities for the coming week. Her other needs were catered for in Aidensfield – there was a village shop, a post office, a church and a pub, for she loved to visit it on a Saturday evening for a glass or two of milk stout and a bar snack (her weekly treat). There she met three lady friends and they sat around a table in the bar to eat, drink, gossip and laugh in a convivial atmosphere. They were part of the Saturday scene in the pub and that is how I came to recognize her.

Part of the village constable's job was to visit all the public houses on his patch, especially on a Saturday night; the purpose was to show the uniform to customers in the belief it would deter any likely outbreak of trouble, but it was also a means of letting the landlord and staff know we were in the vicinity if required. And, of course, there was the law enforcement side of things – we had to make sure the pubs closed on time, that no drunkenness or under-age drinking was permitted and that drivers knew they were likely to be arrested if they were unfit to drive through alcohol.

Most Saturdays therefore, when I was on duty, I paid an early visit to all the pubs on my patch and repeated it later in the evening, as near to closing time as I could. It was during those early visits that I came to know Mabel. She and her friends were always first into the bar on a Saturday; they ordered their meals and drinks, had a good gossip and laugh and usually departed for home before ten o'clock. Whenever I entered in uniform, they would call out cheeky remarks, things like 'Here he comes, I think he fancies you, Mabel', or 'We can't go on meeting like this, Constable, people will start talking', or 'Are you going to show me your truncheon?', or 'I'd like to be arrested and taken down the cells, Constable. . . .'

All good-humoured stuff, and completely normal even if they were all in their seventies.

In time, of course, I learned that one of those ladies was Mabel Lofthouse, that she was unmarried, that she lived in Shepherd's Cottage not far from the War Memorial, and that she earned her living by sewing. That was another small piece of local knowledge which was tucked into my brain, although I could not envisage how it might become useful to me. As time passed, I learned hardly anything else about her – except for a couple of odd habits. One was that she always left her back door standing wide open, even in bad weather, and that it was also left open during the night. In my first months at Aidensfield, I passed the cottage on frequent occasions and would see the door standing open, but paid little attention to the fact because I thought it was an outhouse of some kind.

In time, I learned the door did not lead directly into the cottage; it opened into a small lobby with a stone floor and it contained a number of wellington boots, and outdoors shoes, as well as some coats hanging from wall hooks. There was also an ancient kitchen sink with a cold-water tap and a few shelves bearing surplus kitchen utensils, jam jars and candlesticks. Seeing this, I was torn between two thoughts – first, as a police officer whose duty it was to prevent crime, I should suggest she kept the door closed and locked, especially at night or if she was away from the house, but secondly, I was aware that as a private individual, she was perfectly entitled to leave her door wide open and unlocked if she wished. There was no law against it.

As the months passed, I discovered her second habit or custom. In the upper part of her house, probably at the level of her landing on the first floor, there was a circular window. It overlooked the village street and at night, it always contained a light, an oil lamp. This glowed in the darkness like some kind of beacon and, as I patrolled the outskirts of the village, I could see Mabel's oil lamp from high on the moors. As you drove into Aidensfield from the Eltering road on a clear night, the light could be seen from almost two miles away. It glowed like a candle in the distance, a tiny flicker of light in the pitch darkness of the moors. I wondered why she lit it every night, without fail, and why did she use an oil lamp? Mains electricity had come to the village some years earlier and her house was connected – there was an electric landing light which showed on occasions when it was illuminated. And yet she persisted in lighting her oil lamp night after night, year after year and it never occurred to me, in those early days, that the two practices might be connected in some way.

Her behaviour puzzled me but was not sufficient for me to make enquiries; it was the sort of thing that might crop up in conversation at some stage and I was content to await clarification. I did though make one or two tentative enquiries from people I knew well, but none could say – or would say – why Mabel persisted with her ever-open door and night light. Fairly recent arrivals in the village were not unduly intrigued – the fact there was always a light in Mabel's round window was thought to be her idea of making the house look attractive at night.

For similar reasons, some people always leave a porch light burning through the night either to show they are at home, or to pretend to would-be burglars that they are at home. As a consequence, few thought Mabel's light was particularly unusual and the ever-open door was not especially odd in a village – most of the local people never locked their doors. As I began to gain the trust of the older residents, I tried to elicit from them some kind of explanation for this behaviour, but they did not like to talk about it, so I was told. I was reminded that it was Mabel's affair, a personal thing and nothing to do with anyone else. In other words, I was politely advised to stop poking my nose into other people's business. And in that reaction, I sensed some kind of intriguing reason. It made me more determined to find out.

Many months later, an opportunity presented itself because Force Headquarters, in its wisdom, decided that police officers should do much more to prevent crime and so a North Riding Constabulary Crime Prevention Campaign was launched with coverage in the local papers and leaflets made available in places like shops, pubs, post offices and hotels. In addition, we were instructed to visit people whom we felt would benefit from crime prevention advice, such as shops where barred rear windows were advisable, village post offices where similar protection was suggested and a host of other private and business premises where all manner of advice was proposed. We were told to advise drivers to lock their car doors when leaving them unattended, to buy chains to secure their bicycles, to leave lights on in their homes if they were absent for lengthy periods or at night. However, we told them not to leave lights burning in the porch as a deterrent to burglars – it is a ready signal that the occupants are out, for who lives in a porch? Leave a light on in the kitchen or bathroom or lounge. And so, in my own way, I went about delivering crime prevention advice in Aidensfield. I had a pile of leaflets to leave at every house and business premises, but top of my list was Mabel with her open door. With my briefcase full of leaflets, I went to her delightful house one Wednesday morning when I knew she would be at home; I knew I'd chosen correctly because smoke was rising from the chimney and her ginger cat was sitting in the garden, not stirring at my approach. Both told me she was at home. I went to the back door, the one that was always standing open, and rattled the knocker, an iron one made from an old horseshoe, then shouted to announce my presence.

'Don't stand there shouting,' called a woman's voice from within. 'Come in, the door's open.'

I stepped into the back lobby, opened the inner door and found myself in a comfortable kitchen with a coal fire burning in a black-leaded York Range. A kettle was singing on the hob, steam was rising from its spout and the lid was rattling as the power tried to escape.

It was quite dark in the kitchen but Mabel was sitting at the table which was directly in front of the window, working on a sewing project of some kind; whatever she was doing, it was being done by hand for her machine was standing idle in a corner. In these houses, the kitchen was the living-room; people lived and socialized there and things like washing the clothes or crockery were done in the scullery.

In Mabel's house, there was a small scullery at the back of the kitchen which I could see as I entered.

She was a stout woman with a mass of thick white hair tied up with a blue ribbon. With half-rimmed spectacles and a round, rosy face she was the epitome of a true country-woman as she wore a grey jumper and blue skirt, over which was a floral apron. Several needles containing different colours of thread were sticking into her apron, ready for use when required.

'Well, fancy this!' she smiled at me and laid down her work. 'Folks will talk, Mr Rhea, with a young chap like you visiting me! Wait till I tell my friends you've called ... I've no idea what you might want, but you're welcome to a cup of tea and a bit of cake. The kettle's on. Sit yourself down over there.'

I settled in a Windsor chair beside the fireplace and without waiting for an answer, she left the table, found the teapot and began to make the tea. As it was brewing she put two slices of homemade fruit cake on some plates, placed them on a tray on a sturdy coffee-type table. I did not try to explain the reason for my presence as she pottered about, but soon she was sitting opposite in another Windsor chair.

'That's your cake.' She pointed to the largest slice. 'Help yourself. Now, what can I do for you, Mr Rhea?'

I explained that the Constabulary was conducting a crime prevention campaign throughout the county with the intention of making the populace more aware of the risks of crime. After a short explanation of our purpose and adding that a few simple precautions to safeguard one's belongings, I produced a leaflet which I handed to her. After a brief glance, she placed it on the table.

'So what's all this got to do with me?' she asked. 'We don't have burglars and thieves in Aidensfield.'

'I'm visiting all the houses in the village,' I told her. 'If people are not in, I'll drop a leaflet through their letter box, but it's so much nicer to talk to people. In lots of cases we can make simple suggestions, like locking the garage or garden shed at night, bringing bikes and children's toys in off the street, not leaving car doors unlocked when there are valuables inside, that sort of thing.'

'Aye, well, I suppose folks do sometimes ask for things to be stolen from them, but not me, Mr Rhea. I haven't a lot of stuff worth stealing; I've no car, no children, no valuables in the house, no money lying about. And there's not many times I'm away from the house.'

'You do leave your back door open, Mabel, all the time. That could be an invitation to a thief.'

'Aye, I do, and I leave the kitchen door unlocked an' all, Mr Rhea, always have done and always will. The house is never locked, not at night and not even when I go to Ashfordly on a Friday or the pub on a Saturday night.'

'It's that kind of thing we are trying to avoid, Mabel. Open doors are an invitation to a thief, and I'm sure you know that even if we don't have thieves and burglars in Aidensfield, there are travelling thieves now. They've got access to cars and drive out from places like York, Scarborough, Hull, Leeds and Middlesbrough especially to raid country homes and properties, looking for anything that can be sold quickly in second-hand shops and so on. They can break into a house and steal portable property, then be miles away before the alarm is raised. All we're trying to do is to persuade house-holders to lock their doors and protect their belongings.'

'I've nowt to protect!' she chuckled. 'I'm not rich, you know; I've nowt worth pinching even if I am a bloated capitalist!'

'You've got your sewing machine,' I said, indicating with a nod of my head the large treadle machine on its cast-iron stand. It was the kind used by tailors and dressmakers. 'That's your living, Mabel. If they took that, you'd find it difficult to earn a living.'

'Who's going to steal a thing that size, Mr Rhea? Besides, it's older than you I imagine, an antique. No one in their right mind would steal that, and anyway, it would take two strong men to lift it.'

As I munched her excellent cake and drank the tea, I could see I was not likely to make much headway with Mabel but I knew I had to make one last reference to her ever-open back door.

'I think you should reconsider your decision not to lock your back door,' I said.

'I couldn't lock it if I wanted to!' she snapped.

'You mean you've lost the key? You could bolt it from the inside at night when you're at home, or get a new lock fitted.'

'It's nowt to do with locks and keys and bolts, Mr Rhea,' she was becoming slightly emotional now. 'It's just that it's always open and always will be. For Geoffrey.'

For the briefest of moments I wondered if she was referring to her cat, the one I'd noticed outside, but could hardly imagine a down-to-earth countrywoman naming her cat Geoffrey.

'Geoffrey?' I asked wondering by this stage whether I was being intrusive; the name had clearly caused her to show some emotion, something I'd never seen in her until now.

'I don't often talk about it, Mr Rhea.' She lowered her head and stared into her cup of tea. 'Not now. But mebbe you should know, to stop you worrying about that door. He was my boyfriend, a long time ago. Geoffrey Calvert. His dad had a haulage business in Elsinby. A nice family.'

I waited, wondering what was coming next while not wishing to prompt her in any way.

'He was called up for the war, the First World War that is. In 1916. We weren't married, not even engaged, Mr Rhea, but he was my intended and we said when he came back, we would get engaged . . . he said he would come back for me but he never did. 1916 it was when he went; he got the train down there at the station, went to York to join up and the next thing I knew he was in France. Eighteen he was, a real fine lad. He cried when he got on that train, Mr Rhea, I did as well. I was only seventeen. I went with him to the station and he said he would come back for me. I said I would wait. I said my door would always be open for him and my mum and dad agreed; this was their house then, you see but it would be mine one day and they liked Geoffrey. That's Geoffrey's coat hanging in the lobby; he left it here one day . . . so that's why the door is always open, Mr Rhea, ready for when Geoffrey comes back, whatever time of day or night he returns. It's open for him.'

'So he was killed in action, was he?' I asked gently.

'Nobody knows, Mr Rhea, he just vanished. Lost without trace. His name's not on the War Memorial and one of the vicars in the past wrote to the War Office to see if his name was recorded anywhere among the casualties, but it wasn't. He went down as Missing in Action. I was never told anything, not being next of kin, then his parents moved away, down to Suffolk and I lost touch with them. So I don't know what happened to Geoffrey. Nobody does, so it seems.'

'But you are still waiting in case he returns?'

'Yes. There's always hope, Mr Rhea, you must always have hope.'

'Yes, you must. And the light in that round window upstairs?'

'To show him I'm still here, if he comes over that moor at night. I light it every night, Mr Rhea. Folks must wonder why and I'll thank you not to spread it around the village. Folks might think I'm soft in the head, waiting all this time, never giving up, but what else can I do?'

'I'm sure they would not think that at all, Mabel, they'd be proud of you. So I won't pressure you to lock your door! I'm sorry I've bothered you over this . . .'

'No need to be sorry, Mr Rhea, you have a job to do, just like Geoffrey had, and your job doesn't include silly old ladies who are still waiting for their lover to return after all these years.'

'I wish I could do something to help you find out what happened to him.' I did not know what else to say.

'I've tried, many times over many years, and I've had all the help I've needed, Mr Rhea. Folks have been very good to me, writing letters to the War Office and the French authorities, with no result. That's the worst bit, Mr Rhea, not knowing. So I just keep hoping. And I will until I die.'

And so I left Mabel in her cosy house, still waiting for Geoffrey and still with the back door standing open.

As I patrolled the moors in the days, weeks and months that followed, I could see that little light in the circular window and now knew why it burned in the darkness. Sadly, I knew that one day it would be extinguished.

# Chapter 9

When Miss Felicity Forbes of Moordale House, Aidensfield asked Claude Jeremiah Greengrass to look after her green parrot, Pedro, for just a few days, it created within Greengrass a train of thought which suggested there was money to be earned in accommodating other people's pets. He realized that people with pets were often prevented from going on holiday or even short-term breaks like week-ends or days out because no one would care for their nearest and dearest. He reasoned that if he offered board and lodgings for pets, the scheme might provide him with a very useful extra income.

It all began one Monday morning in February when Felicity, a woman with a strong personality, plenty of money and a large house, arrived at Greengrass's door to ask that favour.

'A parrot?' he growled. 'I know nothing about parrots, Miss Forbes.'

'There's nothing to know,' she assured him. 'All you have to do is feed him, let him out for a fly around in the kitchen from time to time, and clean his cage every two days. I would pay you well, of course.'

'Pay me? Oh, well, in that case I might just find time to look after him.'

'I do hope so, Mr Greengrass. I would not entrust Pedro

to just anyone, you know. He needs love and affection, dedication and companionship, and I know you are so good with animals. All one has to do is to look at Alfred to know how well you care for dumb creatures. I know Pedro will be very happy with you.'

'Aye, well, I suppose I could if that's all that's required. When do I start?'

'Well, this afternoon actually. Can you come round and collect him?'

'Collect him? I thought all I had to do was come to your house and look after him there . . .'

'Oh, no, he likes to see different places, Mr Greengrass, and he does love to explore other people's houses. So, shall we say half past twelve? If you could call at half past twelve, with your lorry, I will make sure he's ready in his cage. I'm catching the train to York at three o'clock and shall be away for the week. I will contact you when I return and make sure there is plenty of food and cage lining available . . . this is so good of you, Mr Greengrass. Half past twelve then?'

'Yes but I've got to go to Eltering this afternoon, I've an appointment . . .'

'Oh, no trouble, Mr Greengrass. Pedro will be quite happy to sit in his cage in the back of your lorry or even on the front passenger seat if the weather is bad, and you can go about your business without interruption. I'm sure he would love a drive across the moors, Mr Greengrass, fresh air never harmed anyone, not even a parrot.'

And so it was that, after agreeing to the terms, Claude Jeremiah Greengrass found himself committed to caring for Pedro the parrot. What he did not know, however, was that Felicity had earlier approached many other people, so-called friends of hers, with the same request but all had turned her down. None had wanted the responsibility of caring for Pedro and none had stated a reason for not wanting him in their house, but there was just a suggestion that it was due to his foul language. Pedro could utter the most dreadful of curses which could be highly embarrassing when one had guests, although that did not appear to worry Felicity.

Indeed some thought he had picked up his rich vocabulary from her.

On that chilly day, Claude and his truck, minus Alfred the dog, arrived at Felicity's house to collect Pedro in his cage. He arrived at 12.30 but Felicity, who was upstairs getting ready, opened the bathroom window and shouted down to him to ask if he would just wait a few more minutes because she was not quite dressed but wouldn't be long. Claude made it clear that he could not delay things too much because he had to be in Eltering before two o'clock that afternoon and he stressed he wanted to deliver Pedro to the Greengrass Ranch at Hagg Bottom before heading across the moors. But it was one o'clock by the time Felicity came downstairs in her going-on-holiday outfit and quarter past before they had hoisted the huge cage into the rear of Greengrass's truck. During this manoeuvre, Pedro had been surprisingly quiet, even though he had fluttered about in alarm at the sight of Greengrass and his truck, but there is so little a parrot in a cage can do to disengage himself from what happened around him. And so his cage was firmly placed behind the driver's cab, then covered with two or three hessian sacks to shield Pedro's eyes from what was about to occur. Finally, it was strapped to the floor with a couple of ropes while his food and cage liners were placed in Claude's cab.

'He'll have to come to Eltering with me,' Claude told her. 'I must be off, time's short and I don't want to be late.'

'Thank you *so* much, Mr Greengrass,' she had oozed. 'I do hope you and Pedro have a wonderful time together. I shall be thinking of you when I am in Paris. Don't take any nonsense from him.'

And she retreated into the house to finish her packing.

Claude's anxiety to reach Eltering, a small market-town at the other side of the moor, arose because only the day before, Sunday, he'd spotted a grandfather clock for sale in an antique shop. The shop had been closed on the Sunday and a note said it would open at 2pm on Monday, then be open all day Tuesday, Wednesday and Thursday from 9 a.m. until 5 p.m., to close at 11 a.m. on Friday. It seemed the owner lived some distance away during the weekend and needed time to travel, hence the odd opening times. The clock in question looked exactly like the one Claude's mother used to have in her sitting-room which was why he wanted to be sure to examine it before it was sold – and if necessary, buy it. It might be a Greengrass heirloom.

As Claude left Aidensfield for the forty-minute drive across the moors into Eltering, he was half an hour later than he'd planned, and then the weather deteriorated. The temperature dropped and the rain came down, and then it turned to sleet. He was snug and dry in his cab and in concentrating on his journey as he raced against time while focusing his mind on the grandfather clock in that shop, he forgot about Pedro in the rear of his truck. When he reached Eltering Antiques, however, it was 2.25. He was twenty-five minutes late! And the clock which had been in the window yesterday, had now gone. Claude, panting, soaked and cold from trotting from the lorry park, was devastated – all his efforts had been in vain but, he reminded himself, this might have been a valued Greengrass heirloom, and so he decided to pursue the matter. He stomped into the shop, dripping water all over the place, and asked the man who greeted him, 'That clock, the one that was in the window yesterday, have you sold it?'

'I'm afraid so, sir, yes. It left these premises less than half-an-hour ago. The man inspected it on Thursday, made up his mind on Friday and arranged to collect it today. He's only just left. I'm so sorry.'

'Who's got it?' asked Claude, his anxiety showing in his panting and general restlessness.

'I'm not really at liberty to say, sir . . .'

'I think it belonged to my mother,' interjected Claude. 'My name is Greengrass, Claude Jeremiah Greengrass from Aidensfield and when I saw it yesterday, I recognized it as a family heirloom and if someone has bought it, I'd be prepared to pay extra to get it back into the family bosom, as it were.'

'Ah, well, in that rather exceptional case, I think I can provide you with the buyer's name because he is a dealer. You will have to pay more than I would have asked, Mr Greengrass, but that is the penalty for buying antiques from dealers . . . and grandfather clocks have suddenly become very much in demand. Longcase clocks, to give them their real name, are now highly collectable.'

Claude was given the name and address of a dealer in Scarborough, a man called Alan Baseley, and promptly returned to his truck to drive to the fellow's premises. In driving sleet and rain, it was a journey of about an hour and he arrived at 3.30. He had to park in a public car-park and walk to the premises in Westborough and when he arrived, once more wet, cold and breathless, he burst into the shop and asked the man behind the counter, 'Are you Alan Baseley?'

'No, he's not back yet,' said the man. 'He's out collecting recent purchases. I'm not expecting him back for a couple of hours, around half past five. Can I help?'

'Well, no, not really, it's him I want to see because he's bought summat that I wanted, from a shop in Eltering, and I was hoping to do a deal with him. The name's Greengrass.'

'All I can suggest, Mr Greengrass, is that you go for a cup of tea then come back here, say, for five o'clock, then you'd be sure of catching him. He always comes back here after one of his collecting days, and we don't close till half past five.'

'Aye, right,' said Claude seeing no alternative. He walked into the town centre and found a café where he bought himself gammon, chips and peas plus a cup of tea – something that would serve as the day's evening meal. After his meal and a time-passing stroll around the town-centre shops, he returned to Baseley's shop just after five but the fellow had not returned. This time the attendant found a chair and allowed Claude to remain. At least it was warm and dry in the shop. Not long afterwards, a van eased to a halt outside and Alan Baseley emerged. The shop attendant smiled. 'Here he is, Mr Greengrass.'

When Baseley walked into the shop, his assistant made the introductions but Claude was already on his feet waiting. He said, 'Ah, Mr Baseley, glad I caught you . . . you bought a clock in Eltering, a grandfather, a longcase as they're called. This afternoon.'

'I did indeed, and a very nice specimen it was too.'

'I'd like to buy it from you.'

'I'm afraid that will not be possible, Mr Greengrass. I've already sold it on.'

'Sold it on? Who to?'

'A private collector who lives in Scarborough. He would not wish me to divulge his name.'

'But look, I think it might have been a family heirloom, my mother had one just like it in the house when I was a lad and when I saw it in that shop window in Eltering I knew I must have it.'

'I rather think you were mistaken, Mr Greengrass. The private collector who has just bought it from me knows its history. He asked me to be sure to obtain the clock for him. It came from a house in Staffordshire, the home of a gentleman called Sir Stanley Freeborough, and it had been in his family for generations. Its history is well documented, Mr

Greengrass, and I can assure you there is no reference to the Greengrass family. I am very sorry, but clearly it is not your heirloom. But if your family has a background in this locality, then I can keep an eye open for any similar clocks which might have come from your ancestors. These clocks are now proving very popular indeed and some fine examples are coming on to the market. Shall I take a note of your address and telephone number?'

'Aye, right,' said Claude dejectedly. 'Thanks, summat might just turn up . . .'

'Not necessarily, Mr Greengrass, I can't guarantee it. All I can do is to promise I'll keep you in mind. I specialize in longcase clocks and if anyone is likely to come across the one which came from your family, then it will probably be me.'

'There's money in clocks, then?' asked Claude.

'There is, if you know what you're doing. Some are little more than rubbish, but if your clock is remotely like the one I have just sold, I shall recognize it and shall contact you immediately. And, Mr Greengrass, I will hold it until you have had an opportunity to view it. I can't be fairer than that.'

And so Claude, dejected by the unexpected turn of events and by the sheer waste of time, made his way home. If there was one consolation, it was that he did not have to prepare himself an evening meal. The meal in Scarborough had been most welcome and so, when he arrived home, he parked his lorry in the yard, lit the fire, fed Alfred and settled down with a glass of whisky. Outside, the sleet was turning to snow as the temperature plummeted; it was indeed the foulest of nights.

Then, at half past seven, the telephone rang.

'Greengrass,' he announced, with perhaps just a little slurring of speech, a direct result of trying to drown his disappointing day. Then he thought this might be that

177

antique man with news of a grandfather clock.

'Ah, Mr Greengrass,' said a woman's voice. 'This is Felicity Forbes. I'm in London before crossing the Channel tomorrow and thought I would call to see how Pedro is coping without me.'

'Pedro?' he asked, and then remembered the parrot. It was still in its cage on the back of his lorry, outside in the freezing cold and wet February night. The poor bird would be drenched. The sacking would absorb the water up to a point, but it would soon run right through; it was not very good protection against this weather.

'Oh, he's fine, Miss Forbes,' blustered Claude. 'He had a bit of a ride round the moor but that didn't seem to worry him and he's eaten like a horse . . . well, not really a horse, eaten like a parrot. . . .'

'Well, so long as he is in good hands, and kept warm and dry, he'll be no trouble, Mr Greengrass. Back next week then. Thanks,' and the phone went dead.

Claude hurried outside. It was still pouring with a mixture of sleet and very wet snowflakes, and the east wind was hurling it almost horizontally against the house. Fighting his way through the darkness, Claude reached the truck, climbed in the back and, with the light of a torch, made his way to the covered cage. The hessian sacking was saturated and covered with the beginning of settling snow, and with some trepidation, he removed it. In the light of the torch, he saw Pedro lying on the floor of his cage, his plumage soaked and bedraggled, and his eyes closed. Claude thought he was dead; he looked very dead indeed, but as the light of the torch passed over the bird's face, it revived.

'Where the ******* hell have you been?' squawked Pedro, who scrambled to his feet and then produced a series of filthy expletives which even made Claude blush. 'Where the ******* hell have you been?'

'You'd better come in,' said Claude. 'But don't tell your mistress about this.'

And Pedro swore again and kept swearing until his cage was safely inside the warmth of the Greengrass household. And he swore even more when Alfred barked at him, saying, 'Where the ****** hell have you been?' Then when Claude presented him with some food he repeated his words.

'If you're going to keep swearing at me like that,' snapped Claude, 'you're going to sleep in the barn.'

Pedro's response cannot be repeated here.

It was Claude who told me the story when he came to see me about the legal requirements which were necessary when opening a boarding establishment for pets. He never heard any more from the antique dealer about a possible Greengrass longcase clock, but he had coped with Pedro by placing him in one of the outhouses. As Claude said, 'My Alfred is very sensitive when it comes to bad language, and I didn't want him being upset by a cussing parrot who could turn the air blue at a moment's notice.'

His experience with Pedro did not deter him from opening some kind of animal boarding establishment and I suspect his enthusiasm arose due to the fee paid by Felicity Forbes. He never disclosed the sum to me, but I felt it was such that he reckoned he could make a fortune from similar requests.

'I thought I'd better keep on the right side of the law with this plan,' he told me, his eyes blinking in that sneaky manner which told me he had no real intention of abiding to the letter of the law. I suspect he told me about his scheme because I could recommend his establishment to people in the district; many made sure they informed the police if they were going to vacate their homes for any length of time and care of pets and livestock was always something of a worry. But, to be fair, if his proposed boarding establishment was suitable, then I would recommend it.

But it wasn't even built yet.

'So if I want to make a home for other folks' pets and livestock, what do I have to do?' he put to me.

'One thing is to your credit,' I said. 'It's the fact your premises are well away from the village, so noise and disturbance of the local people won't be a factor. And smells of course. So your place has a lot to commend it, Claude.'

'Aye, well, I wouldn't be here otherwise, would I?' he chuckled.

'I think you should make an approach to the district council first, to see if you need planning permission, but you will need a licence. It's all laid down in the Animal Boarding Establishments Act of 1963, but you won't get a licence if you've a conviction for cruelty, or if you've been disqualified under various other statutes dealing with animal welfare.'

'Cruel to animals? Me? How can you say that, Constable?'

'I'm not suggesting anything like it, Claude, all I'm saying is that you have to prove yourself a worthy person. And if you get a licence, then you'll have to keep a register of all the cats and dogs that come on to your premises, with names and addresses of owners and so forth, and your premises will be open for inspection at any time by a veterinary officer, or someone from the local council.'

'Cats and dogs? I was thinking of other animals and birds, like parrots, ponies and such. Everything.'

'Well, the Boarding Establishment Act only applies to premises catering for dogs and cats. There are special requirements for riding establishments although you don't need a licence to keep a horse.'

'I'm not thinking of setting up a riding stable, Constable, but somebody might want me to look after their horse or pony, eh?'

'True, so I think the local council is your next port of call, Claude, and you'll have to explain you're thinking of including other animals and birds.'

'But if someone wanted their pet lion or tiger looking after, it would count as a cat, wouldn't it?'

'I think there might be special rules for exotic animals or dangerous ones, Claude, but that's not a matter for the police. It's a local authority matter, so it's the council offices for you. See what they say.'

'Aye, well, you've put me on the right track, Constable, so thank you for that. And if want your cat boarding out when you're cruising in the Mediterranean, you know where to come.'

'If I go cruising in the Med or anywhere else, Claude, I'd be pleased to let you look after my cat. With my four offspring and my salary, I'm more likely to need a cheap cottage in the Lake District. I'm not a wealthy entrepreneur like you!'

'I'm not wealthy, but things are looking up, Constable. Right, council offices it is!'

And so it was, that a few weeks later, signs of activity were in evidence on the Greengrass ranch. In the field behind Claude's house, a wire netting compound was being erected, divided into separate units. Running water was being laid into the structure and a new wooden fence was erected along the entire boundary of the field, with wire netting along most of its length and height. As this was going on, I encountered Claude in the village.

'I see you've workmen in, Claude?'

'Aye,' he beamed. 'Things are going ahead just as I wanted. I've got planning permission from the council, and I'm licensed to set up an animal boarding establishment so I'm getting my premises in order. The council chaps will come and inspect it when it's done and if they approve, we're off! I'll open for business the moment I've got the go ahead, so if you can recommend anyone to me . . .'

'I'll have to come and see it first,' I smiled. 'Give it the once-over, as they say, then I can make personal recommendations.'

It wasn't long before a sign appeared outside Claude's premises announcing 'Aidensfield Animal Boarding Establishment, Prop: Claude Jeremiah Greengrass.' I went to have a look, more out of curiosity than for any legal purpose, and found a well-constructed and very sturdy set of animal compounds with facilities both indoors and out, complete with running water, electric lights and neat bed areas in the inner quarters. There was a large stable-like structure too, with a rack for hay and a concrete floor with ridges for easy cleaning. Clearly, Claude was intending to invite animals larger than cats and dogs. But in the doggy part there was already a guest.

'That's Mrs Carruthers's Fifi,' said Claude, pointing to the white poodle. 'She's a pedigree dog. She's my first customer so she gets free board and lodgings, with plenty of walkies and a special line in dog biscuits. She's here for a week while Mrs Carruthers is in the south of France. Alfred's got his eye on her, but I've assured Mrs Carruthers that Alfred won't get near her . . . but he loves having company, Constable, I think he sees himself as Fifi's protector. He spends all day mooning about outside her cage.'

With all due respect to Claude, he appeared to make a success of his new enterprise because people entrusted their cats and dogs to him which all seemed to thrive in his care. It wasn't long before he was getting repeat bookings as people went away for the weekend, confidently leaving their cats and dogs at the Greengrass establishment. I received no complaints about the noise or smell even if some of his guests barked all night or during the day, but he was far enough out of the village for the noise not to be a nuisance. Then other animals began to arrive. During the course of one week, I noticed a donkey in his field and not long afterwards, a Shetland pony. It wasn't long before I saw a beautiful Cleveland Bay horse there and then a small herd of ten Jacob sheep with their distinctive black and white wool. They stayed for only a few days. A turkey was boarded for three days on one occasion, and then a pet goose arrived; I heard too, that he had taken some orphaned pet mice and then an unwanted hamster. Word quickly circulated the area that Claude was very caring and good with animals. Soon it was evident his establishment could and would cater for most animals, pets and domestic, large and small.

The Aidensfield Animal Boarding Establishment was clearly a success and I think everyone was pleased for him, and very impressed by his enterprise. It was one Claude could rightly consider a success.

Until he took in a bull as a guest.

It was a huge, muscular, chestnut-red creature with short white horns and sturdy legs. Powerful and packed with prime beef, he was a fine example of the Shorthorn breed and his name was Gus. At three years old, he was consid-ered the most docile of creatures and had won umpteen awards at agricultural shows in the area. Gus was used for showing and breeding all over the north of England but his owner, a smallholder called Chris Jenkins who lived in Elsinby, had gone into hospital with a broken leg and was expected to be there for at least a month. His wife, unable to cope with Gus among all her other commitments, had approached Claude and, after being reassured that Gus was the most docile of fellows, Claude had taken him in. Claude's paddock was large enough and secure enough to accommodate him, and he had adequate indoor shelter for the beast.

Claude told me all about his new guest and seemed very proud to be entrusted with Gus for he was rather famous on the show and breeding circuit. One day as I was patrolling past, I stopped to have a look at Claude's growing menagerie and saw Gus in the paddock along with a few moorland sheep, another goose and some hens. He seemed very content and very placid. From my point of view, there were no legal implications in Claude providing accommodation for a bull.

There was no public footpath or bridleway through the field, Claude was not likely to use him in a rodeo exhibition, I didn't expect anyone to ride him on the highway and I knew that, in Claude's care, the bull would have the finest treatment. However, Claude did erect a 'Beware of the Bull' notice which he positioned close to the paddock gate, just in case anyone decided to visit one of the more cuddly creatures inside.

Then, one Saturday in June, Jake Harrison, who farmed at Village Farm, Aidensfield, went to a livestock sale near Malton and bought two cows. He was keen to expand his herd, by selective breeding if necessary, or even by purchasing suitable animals, and these two splendid animals were exactly what he wanted. He loaded them into his cattle truck and transported them back to Aidensfield, a drive of some twenty miles. Jake's farmhouse stood on the main street in Aidensfield, but all his fields and buildings lay behind the street, spread out along the north side of the village so that, unless he chose to sell any of his land, the village would never expand in that direction. Some of his acreage lay behind the parish church with an access lane along the side of the vicarage grounds and churchyard, there was more land behind the shop and he even had a small patch of land behind the pub. Should he ever decide to finish farming, he could live in his fine farmhouse and sell his land for building – it should fetch a considerable sum. But Jake had no such idea – all he wanted was to expand his well-known herd.

He arrived back at Aidensfield about four o'clock that Saturday afternoon with his new possessions and drove his vehicle into the village steadily, doing his best not to alarm his precious passengers. It had been a long and rather slow journey but now he was on the final stretch; the village street, he knew, would be quiet and largely devoid of traffic and pedestrians because a garden fête was in progress in the vicarage grounds; most of the villagers would be there, enjoying the games, sideshows, exhibitions, tombola, food and drink. He knew the tea was arranged for four o'clock because his wife was one of the helpers and, as the day was fine and sunny, everyone would be out in the grounds and not crowded into the marquee. A crowd of about 150 was expected for this fund-raising event.

As Jake turned into the village, however, he had to drive past the end of the lane leading down to the Greengrass ranch and as he guided his vehicle carefully into the village, the cows on board noticed Gus among his new friends in the paddock. They could peep through the panels on the side of the cattle truck as it moved along and at the sight of the handsome bull, they both broke into a cacophony of loud moos, which cows tend to do at the sight of a bull. Gus lifted his head, accurately gauged the direction from which the moos were coming, sniffed the air and uttered an almighty bellow. He smelt females, cows to love and cherish, cows to take by force if necessary. And so, bellowing to match their mooing, he set off in hot pursuit. It was the work of a moment to smash down the rather fragile fence Greengrass had built; the wire netting caused no problems at all and within seconds, Gus was lumbering in pursuit of the cattle truck and its harem.

All he had to do was follow the scent and the moos. And so he set off towards the village at a steady trot.

Meanwhile, Jake was unaware of the drama not far behind his vehicle. Although he heard the loud mooing from his two new purchases he thought they must have been momentarily frightened by something. He drove on and turned into the track which would take him past the church-yard and the vicarage grounds and then into his own field. And, of course, the scent of the cows wafted along in his wake . . .

He arrived in his field and parked neatly inside it, almost immediately behind the vicarage. At that point, the air was rent with screams and shouts from the fête just over the wall. Gus had followed the scent, seen the open gate into the grounds of the vicarage, and had taken a direct line towards the objects of his affections. Unfortunately, that was through the marquee with its chairs, tables and banks of side tables with cakes, crockery, tea urns and bottles of fizz. As the people inside scattered at the sight and sound of this bellowing bull, so Gus became alarmed and launched an attack on the nearest object of frustration – the centre pole of the marquee. As he butted it repeatedly, so it crumbled to earth and then he found smaller poles to butt and, as the people ran screaming outside, he decided to follow for the scent was still in the air, not far away. As he made his dramatic exit, the marquee collapsed like a deflated balloon as people scattered and ran for safety, some heading for the inside of the church and others simply running in the oppo-site direction to Gus. Outside, people in flight demolished stands and tables bearing their purchased food. I'm not too sure whether bulls chase people wearing red, but Gus did not seemed interested – all he wanted was to enjoy time with the cows who were just at the other side of the vicarage garden wall.

Meanwhile, Jake had peered over that same wall to try and establish what the fuss was about, saw what was happen-ing and decided he must try to tempt Gus away. Luckily, he had not unloaded his two cows and so he leapt aboard his truck and drove as fast as he could towards a compound near some of his buildings. Gus, meanwhile, was trapped in the vicarage garden but it wouldn't be long before he had demolished the wall. It gave Jake just enough time to get his truck into the compound leaving the gate open for Gus. He then drove into some buildings at the other side, locked the huge doors behind his vehicle and waited for the arrival of the bellowing Gus. It hadn't taken him long to demolish a section of the dry-stone wall.

Being a cattleman, of course, Jake's buildings and fences were stout enough to withstand attacks from bulls and angry cows and, so, thanks to his quick-wittedness, Gus was contained in a bull-proof enclosure, pawing the ground, bellowing and scenting the cows now beyond his vision. Jake would cope with the bull; he'd experienced this on previous occasions, and he would keep the animal secure until it could be rehoused. Greengrass would have to pay, of course.

I was not there to witness this drama but was told about it afterwards. Happily, no one was hurt. Most of the people had been outside the marquee as Gus had vented his anger on the support posts, and he'd been far too keen to reach those cows to worry about chasing human targets. Although the marquee had been demolished in a spectacular fashion, it had not been badly damaged, although lots of cups, saucers, plates and glasses had been smashed, along with many bottles of soft drink. A stretch of the vicarage dry-stone wall had been demolished but that was easily repaired by a competent waller and so, in spite of what initially looked like a major disaster, the whole charade turned out not to be too serious. But the parochial church council were adamant that some compensation was due from Claude Jeremiah Greengrass. After all, he had been responsible for Gus at the material time, and his lack of security had resulted in his escape and pursuit of the cattle truck.

'I'm giving up my boarding establishment, closing down next week,' Claude told me some time later. 'I've spent all my profits compensating folks . . . why can't animals behave like humans?'

'They do,' I laughed.

# Chapter 10

As the national park's efforts to attract visitors became more successful, so the influx of tourists and day-trippers grew from a stready trickle to something akin to a flood. One of the reasons for such a huge increase after the end of the Second World War was the ability of many so-called 'ordinary people' to purchase a motor car. Instead of heading by train or coach for a week or even just a weekend at the main Yorkshire coastal resorts like Scarborough, Whitby, Redcar, Filey and Bridlington, they rearranged their outings into day trips. That was far cheaper and more flexible than boarding for the week, and the advent of the family car meant the whole household could travel to the coast for the day from far-off places like Leeds, Wakefield and other industrial areas in the West Riding of Yorkshire. Similarly, they could head south from Teesside to leave behind the industrial haze which was a permanent fixture in the sky above Middlesbrough, Stockton and Thornaby. The result was that northerly resorts like Saltburn and Redcar, in addition to seaside villages like Staithes, Runswick Bay and Robin Hood's Bay suddenly found themselves with a new lease of life. This spawned lots of flourishing small businesses like ice-cream kiosks, souvenir shops and cafés, and so these changes were of great benefit to the local economy.

Instead of one or two people arriving for a week, a carload would turn up for a day, or for several days in succession, and even if they did not spend the entire week at that resort, they returned time and time again, often at weekends. Day-trippers therefore replaced those who had earlier spent their weeks' holidays in seaside boarding-houses; a new type of tourist was born.

Car-parks were filled on a daily basis, the bingo halls and fish-and-chip shops did a roaring trade, and people selling cheap-and-cheerful souvenirs made a fortune out of trading for little more than three months out of the year. They went overseas for their long holidays in guaranteed sunshine – a type of break the 'ordinary person' was soon to discover.

Instead of restricting their outings to the English seaside, however, many day-trippers discovered the magic and beauty of the North Riding countryside – quite suddenly, pretty villages deep in the moors and dales became tourist resorts, as did ruined abbeys, deserted castles, country houses and pretty dales. Nice little cafés and tea shops sprung up all over; farmhouses started doing bed-and-breakfast, with the added attraction of cuddly live creatures like lambs, calves, chickens and puppies. Village shops began to sell cheap souvenirs, as well as a bewildering range of goods produced by so-called rural craftsmen and women, and to steer the visitors around the district, guide books were published and some tourists even went so far as to purchase maps! In many ways, the seaside resort had moved inland along with the inevitable crowds of people who did silly things like getting lost, tumbling down cliffs, falling into rivers, getting swept out to sea in dinghies, being trapped by the incoming tide, breaking limbs, crashing their cars, losing their wallets or forgetting to bring any money. But all this frantic new activity pleased the national park authority because it helped to regenerate rural areas.

No reference was made to the fact that visitors parked all

over the place and blocked narrow lanes as they sought picnic sites, camping-sites, country pubs with good food, and real life cows and sheep in their natural habitat. It took no account of villagers who were prepared to act the part of a yokel so that tourists could take their photographs. I knew one old character who kept himself in pints of beer at the local pub by standing all day at his cottage gate and letting tourists take his photograph. He would offer to meet them later in the pub to tell them his life story. His popularity might have been something to do with the fact he claimed to be the illegitimate son of a former sovereign. He told a good, well-rehearsed story which could not be checked – and therefore never authenticated.

But if one change dominated the countryside – and continues to dominate – since this fairly modern revolution in mass tourism, it is the amount of litter which is cast away by visitors and left along the verges of the lanes and highways, dumped in villages or on the moors, hidden in woods and even tossed into the gardens and fields of local residents. It can be measured in barrowfuls per week on a single picnic site even though bins are present. Farmers, landowners and country dwellers will, each weekend, search their own premises for tourist litter and clear it away by the sackful. In many cases, things like plastic bags or wrappers can cause fatalities in sheep, horses and cattle if they try to eat them; broken glass bottles can cause fires when the sun's rays are intensified by shining through them and, of course, they can cause injury to children who might step on a piece of jagged glass in a pretty stream.

One of my own daughters, then aged eight, put her foot on a broken bottle which had been tossed into a stream and had to be rushed to hospital for medical care which included stitches in the wound. Tiny creatures like voles and harvest mice will sometimes inspect a piece of rubbish to check whether it is useful as a nest or temporary home, and often get trapped inside. There are untold dangers to people, wild life and the countryside when litter is dumped and so, when this social problem first became very evident, the government took action to prevent it. It passed the Litter Act of 1958 which came into force on 7 August that year, just in time for the advance publicity to be effective during the long summer holidays.

In simple terms, it created the offence of throwing down, dropping or otherwise depositing any kind of litter in any public place in the open air and leaving it so as to cause defacement of any place in the open air. People who dropped cigarette packets in the street or countryside, or who left behind things like chip papers, empty bottles, sandwich wrappers, the remnants of picnics and so forth could all be prosecuted – that's if they were caught in the act. It was most difficult proving anyone had dumped litter unless they were seen to do so by a reliable witness, or caught by a sharp-eyed police officer. One essential part of the new law was that the litter had to be left behind – abandoned in other words – otherwise no offence was committed. If the perpetrator said, 'Sorry, Officer, I was going to take it home with me', or 'Oh, right, I'll pick it up', then there was no evidence of the necessary abandoning of that litter.

The maximum fine was only £10 and so if police officers caught anyone dumping litter – which they did with surprising frequency – they usually admonished the offender and told him or her to pick it up and take it to the nearest litter bin. That was often sufficient to deter the culprit from repeating the offence.

However, there was one major problem with that Litter Act. It did not give the police, or officials from the local authority, any power to demand an offender's name and address, nor did it give the police the power to arrest anyone who refused to provide such details. This much trumpeted law was therefore rather useless in practice and if it achieved a temporary reduction in the amount of litter strewn around, that was probably due to the widespread publicity which it generated, rather than the Act being an effective piece of legislation.

In time, the public came to realize this deficiency and if a police officer challenged a litter lout, the reply was often, 'So what? What can you do about it?' The strictly legal answer was nothing, but I knew one enterpriging police constable who was challenged in precisely this fashion. The lout had thrown away an empty beer bottle and had been seen by a patrolling bobby of considerable experience. The constable approached the lout and demanded he pick up the bottle, which had not smashed, and place it in a waste bin a few yards along the street. The lout, with his mates around him, laughed and said, 'There's nowt you can do, copper!'

'Then I'm arresting you,' smiled the policeman.

'Arresting me? What for? Chucking an empty bottle away?' laughed the lout.

'No, on suspicion of stealing the beer. I suspect you stole the beer from a pub, drank it in the street to avoid detection and then threw away the evidence. You're under arrest, sonny. And theft carries a maximum ten-year sentence.'

'No, hang on . . . no . . . you can't . . .'

And so the man was marched towards the police station, being made to carry his bottle with him, and he was followed by his mates who now started to plead with the constable that he had not stolen the beer, that it was just a bit of silly fun . . .

Before reaching the police station, however, the lout volunteered his name and address, but was told to march through its doors and place the bottle into the police-station waste bin. He was told a summons would follow. It did, and he was fined £10 by the local court. I often wonder whether he ever dumped litter again. He'd had his bit of fun – and so had the policeman.

The ineffectiveness of the Litter Act of 1958 also meant people ignored it when they wanted to get rid of larger items like old cars, refrigerators and household waste such as mattresses, wardrobes and settees; quite simply, it was worth the fine to get rid of such large pieces of junk. They would drive on to some quiet piece of land, often private property owned by a farmer or landowner, to dump such larger items and so the Civic Amenities Act of 1967 became law in an attempt to halt this aggravated nuisance. A few years later in 1971, the Dangerous Litter Act increased the £10 fine of the first Litter Act to a new level of £100. Since then, new laws have sought to deal with the ever-present litter menace, such as the Environmental Protection Act of 1990 and the Refuse Disposal (Amenity) Act of 1978, both of which have superceded the earlier Litter Acts as well as the 1967 Civic Amenities Act. As I compile these notes, a fixed penalty system of fines is in operation under the Environmental Protection Act, but in spite of this, the dumping of litter remains a serious problem, making the countryside both unsightly and, on occasions, dangerous. The problem of how to prevent the public throwing their litter into the lanes and byways, moors and dales, rivers and woods, is one which is exercising the minds of the government, local authorities and police alike. Perhaps, if litter is thrown from a car or caravan, then the offender's vehicle should be confiscated? If such a hefty penalty could be enforced, it would be one way of vastly reducing the amount of motor traffic and caravans on our roads!

When I was the constable at Aidensfield, however, the 1958 Litter Act was a fairly new piece of legislation, and one of my duties was to enforce it as best I could. I did catch a few tourists tossing paper and bottles into the ditches and hedgerows and managed to identify· some of them, although few ever went to court. Either I warned them about their future conduct, having extracted their names and addresses even if I did not have any power to demand them, or else they received a written caution from the superintendent of my division. Although I caught a few offenders, I never really felt the problem was being solved. The more people we prosecuted, the more litter seemed to appear along our lanes and hedgerows; it was almost as if the public were deliberately defying the law. What we needed, we all agreed during a quarterly meeting of rural bobbies in my section police station at Ashfordly, was some kind of widespread publicity. We needed a high-profile case where a person was prosecuted with maximum publicity, and it had to be something which would send a message to visitors and locals alike.

And then such an opportunity arose.

One Thursday morning I received a call from Jonathan Reynolds, the new estate manager for Crampton Estate. He was a very keen and forward-thinking young man, some six feet two inches tall with short cropped black hair, a lean face with high cheekbones and dark eyes which never seemed to be still. A bundle of energy, he dressed smartly in country clothes – a pale-green sports jacket, corduroy trousers and brown brogue shoes were his usual wear, and he spoke with the clipped accent of the aristocracy.

'Reynolds here from Crampton Hall,' said the voice in my telephone. 'Are you likely to be in this neck of the woods in the near future, Nick?'

'I'll be leaving home to begin my patrol in about half an hour,' I said. 'I can make a point of calling.'

'Champion! Say eleven?'

'Eleven will be fine,' I assured him. 'Do I need to prepare anything?' I wondered if he required some kind of legal advice.

'Nope, just a bit of knowledge about the litter dumping legislation. I've some information for you to act upon if you think it necessary,' he said, with an air of mysterv. 'I'll make sure the coffee's on.'

And so it was that at eleven that morning, after swotting up the provisions of the Litter Act, I drove into the magnificent grounds of Crampton Hall and parked my Mini-van outside the estate office. It was in an old part of the Hall, a spacious and comfortable office furnished with antiques and sporting a wonderful beamed ceiling, a massive open fireplace and mullioned windows.

'Glad you could make it, Nick. Coffee?'

'Thanks, Jonathan, milk but no sugar.'

As his secretary busied herself with the coffee, we chatted about inconsequential things such as how he was settling into his new post, how he enjoyed living in Crampton, how his children liked the primary school and so forth. Eventually, the coffees and a plate of chocolate biscuits arrived on a tray and his secretary left us alone for our discussion. When she closed the door between her office and ours, I wondered if there was some degree of secrecy or confidentiality in this meeting? But perhaps this was nothing more than the policy of Jonathan Reynolds?

'Nick,' he said. 'The Litter Act. I read something about it in *Country Life* I think it was, but does it only apply to public places?'

'It's a bit broader than that,' I told him. 'For the offence to be complete, the litter has to be deposited in, into or from any place in the open air to which the public are entitled or permitted to have access without payment, and it has to be left in circumstances which cause, contribute to or tend to lead to defacement by litter of *any* place in the open air.'

I could see him pondering the full meaning of this, so I added, 'It means the place which is defaced does not necessarily have to be a public place, or even open to the public. It could be someone's private garden, for example.'

'So the clause about free public access is only a factor so far as the act of depositing is concerned?' he frowned.

'Yes, a good example might be a public footpath running alongside a private wood. If someone on that footpath tossed an empty beer bottle into the private area – the wood – and left it there, then the offence would be complete even though the defaced place was in a private area.'

'Right, I understand,' he nodded.

'You'd get a similar result if someone was driving along a public road and threw a bag of rubbish out of the car and into a private wood, that would constitute an offence too.'

'Right,' he smiled. 'I can see, in both those cases, the offender has deposited litter from a place to which the public has access without payment, and the effect will be to deface a place in the open air.'

'Yes,' I said. 'It's important that it doesn't matter whether the place which is defaced is open to the public. For example, if someone is walking down the street and tosses a fish-and-chip paper into someone's private garden, then the offence would be complete. But it doesn't include a neighbour who tosses rubbish from his own garden into the one next door – in that case, the litter has been tossed from a private place!'

'I understand,' he said. 'I can see how it fits our circumstances. Now, Nick, we've been having sacks full of household junk tossed into one of our woods. It's been happening on a regular basis, fortnightly we think. You know that track along the Crampton Rigg?'

'I do,' I nodded. It was a public right of way through part of Crampton Estate and although it was unsurfaced, some people took their cars along the track, usually Landrovers rather than smart saloon cars, although horse riders, ramblers and dog walkers also made use of it. It offered spectacular views across the landscape around Crampton and, as it descended from the heights of the Rigg, it passed through some lush woodland. It was very popular and Crampton Estate had never attempted to prevent people enjoying it.

'There's a small path which leaves the main route and dips down the hillside,' he said. 'It's about a mile from the eastern end of the track, at the point where the woodland begins, and it leads into an old disused quarry. The quarry is well out of the sight of people passing through the wood, you have to make quite a detour to find it.'

'I don't know the quarry,' I admitted. Although I had walked the path in question, I had not diverted from it because there were plenty of signs saying 'Private Woodland' followed by the words 'Crampton Estate'.

'It's not been worked for decades,' he told me. 'But in recent weeks our gamekeeper has found rubbish in the quarry. Obviously, it's been dumped there without any permission on our part, and for the first few times, all he did was put the sacks in the Landrover and get rid of them through our own channels. But it's become a regular thing, Nick; somebody is using our quarry as a dumping ground, hence my enquiry.'

'And do you know the identity of the culprit?'

'We do, Nick, which is why Lord Crampton wanted you to be informed. That particular gamekeeper, the one who found the sacks, is Peter Fisher. Once he realized this was happening regularly, he kept watch and eventually saw the culprit park his car just off the track and carry a sackful of rubbish into the woods. He comes on Wednesday afternoons, not every Wednesday though. He threw the sack down the cliff into the quarry and then left. Peter took the number of his car, a Volvo, and then recognized it. It belongs to Michael Britton.'

The manner in which he revealed the name suggested he expected me to recognize the name, but I didn't.

'You know him?' I asked.

'Not personally,' admitted Jonathan. 'But he is well known He runs a newsagents and stationery shop in Ashfordly. Brittons.'

'Ah!' I realized who he meant. 'So why would he get rid of his rubbish in such a furtive way? There are plenty of places in Ashfordly where he could take it.'

'Exactly,' said Jonathan. 'That's what we found curious. When Peter saw him dump the last sack, only yesterday, he had a look inside – on previous occasions, he just collected it and took it to our disposal area, but this time he wanted to know what the fellow was tossing away so secretly.'

'We're talking of sacks, are we?' I interrupted. 'Not just bags?'

'Sacks, yes, those big hessian sacks, the sort that will hold a hundredweight of potatoes. Until yesterday, he thought it was just household waste. Anyway, he opened it.'

'And?' I wondered if he was going to say it contained parts of a chopped up human body.

'Filthy magazines, Nick. It was full of out-of-date magazines, indecent ones, going back years. Pornographic stuff, the sort that would be hidden under the counter. That's why Lord Crampton wanted you to be informed. He thinks you should take action against Britton.'

'For dumping litter, or for selling obscene literature?'

'That decision must rest with your senior officers, Nick. The sack is still there, Peter can take you to it, and Lord Crampton has assured me that he will permit Peter to give evidence of identication of the man who deposited the sack in our quarry. I might add that he regards obscene literature as one of the curses of our society, Nick.'

'If we are to prosecute him for selling the stuff, we'd have to catch him in the act and that might mean a raid on the shop. This is a matter for someone of higher authority, Jonathan; I'll have to refer it to my sergeant. But I will recover the sack today, with Peter's help, and that should give my bosses enough evidence to take whatever steps they feel necessary.'

'We think that when some of the magazines remain unsold, he daren't get rid of them through the usual channels, as the dustmen and their colleagues might talk, so he decided to find a secret dumping place. That's our theory, Nick.'

'You could be right, although I thought unsold magazines and newspapers were returned to the wholesalers?'

'I believe they are, under normal circumstances. There might be some other reason for his behaviour. And there is just one other thing that might have escaped your notice,' said Jonathan. 'Lord Crampton reminded me about it.'

I could sense that something not very pleasant was to follow and was right.

'Tell me,' I invited.

'Michael Britton is married to Joyce,' he said quietly.

'Oh crumbs!' I realized now just who this man was. 'She's one of the newly appointed magistrates for Eltering Petty Sessional Division, isn't she?'

'Right,' he said. 'You can see why this needs very careful handling, but Lord Crampton feels he must do his public duty by reporting this, hence this meeting.'

'It is not an offence simply to be in possession of obscene literature,' I explained. 'The offence occurs when someone sells it, sends it through the post, distributes it, lets it on hire, circulates it and so forth. If this man kept this sort of stuff for his own personal use, then there is no offence – but if we have reason to suspect he has been selling it in his shop, then we can raid the premises, seize any obscene material we find there and then let him show, in court, why it should not be confiscated and destroyed.'

'I'll explain that to Lord Crampton. So you are saying he might not necessarily be prosecuted for possessing obscene literature?'

'Right,' I said. 'But we could prosecute him for depositing litter, and I am sure the nature of the litter thrown away would be mentioned in court!' I laughed. 'I am sure the Press would love that story, especially as his wife is a magistrate – they do get advance notice of cases which are due in court. That way, I think, we could get some very useful publicity while achieving our purpose in telling the world what filthy stuff he's been selling.'

And so it was that Peter Fisher, a bearded man in his mid-fifties who wore plus fours and spoke with a strong Scottish accent, took me to the quarry where we recovered the sack of dirty magazines. I obtained a witness statement from him in which he identified the culprit and gave his account of watching him dump the sack and its contents, then drove immediately to Ashfordly Police Station to find Sergeant Craddock. After explaining the story to him, he said he would speak to Inspector Breckon at Eltering before any further action was taken. He locked the sack in one of the cells and kept the key because he did not want us to sneak a look at the juicy contents!

I was to learn that a detective, unknown to Britton, had subsequently entered the shop in an attempt to buy a filthy magazine, but had not been successful, so there was very little evidence that Britton was actually selling the stuff. We maintained careful observations on his premises for a few days afterwards but found no evidence of obscene material being sold.

We did learn, however, that he was receiving lots of large brown envelopes by post and had been for some time. This evidence suggested he was buying the magazines for his personal use and so the inspector decided we should go ahead only with a prosecution under the Litter Act. I got the job of interviewing him and then informing him that he would be prosecuted for depositing litter in the open air – and I told him we knew what was in the sack. He was very anxious that the nature of its contents should not be divulged in court and assured me he had never sold such material in his shop, buying the material for his own personal use and then being unable to dispose of it in secret. He said he would plead guilty in the hope the nature of the contents was not made public.

When the case came to court, it made a headline in the local *Gazette* but only because Michael Britton's wife was a magistrate. He was fined £10 for depositing litter in the open air and the whole area talked about his silly action especially when married to a magistrate and moreso because there were other ways of getting rid of unwanted paper. No mention was made of the precise contents of his sack.

But it prevented him for depositing more litter and, I think, deterred a few others who might be tempted to throw their offal into the lovely countryside.

It did not stop Solomon Plott, however, probably because he was far too mean to buy the local *Gazette*. I am sure he did not read about the Britton saga and would probably never hear about it; whether or not such knowledge would have affected his way of life or behaviour is something I cannot answer.

Solomon was the local miser, a fact well known to everyone living in the Aidensfield district. He lived alone in a tiny cottage along the Elsinby Road at Aidensfield, being too mean to get married or raise a family. He did not even keep a cat or a dog – they would cost money. His house cost him little in upkeep and rates and had been left to him by his equally thifty parents. In my time at Aidensfield, Solomon, then in his mid-sixties, would rarely leave the house except to potter along to the shop for his weekly groceries, or to ride his peculiar bike-trailer into the countryside. For his groceries, he would allocate a certain amount of cash each week, calculating down to the last halfpenny just how much he would need to spend. He existed on a fraction of what a normal man might spend, usually through buying his requirements just as the shop was about to close for the weekend and thus getting things at dirt cheap prices.

So far as anyone in the village knew, Solomon had never had a job, preferring to exist on money left by his thrifty parents and struggling to make it last throughout his remaining life. He sat alone on cold nights without bothering to light a fire; he bought his clothes at second-hand shops, or was given them by friends whose relatives had died, and he could make a loaf of bread last until the final slice was going mouldy.

Some people felt sorry for him and gave him their own unwanted gifts, like sweaters, socks, shirts and coats. Sometimes one of the village ladies took him his Sunday dinner, or made him a cake; others might darn the hole in the sleeve of his cardigan, or gave him a pair of old shoes or unwanted wellington boots. That he was dreadfully poor was never in doubt, but some of the menfolk thought he could help himself a little more by doing some kind of work, like helping out on farms or labouring for local builders. But Solomon had no intention of working; he preferred to stay at home, eking out his meagre income without buying any unnecessary thing. To go out to work would cost money, he had once told a friend, he'd need extra clothes for that.

There was one story of him going out regularly early in the morning, taking a selected newspaper from the letter-box of a house, reading it quickly, and then replacing it before the occupant drew it inside. It was said he could calculate the cost of cooking a single potato, or lighting his cottage by oil lamp for a mere half an hour. It was a standing joke in the village that Solomon stayed at home so that he could count his savings by the light of a single piece of coal smouldering in the grate; he was, in fact; the Ebenezer

Scrooge of Aidensfield, except that he was never likely to reform.

As a mode of transport, however, he excelled in that he had an old bicycle which had been owned by his father and he would often go off on it. I was never sure where he went on his bike because many of his trips were in the very early hours. The bike had a small trailer which could be attached to the rear. Most of the time it was fixed to the bike, making it look rather like a pedal-operated tractor and trailer.

Some people said he was careful about the number of times he rode his bike because each outing would cost money by wearing down the tyres just a little. I knew, however, that from time to time he would journey into the woods beyond Aidensfield along the Briggsby Road to collect timber and kindling. These early morning outings for timber cost him nothing and helped, quite literally, to keep his home fires burning. The wood was there for the taking, it cost him nothing. So far as I knew, that was the sole purpose of using his bicycle-trailer but did he go further? Did he go elsewhere on bike? If so, where?

Solomon was a master at surviving without money. Although he rarely featured in any of my duties, nonetheless, I kept an eye on his cottage, thinking that one day he might be found dead among his meagre belongings, or that he might need help of some kind, especially if he became ill. But I never made an open approach to help him – he wasn't the sort of man who'd welcome a police officer into his dismal life. But, a considerable time after I had been appointed the constable of Aidensfield, I found myself having to interview him on suspicion of having dumped litter on the moors.

A recent arrival in the village, a retired dentist from Wakefield called Ronald Stanway, was walking his golden retriever on the moors above Aidensfield when he came across a stream which was blocked. The route was part of his daily walk with Rufus and was a wide bridlepath popular with horse riders and pedestrians alike. On this occasion he was surprised to see the stream was overflowing.

It appeared to be blocked somewhere downstream beyond his vision because the water had backed up to form a large pool near the footpath and in places it had spilled across this stretch's low-lying banks. The stream, known as Briggsby Beck, rose somewhere higher on the hills and by the time it reached the point in question it was about twelve feet (4 metres or so) wide and flowing quite rapidly over courses of rocks and through peat beds. From time to time, its course did get blocked with fallen trees or dead sheep, or sometimes because rocks on its banks had become dislodged by a heavier-than-normal flow. On this occasion, however, Ronald knew of no such event. There had been a long spell of fine dry weather with the water level falling, not rising, consequently the flood was very much out of the ordinary. He decided to investigate.

Within a matter of yards, he came to a point where a dry-stone wall crossed the beck, this marking the boundary of a farmer's land. The beck tumbled down a steep slope just beyond that gap in the wall, and ran through the farmer's land before levelling out on the plain below. There was therefore a wide gap in the wall where it crossed the beck. The farmer, however, to prevent his livestock straying on to the moors by getting through the gap, had stretched several strands of barbed wire across it. They were well above water level but high enough to obstruct any of his adventurous cattle and sheep. However, whenever a flood occurred, large objects such as dead sheep, boulders or branches from trees would get swept downstream by the powerful water and then become lodged against the wire. All manner of other debris would collect around the obstruction and very soon, the beck could be reduced to a trickle immediately below the barrier while flooding across the landscape on the high side. On that high side, the land was almost level with the surface of the water and the banks were low. Even with a slight obstruction in its flow, the water would spread across the ground to eventually find an escape route else-where – perhaps one of the wall's smout holes – and so find another route into the valley. Usually, the farmer would quickly realize what had happened and would rush to clear the obstruction before the new water course created damage or destruction. (A smout hole, by the way, is a small passage through a dry-stone wall at ground level. A small one will permit rabbits and hares to pass through while preventing sheep, cattle and horses; a medium smout hole will be large enough to allow sheep to pass through while obstructing cattle and horses).

When Ronald arrived at the barbed wire fence he could see that something was blocking the stream to make the water back up a considerable distance before overflowing and when he inspected the material, he was astonished to find a mass of paper in the form of newspapers, magazines and periodicals. They appeared to have been dumped *en masse* somewhere upstream before being swept down to this point; some earlier obstructions against the wire – large branches and roots of heather – had prevented the papers from going any further. As more papers had arrived, so the flow of water had been interrupted by the highly effective paper dam until it had been reduced to a mere trickle – and the surplus was now flooding the banks.

Ronald struggled to clear a waterway through the mass of paper but had found it impossible to clear the lot due to the weight of the wet paper and the pressure and depth of water which was constantly bearing down upon it. Furthermore, he was not wearing wellington boots and so he had decided to inform the farmer on whose land it was. Sadly when Ronald arrived at High Farm house the farmer was out – he'd taken some livestock to the market – and his wife was an invalid who could not help, other than to suggest he sought help elsewhere. And so as Ronald hurried homeward to find someone to help, he chanced to see me standing beside the telephone kiosk in Briggsby, making what was known as a conference point. Even though my vehicle was radio equipped. I was still expected to make hourly points at telephone kiosks in case the office needed to contact me. Daft I know, but old habits die hard!

'Ah,' he said, when he reached me with Rufus at his heels. 'Just the man!'

'Hello, Mr Stanway, and Rufus.' I knew him by sight and patted the tail-waving dog. 'Out for your constitution as usual?'

'I am, Mr Rhea, and I have a slight problem. Not an emergency, I may say, but something that needs attention,' and he told me about the blockage in the beck, adding, 'It's caused by masses of paper, Mr Rhea; it looks as if some shop or other has dumped all its unsold newspapers and magazines up there. I tried to clear a way through them but I've no wellingtons and the water's almost knee deep. Besides, there's a heavy weight of water bearing down on them.'

'Can I get my van up there?' I asked.

'Oh yes, there's a wide track leading on to the moors. You'll see the flood water; its spreading close to the track about a mile from High Farm.'

'Right, I'll go and have a look.' If a shop had dumped its stock of unsold papers here it would be most unusual because I understood that unsold periodicals and papers were returned to the wholesaler so that credit could be given. As I drove the short distance, I realized I might need a tool of some kind. I called at High Farm, borrowed a corn fork and a pickaxe, and soon found myself at the blockage. Ronald was right – it was a dam of paper magazines and it was proving highly effective and so, with my wellingtons on (I always carried wellies in the rear of my van, among a mass of other potentially useful things) I waded into the water armed with the long-handled two-pronged corn fork. The prongs were slightly curved and I thought this would enable me to lever the paper away; if not, the pickaxe might be necessary.

Large chunks of slippery paper such as wet magazines are not easy to manipulate but more by good luck than skill, I managed to dislodge a particularly large batch of paper – magazines which appeared to be lashed together in a block with string – and this allowed the ever-pressing water to find its escape route. The level dropped quickly and this allowed me to dislodge more. Very soon, I was able to wade into the depths and manhandle the batches to the banks; in some cases, several magazines had been tied together to form a bundle but in others they were quite separate, being held together by their wetness and pressure of the water. As I laid them on the banks, I realized they were all financial magazines. Intrigued, I examined several of them. I noted *Investors World, Personal Finance and Money Manager, Economics and Investments, Banking Worldwide, Stocks and Share Markets, Gilt Edge Investments, Business in Britain, Insurance Broking* and others, including newspapers like the *Financial Times* and *The Economist.* Closer inspection showed they were out-of-date by several weeks and months and, as I was wondering who might have dumped this lot in the beck, I saw a name scribbled on the front page of one of the periodicals. Solomon Plott. My own newsagent, the Aidensfield Stores, scribbled my name on the top of each newspaper delivered to my home, but this handwriting was different. These had not come from the Aidensfield Stores but from some other source. In Ashfordly perhaps? But had they been dumped by some errant newspaper lad before reaching Solomon? Or had Solomon dumped them? Would Solomon, with all his miserliness, actually buy financial papers? Yes, I said to myself, he would. People like him did just that – they lived in misery and penury while amassing a fortune in stock and shares. And, I knew, Solomon's parents had left him the house and probably some money which would require careful management if it was to keep him for the rest of his days. I removed sufficient paper to permit the water level to drop and the beck to flow as near to normal as I could in the time available, returned my tools to High Farm and then went to see Solomon. I took one of the wet magazines with me, one which bore his name on the front.

He saw me approaching and came out to meet me. I knew he'd not offer a cup of tea or coffee, which would cost too much, and besides, I was not here on a social call. This was business, police business.

' 'Morning, Solomon,' I said, holding the magazine before me. 'Can I have a word?'

'Aye, Mr Rhea,' he said without inviting me inside. 'What is it?'

'This magazine was found in Briggsby Beck,' I said. 'There were hundreds more with it, some loose and others bound in bundles. Thrown away, I suspect, Solomon, and they were blocking the beck. A really effective dam, Solomon.'

'Oh, aye?' he frowned as he stared at the magazine in my hand without making any further comment.

'This one's got your name on, Solomon. And lots of the others have your name on. I think you dumped them there.'

'And you say they all got stuck?'

'They did, where the stream goes through a wall, there's barbed wire stretched across, like a gate. They were caught in a tangle of other things which had become trapped by the barbed wire.'

'Well, they've never done that before, Mr Rhea.'

'You mean you've done this before?'

'Oh, aye, I've always got rid of my magazines like that, drop 'em in the beck and the water carries 'em off, Mr

Rhea. They get broken up on the rocks, so my old dad would say. He always got rid of his old paper like that, he got the idea when flush toilets became popular. You pushed your waste paper down the bowl and pulled the chain and it all disappeared. He was quite taken with that, was my dad.'

'Those kind of toilets aren't for getting rid of waste paper, Solomon!'

'Well, they seem to do it very well,' he smiled. 'My dad reckoned the sticklebacks way downstream would make nests out of the shreds and if they got past the sticklebacks, it would all go underground. That beck goes underground you know, in the village. Just like the toilet water. We've been doing it for years, Mr Rhea, me and my dad, and there's never been trouble before.'

'You mean your father did this too?'

'Aye, all his life. Us Plotts have always got rid of our paperwork like this, Mr Rhea.'

'Can I ask why? Why don't you put it in the dustbin?'

'Secrets, Mr Rhea. My old dad hated the notion that somebody might know what he was up to, in his share dealings and so on. He marked the shares he bought, you see, and then got rid of the papers . . . he wouldn't put 'em in the dustbin, Mr Rhea, in case folks snooped on him. So he put all his magazines in yon beck, so they would be carried off and ripped to shreds by the water and then it would all go underground. Can you think of a better spot for getting rid of very personal papers? Once down there, they'll never surface again. Just like the stuff we flush down our water closets. Them papers are too big to go down my toilet, you understand.'

As I quizzed him, it seemed he had once been in the practice of tossing one or two magazines or periodicals into the beck at each time, taking them there in his bicycle trailer while *en route* to collect the next batch of magazines from a newsagent in Ashfordly. He arrived at the newsagents before six on a morning while the day's papers were being sorted, for he did not want anyone in Aidensfield to know his business. To maintain his secrecy, he was prepared to cycle the four miles into town at the crack of dawn, destroying old magazines *en route* and collecting the latest before his return home. And to hide them in the base of his trailer, he covered them with logs and sticks gathered from the wood.

'I need them to keep up with my investments,' he told me, 'But I don't want folks knowing my business, Mr Rhea, and I shall be pleased if you will keep this to yourself. I know you're bound by the Official Secrets Act and I'm only telling you because I don't want it to go any further.'

'You could always wrap your papers in brown paper and tie them in parcels, then put them in the dustbin,' I suggested.

'That would cost money, Mr Rhea,' was his reply.

'What would?' I asked.

'The string and brown paper,' was his answer.

'Solomon,' I said. 'It's illegal to dump rubbish in the countryside it's been illegal since 1958 and if you persist in doing this, you could finish up with a fine of £10, and a court appearance.'

'Illegal? Ten Pounds? You can't be serious! We've done that for years, Mr Rhea, me and my dad before me.'

'Well, it's got to stop as from today. You'll have to find some other way of getting rid of your old magazines, newspapers and periodicals. And, I might add, I should really prosecute you for this episode – but I won't. On two conditions.'

'What's that, Mr Rhea?'

'That you clear every scrap of paper from that beck before it causes more problems, and that you never dump it there again. Next time it happens, there'll be a fine of £10 and a court appearance. And the same every time you repeat it.'

'Well, there's no way I can afford to be fined, Mr Rhea, so right, I'll get up there tomorrow morning and clear the lot.'

And so he did. When I checked two days later, every scrap of paper had been removed and, as I repeated my checks over the months, no more appeared. I don't think he disposed of his papers down the toilet either, and must admit I do not know where or how Solomon disposed of his financial magazines after that episode. I told Ronald Stanway what I had done, and the reason behind my actions. He was quite happy with my handling of this tiny incident, but more than intrigued about the cause of the flood than possessing any desire to prosecute Solomon.

Years later, Solomon died. He left more than £650,000, a huge sum in the 1970s. He had no relations and left no will. What a sad waste of money. Just think about it – I'm sure Solomon could have blocked that beck with pound notes if he'd been so inclined but I don't think he would have flushed any of his money down the loo.

# Chapter 11

Elsinby Grange, situated on the former estate of the Marquis of Elsinby, featured in an earlier collection of tales (*Constable Over The Stile* – 1998). At that time, it was a very upmarket hotel catering for very special people, being more of a country club or posh guest house because members of the general public were unaware of its presence. Its guests were privileged people who were invited by the owners to make use of its ample facilities, for payment of course. That ensured it was very exclusive indeed. Virtually everyone who stayed there was an invited guest of the owners – you did not ask to stay at Elsinby Grange. You were invited.

In its former days of glory, however, the marquis had lived in Elsinby Hall which was set high on an escarpment among acres of copses, scrubland, meadows and gardens. When he died, the estate was sold to pay horrendous death duties. Shortly afterwards, the Hall was destroyed by fire and the estate lay derelict for some time until it was purchased by a development company from London. They did not rebuild the Hall but instead modernized and extended Home Farm, one of the estate's large surviving properties, and turned it into that very fashionable private guest house. But eventually, due to their age, the owners decided to retire and give up their thriving business and thus Elsinby Grange was once again put on the market. It was very quickly purchased by a trust who turned into a private hospital – Elsinby Cottage Hospital. In the space of a few years – no more than twenty – The Grange had seen service as a busy working farmhouse, an up-market country guest house and now a private hospital. It had been functioning as a hospital for almost a year.

It had probably been a farm for hundreds of years before that and I wondered how its earlier occupants would regard its modern role. Now, on its splendid site deep in the countryside, its resident medical staff performed fairly common operations but seemed to specialize more in old folks who came to rest and recuperate; just like the hospital's former role, people were prepared to pay for the privilege of staying there. I recall thinking it was more of a convalescent home than a hospital.

Because it was a new venture on my beat, I ensured my presence was known to the hospital secretary and registrar, and to various members of the regular staff, and I made a point of calling at least once a week. If the administrators and staff had any problems of the kind I could solve, then this was one means of learning about them or perhaps dealing with them on the spot. The small hospital's isolation on its hilltop site and its potential for attracting very exclusive patients meant there were few problems which demanded police attention. In spite of that, I knew I could make use of its facilities in an emergency – such as coping with a road accident victim suffering from severe injuries – but such occasions were rare indeed.

It was during one of my periodic visits that Dr Adrian Matthews, the registrar, asked if he could have a quiet word with me. Tall, distinguished and with a good head of silvery grey hair, he led me into his office, arranged a cup of coffee via his secretary, and spent a few moments chatting in an amiable way. He asked about my family, my work and my ambitions and seemed genuinely interested in my career and responsibilities, then reiterated his willingness to help should I ever need his services. I was later to learn that he specialized in tropical diseases but felt that skill had little potential in this part of the North Riding! But we were here on more mundane business.

'I'm pleased you called in,' he smiled. 'I don't want to make a fuss about this and most certainly would not want it known around the village, or among our patients, but I fear we have a prowler, PC Rhea.'

'Oh dear!' I sighed. 'Right out here? I'd have thought the hospital was too far from civilization to attract that kind of nuisance.'

'So did I, I must admit. We often get that kind of nuisance around town and city hospitals, especially when there are nurses' homes nearby. They attract peepers and similar weirdos, including young men who think they are daring but who are, in truth, rather stupid after a few drinks. I must say I didn't expect that kind of behaviour out here.'

'You've seen him?' I asked.

'No, I must admit I haven't. I've had one or two reports from patients who've noticed someone outside the windows at night and the night porter has mentioned it to me as well. He heard someone outside – a plant pot was knocked over beneath one of the windows – but he had gone by the time he got outside. I've no description I'm afraid, PC Rhea, except one old man thought it was a ghost!'

'Did he give a reason for thinking that?' I smiled.

'Not really, he just got a fleeting glimpse of something grey outside his window; his eyesight's not all that good, I'm afraid.'

'Grey? You mean a grey coat?'

'I can't be sure what he meant. He said he only got a very brief glimpse of something. Due to his poor eyesight, I'm afraid we took that report with a proverbial pinch of salt. It was a ground-floor window, I ought to add!'

'But you do really think there is someone about?' I had to ask.

'I had my doubts when the suggestion first arose. People do hear things and see things, or think they hear things and see things. Foxes, badgers and hedgehogs can make an enormous noise when they knock things over. Foxes overturn dustbins at times looking for food, or knock the lids off, and hedgehogs can skittle over milk bottles, so there are often strange noises at night, PC Rhea. And the hospital itself is noisy at night, staff moving about, water cisterns operating, doors opening and closing, there's always noise of some sort. But in spite of that, I do think someone is prowling. That plant pot that got knocked over, for example – no fox or badger could have done that. It's quite a large one and it was full of earth with a miniature rose bush in it. It would take a hefty kick or knock to move it, and I reckon it was overturned during a rush to flee from the scene, it's right under one of the windows where a sighting was reported. Then one morning I found footprints in the dew crossing the lawn as if taking a short cut from the drive to Ward 2 – that's on the ground floor to the right of the main door. None of our staff made those marks, I checked. They weren't distinct marks, by the way, just a disturbance in the dew, a single line of them, but footprints nonetheless. It's one person, PC Rhea, I'm sure of that.'

'Right, thanks for that. So there were no sounds of a car? Or a motor bike? Vehicle of any kind? Torch flashing in the darkness? Voices calling to one another?'

'No, nothing. I've asked the night duty staff – nurses, sister and porter – to keep an ear and an eye open, and although there have been noises and hints of someone around, we've never caught anyone or even seen anyone.'

'Are the sightings regular?' was my next question. 'Once a week perhaps? More or less? On a certain night? At a certain time of night? Fridays or Saturdays after the pub turns out perhaps? Midnight, say, or shortly afterwards?'

'All the visits I know about have been during the night time.' He was adamant about that. 'Late too, probably after midnight; one or two in the early morning even. They were not on any particular night so far as I can ascertain. One was a Sunday, or the early hours of Monday, another was Thursday. There's no discernible pattern to the visits, PC Rhea.'

After quizzing him at some length, and later speaking to those who thought they had seen something, I came to the conclusion that someone was paying unauthorized nocturnal visits to the hospital grounds. Clearly, it was someone on foot for there had been no reports of vehicle lights or noises and no sign of tyre marks; there was that trail of footprints in the dew too, and the knocking over of that plant pot. A human foot colliding with it in the darkness could have achieved that. And there was no knocking over of dustbins or removal of their lids so I felt the culprit was not a wild animal; I came to believe we did have a human prowler at Elsinby Grange.

The problem was what to do about it. One simple solution was to conceal myself somewhere about the premises so that I could maintain a watch on the approaches to the hospital and the exterior of the ground-floor wards, but I could not afford to spend every night waiting for hours and hours just on the off-chance that someone would arrive. I had other things to do, other responsibilities. If I could be sure that chummy came very obligingly, say, every Friday between eleven at night and two the following morning, I could justify being there, but things were rather more vague. I needed some rather more precise timings before I could commit myself to a pre-determined period of observation.

I decided that one tactic was to drive up to the hospital in the police van on regular occasions, even with the blue light flashing, in the hope that chummy would see my presence and so be deterred from revisiting, but I had to be sure my lights and vehicle noises would not unduly disturb the patients. Or, of course, I could pay regular visits on foot, preferably under cover of darkness while in uniform, in the hope that my presence would be noted by the prowler and so deter him. One danger with that tactic was that I might be mistaken for the prowler . . .

Furthermore, I could not ignore the possibility that the culprit might be a member of staff or even a patient sneaking outside for reasons best known to him- or herself, perhaps to have a crafty cigarette, or even just to get some fresh air. The possibilities were numerous and the chances of catching the culprit in the act were, I had to admit, somewhat remote. I realized I would have to depend greatly upon a sheer chance encounter!

For that reason, deterrence by my visible and unannounced arrival and presence seemed the wisest option and I could reinforce this by making discreet enquiries in the nearby village in the hope I might learn about someone walking alone at night. Even a dog walker! People did walk their dogs at night, often for quite long distances.

I put these ideas to Adrian Matthews and he agreed with my decision, so I told him that if I did visit the hospital at night with the intention of concealing myself on the premises, I would inform him in advance, and I assured him I would do my best to let him know when I would be making both overt and covert visits. There would be times, I explained, when I would call without warning; it was all part of a plan to try and either trap the prowler or warn him off. I had to be as unpredictable as the prowler. In return, Matthews would let me know of any further visits by the prowler and would do his best to obtain a description along with more accurate timings of his presence. With those assurances in mind, I left Elsinby Grange with a determination to identify and catch the villain.

In reality there is little the police can do in such circumstances because although such people are a nuisance and even create alarm in others, they are committing no crime by snooping through windows, or prowling in the hope of catching sight of someone without any clothes on. To deal with them, and to attempt to stamp out the nuisance, we relied on an ancient statute dating to 1360 which was enacted during the reign of Edward III. This allowed all disturbers of the peace to be bound over to be of good behaviour, and one huge benefit was that it need not be proved that such disturbers had put others in fear. That old statute was useful because it catered for a broad spectrum of unspecified social nuisances and bad behaviour for which no specific provision had been created in law, and it allowed the courts to bind over such people either to be of good behaviour or to keep the peace. In short, it was a superb piece of legislation in spite of its age.

Sometimes the period of good behaviour was specified by the court, say two years, and sometimes the court said that if the person repeated his conduct, he would forfeit a surety of, say, £20 or more. If and when I identified the Elsinby prowler, therefore, that kind of response would be his fate.

In the days and weeks which followed, I made very discreet enquiries around Elsinby and in the nearby hamlets in an effort to find out whether anyone was known or suspected of prowling at night. I knew that some poachers – Claude Jeremiah Greengrass among them – were prone to wandering at night in pursuit of pheasants and other game, but the visits to Elsinby Cottage Hospital did not seem to be that kind of outing. I could not imagine a poacher wanting to seek game within the hospital grounds. Neither did it appear to be a late-night courting couple looking for somewhere quiet. All my discreet enquiries produced no useful information and not a hint as to who the culprit might be.

And then I had a stroke of luck.

One Thursday tea-time, there was a knock on the door of my police house at Aidensfield and I opened it to find my caller was a mature lady. Quite sturdy in build with neat grey hair and horn-rimmed spectacles, she asked if she might have a word with me. I noticed her car outside and invited her into the office at the side of the house, then offered a cup of tea which she declined.

'I can't stay many minutes,' she said. 'I'm on my way back to Wolverhampton this evening. I must leave soon, but thought I'd better have a quick word with you about my mother.'

'Your mother?'

'Mrs Buckley, Alice. She lives in Castle Drive in Elsinby, number seven.'

'Ah, yes!' I knew the house and had seen the elderly Mrs Buckley in Elsinby on many occasions, doing her shopping or merely chatting to friends. In her eighties, she was a familiar figure around the place and as I looked at her daughter, I could see the family resemblance. 'So how can I help?

'She's taken to wandering at night, Mr Rhea. I've been staying with her and I woke up one morning in the early hours to find the back door standing open and her bed empty. Luckily, she hadn't got far, I found her walking up the street, just beyond the Hopbind Inn. I've suggested she might like to come to live with me, but she won't hear of it. I've got to get back to Wolverhampton for tomorrow, work you know. My reason for calling on you is to let you know she's liable to go off like that from time to time; perhaps you could keep an eye open when you're on night patrol and let your colleagues know? I have told as many people in the village as I can, and they've all promised to look out for her and take her back to her house if they find her wandering, but it is a worry. I've no idea how far she might go or what might happen to her if she's not found.'

'I'm sure we can cope,' I smiled. 'The people of Elsinby are good in that kind of situation. I'm sure she'll come to no harm.'

Finding such wanderers was not all that uncommon for police officers on night duty and mostly we had no idea who they were, but in this case I was already thinking of the Cottage Hospital prowler.

'I'm sorry to be a nuisance,' she was saying, 'but I can't see any other solution just now. I am trying to persude her to come to live with me, and when I retire I might move back here, to be with her. This is just a temporary measure, I hope . . .'

'Yes, yes of course I'll keep an eye open and I will notify my colleagues. Rest assured we'll take her home if we find her, but do you know if she wanders far? Or where she goes?'

'It's hard to say, to be honest. I've a feeling she goes out at times without anyone realizing. I'm sure she's slipped out sometimes while I've been upstairs asleep, but so far she's always come home, Mr Rhea. I've stayed with her several times in recent months, weekends mainly, and have discovered that when she goes out, she puts an overcoat on and her shoes and wraps up, then disappears. I've no idea where she gets to but as I said, she always returns. I've tried to stop her, telling her it's dangerous and silly and inconvenient to others especially late at night but she seems determined to go as she wants.'

'That's one of the privileges of growing old!' I laughed. 'Defying one's children!'

'Don't I know it! But I just thought you should know, in case you come across her at some ungodly hour. She's getting more clever at it now; she sneaks out without me knowing while I'm doing something in the house during the daytime. If you do find her, night or day, just take her home, Mr Rhea. That's all you can do, She's not insane, I should add, we can't have her locked up under the Mental Health Act; section 136, isn't it? You could perhaps let me know if you have problems. My married name is Williams. Sylvia.' And she gave me her address and phone number.

'I think I know where she goes,' I told Mrs Williams having listened to her account. 'I've been getting reports of a prowler at the hospital, Elsinby Grange. You might know it?'

'Oh good heavens . . . yes. That could be it . . . I never thought of that! It could be where she's going. It used to be her home, you know, for most of her life, before my dad died. It was called Home Farm then, part of Elsinby Estate, and Mum and Dad were tenant farmers. She was born there; it was her family home. She's always said she'd like to go back and look around but no one's ever invited her. Oh dear, has she been making a fool of herself? What's she been doing?'

'Just visiting in the early hours,' I said. 'Peeping through windows, walking around the grounds, seeing what's going on, so it would seem. Nothing nasty, nothing sinister – we thought it was a man snooping – but having heard your story, I bet it was your mother.'

'She was always very disappointed that no one had ever invited her back to the farm, not even when it was an hotel, and I know she'd love to see what they've done with it, but I don't know what to say about her nocturnal visits. Except, knowing her shyness, I think she would want to return in secret, not be a nuisance to anyone.'

'Suppose I arranged for her to have a look around Elsinby Grange?' I said. 'I could speak to Dr Matthews, the registrar, and I'm sure that once he learns the reason for this, he'll be more than pleased to invite her in to have a proper look around. He'll have had no idea of her links with the Grange. I'm making great assumptions that the nocturnal visitor is your mother of course, but in the circumstances it does sound highly feasible. Even if she is not the prowler, I think she'd still welcome an official visit to the Grange – and it might stop her wandering!'

'Yes, she would love that, it would really make her happy. She once said she didn't like to go there uninvited, but I had no idea she might do it so secretly under cover of darkness! I'd take her myself if she was invited, but right now, I have to get back for work . . .'

'Maybe next time you are here?' I suggested.

'Yes, yes, well, thank you. If she is that late night visitor, it's put my mind at rest. I did not want her to go wandering off and get lost or injured, old people can soon be affected by the cold at night.'

I called on Dr Matthews and told him about Mrs Buckley, expressing my belief that she was the phantom visitor. He listened with amusement and said, 'Mr Rhea, she must come to our anniversary party.'

'Anniversary?'

'Yes, we'll be celebrating our first year in these premises in six weeks' time, and she could be our guest of honour! And her daughter too. Would you mind if I went to talk to her about it?'

'Not at all,' I said. 'I think it would be a great idea.'

'And you must come too, with your wife and family. Yes, it would make it a really happy occasion. But, one final thing and on a more serious note, do you think Mrs Buckley is capable of living alone?'

'That's something you must discuss with her daughter,' I said. 'I have her name and address, and I think she might be more than pleased to discuss things with you. I'm not really sure how dangerous this wanderlust really is; I must say I am not very happy about an old lady wandering at night, even if she has a purpose. But if she visits the Grange, her wanderings might stop. Who knows? Is there some way you can help?'

'We have a special fund, Mr Rhea, for deserving cases. It's called the Foundation Fund and it was set up by a wealthy benefactor; it's never been used yet. We could accommodate Mrs Buckley free of charge if she cannot afford our fees and surely a lady who once lived here and who is now in need of help is a very deserving case? She doesn't need to be ill for us to admit her, you know, just in need of care.'

'You could have found your first candidate,' I said.